"Not since Denis Johnson's *Jesus' Son* have I read a book of stories that so resonated in my soul. McLean's prose sings with a fierceness that is ornate and sparse, spiritual and secular, peaceful and violent. These are stories that remind of Annie Proulx, Joy Williams, and Flannery O'Connor: surprising in the fundamental weirdness of mundane life pressed inextricably into the borderlands. The best collection of stories I have read in years."

CHRISTIAN KIEFER

"I challenge you to point to another writer like McLean. She is voracious, and her vision is brutal, yet hilarious. We will see her everywhere. These brilliant tales are so surprisingly original, so strange and moving, so funny, so irreverent, I swallowed them, I ate them whole."

DEB OLIN UNFERTH

"These stories, they churn and turn with ferocious pace and a brute subject-verb force. McLean is a writer of pure conviction, unafraid of risk, unconcerned with convention, objective but deeply humane, alive to wonder and strangeness. This collection, like her first, is beautiful and harrowing. I'll say it again and again: Nobody writes like Robin McLean."

CHRIS BACHELDER

"Robin McLean has always excelled in narrators who communicate their own self-sufficiency even as they inadvertently reveal the extent to which they're actually barely holding it together.

They live in places where a bed frame and box spring are just a dream. They remind us that they're still evolving . . . And yet somehow in the face of all of that, her protagonists summon lift, and generate that tenderness necessary to continue. The results are fictions that unite the personal and the political in ways that we need now more than ever."

JIM SHEPARD

"Deeply engaged with the rural, with people on their way off the grid, Robin McLean's fiction is at once fantastical and intensely observed. These are stories about human frailty and darkness, shot through with small moments of glory . . . "

BRIAN EVENSON

"Where so many American writers balk at genuine human darkness, Robin McLean steps inside with a poet's eye and an ill-used gavel she swiped from the decaying desk of some corrupt, abusive judge. The results are gripping, chilling, and far too realistic for the term. These ten modern parables lay bare our species' manifold predicaments here in the dimming light of imagined futures. An unforgettable book."

KYLE BEACHY

"Robin McLean writes with a kind of tender violence, her sentences aimed like fire hoses at a burning world. I loved this collection, and its cast of extraordinary characters will haunt my dreams."

DANI SHAPIRO

"I loved these brilliant, atmospheric and original stories – Robin McLean is such an exciting writer, and this is her best so far."

JOANNA KAVENNA

GET 'EM YOUNG TREAT 'EM TOUGH TELL 'EM NOTHING

ROBIN MCLEAN

SHEFFIELD – LONDON – NEW YORK

First published in 2022 by And Other Stories
Sheffield – London – New York
www.andotherstories.org

1 3 5 7 9 8 6 4 2

ISBN: 9781913505530
eBook ISBN: 9781913505547

Editor: Jeremy M. Davies; Copy-editor: Jane Haxby; Proofreader: Sarah Terry;
Typeset in Albertan Pro and Linotype Syntax by Tetragon, London;
Cover Design: Anna Morrison; Printed and bound on acid-free,
age-resistant Munken Premium by CPI Limited, Croydon, UK.

And Other Stories gratefully acknowledge that our work is supported
using public funding by Arts Council England.

For all the kids—

(especially)
M, C, S, K, L & E

I shake my two hairy fists at the sky
and I let out a howl so unspeakable
that the water at my feet turns sudden ice
and even I myself am left uneasy.

—Grendel,
JOHN GARDNER

CONTENTS

BUT FOR HERR HITLER

Iris got her name from a great-aunt, whose phone was tapped during the Red Scare. Agents took pictures of the house through gaps in the fence. Great-Aunt Iris spoke pig Latin on the phone and buried cigar boxes under the cabbage and spinach.

"They get salary," she said to her namesake later. "So they must vork for it."

Iris thought the name was old-fashioned. Eric liked old-fashioned. "Iris, yes, Iris." They met on opposite sides of a bowl of peanuts. She said he looked familiar. She liked his crew cut, his right arm without a hand, and the smell of his earlobe when she leaned in, speaking into him over the crowd. Iris set his hook on the bar by her beer. A punk band played over his shoulder. He watched her eyes drift from bass to drummer. She rolled his sleeve back to the bicep, revealing a Norse god blurred at the edges.

"Thor," Eric said.

"You're kidding," Iris said, and crossed her fishnet legs.

"Gods are handy," he said. "If he comes in, I'll introduce you."

"Where'd the hand go?" she said.

"Some raghead's got it," Eric said.

They fucked the first night in her little blue car, yes yes, whatever you want—his hand on her inner thigh, her finger on his defenselessness. She climbed on top.

"What are you?" he said. "You're perfect."

She gazed out the back seat window. The alley, lit by a security spotlight, was only average filthy, beer-can scent and rotting fish. Puget Sound sloshed between buildings. The dumpster was empty. The garbage strike was finally over.

"Let's run away," she said. "To some big shiny life."

He crawled out from under.

"A big life," he said. "Someplace big."

His father had said, *Think big or stay home*, one then another apartment in the projects.

She got pregnant the third or fourth time.

The car had dents in the fender, cracked and wilting wiper blades.

"I couldn't find the pills," she said.

He took the key. He slid into the driver's side. The car had come to her when Great-Aunt Iris died. "She refused to eat," Iris told him. "She pushed the tray of mashed potatoes off the bed, shook her head sorry for the mess, asked for her stash of pills from her political days. Tried to tell me with her eyes where the pills were."

"I want land," he said. "Lots of it."

"Fine," she said.

"The smell of pine."

"Wonderful."

She strapped the seat belt over her belly, pulled the visor to block the sun. They left Seattle.

"We'll buy it from an old man with whiskers," he said. "Shotgun on the porch, dogs in the yard."

She petted the bristles on his neck. "Just get me out of here."

The road crossed into Canada, cut through a thousand miles of mountains, then a thousand more of marshy flat, a continent of black spruce. Her earrings hung to her clavicles. They swung at ruts, knocked her jawbone.

Dead bugs slicked the windshield. They stopped at creeks to scrub the glass. "I want a hot tub," she said, knee-deep in ferns. "I want sliding doors to the patio."

"You will be a queen," he said.

They crossed out of Canada at Beaver Creek, which consisted of low, scanty prefab clusters. Border City was smaller. A gas pump and an American flag. The road was potholes and humps with washed-out places. The land was too wide for cameras. Signs on gravel roads pointed to national parks she'd never heard of. They passed log cabins and stick-frame houses with airstrips and small planes in driveways. They passed Moose Creeks, Bear Creeks, Bad Luck Rivers. They passed teepee gift shops with split-rail fences and twenty-foot chiefs standing with hatchets, warpath feathers, and painted foreheads, cheeks, and noses—gold, white, and blue—their right hands raised in peace signs.

She sniffed the big sky stretching to the far-off mountains. "I don't smell anything."

Telephone poles were very thin men walking in line.

Trees were trees. Trees. Trees.

"Who could live in all this *nothing*?" she said.

"The pioneers," he said.

The tire blew at Tok. She handed him a lug wrench. He lay on the shoulder. They rolled the tire to the liquor store, past a double-wide church, a hardware store, and a tiny pet shop CLOSED FOR THE SEASON. They shared a bottle of rum on the step. An Athabaskan boy patched the puncture. He was slow to speak, to answer questions.

"I don't think he likes us," Iris said, sipping backwash.

Eric spat at the gravel between his boots. "Why would he?"

They'd heard land was two hundred an acre near Delta. They borrowed the money from Iris's mother. "We'll pay back every penny."

They bought eighty acres with a butte at half price. Iris wanted the butte for the view.

"An impossible driveway," the real estate agent warned, but he'd come from California.

Eric bought dynamite. On weekends, he rented a pile driver and bored holes, set fuses behind boulders. A neighbor came with a Bobcat and cleared the rubble. "No better reason for a party," he said and slapped the backs of new arrivals. Others brought shovels and earplugs. They sat on tailgates, muddy boots dangling.

More people arrived. Blasting rock walls for new roads seemed the best kind of entertainment. Iris stood on the double yellow lines with the other onlookers. They all knew each other. There were few cars, but the cars that came flashed their brights, slowed, and asked Iris her due date.

One neighbor woman came on foot, appeared through the trees, up the trail from the glacier. Her kids followed, scattered.

"Blast away," the woman said. "Welcome to the neighborhood."

Trucks pulled in. Engines ticked and cooled. Evening was blue, full of blast dust.

"Need a hand?" someone called.

Eric waved his hook. She'd never seen him laugh like that.

"My advice," said the woman, pointing at Iris's belly. "School that baby at home. No one comes to Alaska for other people's opinions. Learn to love moose and salmon."

The woman slugged Coke from a two-liter bottle. She swatted her kids when they begged for a sip. The sun was pink well after dinnertime. Scorched leaves, pulverized rock, sweat, bug spray, a whiff of sulfur. It was still midsummer, but new snow dusted the peaks and saddles.

"You like it here yet?" the woman said.

"I hate bugs," Iris said.

"Too bad for you," said the woman.

"We're living in a tent," Iris said.

"Everyone starts in a tent."

The woman offered Coke, and Iris drank some. When parts of the wall exploded, the noise echoed off distant cliffs. Men leaped and laughed in the showers of dust.

"All the quiet's the hardest getting used to," said the woman. "And if you don't like trees, best divorce him now."

"I like trees," Iris said.

A trooper rolled by. Men leaned in his window, played with his radio.

"Dark winters," the woman said. "Some people blow their brains out. Drink."

"I don't mind the dark," Iris said. "We get along."

"Don't get fat," said the woman. "Don't get ugly."

They swatted mosquitoes. They sat in lawn chairs at midnight. The sun rolled across serrated peaks. Kids leaned under hoods in headlights. They poured jugs of water on steaming engines. They threw snowballs from patches left in ditches. Eric in the middle of everything, pointing and directing—taller than ever before, she thought.

They were drinking coffee at six. Someone had brought a potful from the lodge. The woman was counting kids, finally heading home. A happy, tired family.

"Why in hell do you live here?" Iris said.

"Come see my glacier," said the woman.

⚬ —— ⚬

Once, Great-Aunt Iris apprehended a masked intruder, cornered him in the bathroom with a dog and mop. He dropped his sack. She cuffed him with antique handcuffs, Berliners with an oval-key top. She marched him though the yard. In the garage, she duct-taped him to a chair by the mower, round and round till the roll ran out. She locked the door. After twenty-four hours she let him go but didn't uncuff him. He smelled of piss and shit. She pressed twenty dollars in his pocket.

She said, "Never try such nonsense again!"

⚬ —— ⚬

The chainsaw was designed for handless veterans by the VA. When Eric signed for the crate at the PO, he thanked the clerk, refused help getting it to the truck. The blade sliced trees along the easement. He walked behind it, kicked the rounds apart with his heel. He counted trees until he stopped counting. If his father ever came to visit, the old man would approve of the overall plan. He'd approve of Iris too, since his father preferred tall women, said small-women men got it all wrong since a tall woman fits best, pushes back, enjoys herself. His father would never make the trip, Eric knew. He watched Iris drag the slash to the burn pit. The baby napped on a stump in the car seat.

The house Eric built was a shack at first, stick frame. A generator for light, wood for heat, and a gate round the woodstove. He dreamed up names for the parcel: Irisville. Iris Junction. At first, they played chase in the trees, rode the dogsled when the snow got good, ate goat cheese until the goat died. He got part-time work with the state troopers. Wolves at night. Bears. Coyotes. The second child was a girl. The mud was worse than imagined. Iris's city clothes were ruined quickly, her earrings lost. Before the well, they bathed in a lean-to by the creek: fire, suds, and steam on rock.

"There's no way to get cleaner," Eric said in a cloud.

They sponged each other's backs, rinsed with water from plastic jugs.

"I want running water," she said, pushed out the flap into the snow, walked to the house naked but for boots and the baby.

"Snowing again," said the boy, stepping carefully in his mother's tracks, followed by Eric, who crushed her footprints with his big wide boots.

The floor was often unswept. The laundromat was thirty miles. He had believed she would be a better mother—canned jam and aprons—and that motherhood would make her softer. Her belly softened. Her hips widened. He saw her kneel, sometimes, take the boy's head in her hands, and whisper to him. The boy laughed and touched his ear for more. A good sign, Eric thought. Sometimes he found them curled like cats, the baby in the middle of the bed. They looked up at him, the intruder.

"Of course they love me," she told him. "Of course I know how."

Bugs blackened the screens all summer, a patient army—drumming, drumming. Let us in. On their chains out in the trees, the dogs whined.

"Poor things," Iris said as she dragged out the dog food.

Eric carried a bucket of water in each fist.

"Use your mind," he said. "Block out the minutiae."

He watched the bag spill when she dropped it, then Iris running from dog to dog, slapping herself, slapping the dogs, bugs flying up from their naked noses, Iris swatting, "Get the hell away from us!"

She missed traffic, bus exhaust and smog, and the burning rubber at car crashes. She missed urine-scented doorways, nail-polish remover, perfume aisles.

"Damn it," Eric said. "Think of all we do have."

She let the hippies at the creek braid her hair. They rubbed her feet, and she rubbed theirs, though she was no expert. They hopped across the creek to dry-topped boulders. They crouched and talked about the water shortage. She rocked the baby, who had colic, lifted her blouse to give the mouth a nipple. They offered medicinal herbs for the colic. The king salmon rested below the falls. The biggest were four feet long, turning red, mouths frowning, almost panting.

"Spawn till you die," said a man with a blond braid, watching her.

The boy threw a big stick that floated by the kings. The fish bumped each other at the disturbance.

Iris kissed the baby, who rejected the nipple, cried and cried.

The boy covered the nipple with her blouse.

She smiled at the hippies and kissed the baby, saying, "Sometimes I want to throw this baby out the window."

The hippies approved of the cliffs, pointed to notches where clever birds lived.

Potatoes grew in a line of old tires. In September, the last month he could take his shirt off, Eric flipped the tires and dug. His father had died by then. Eric didn't go to the funeral. "The flight is six hundred," he said, but thought, Dad would not have come to mine. He imagined his own burial, in his own woods, in a grove just off his easement, snug between his trees, no death certificate, no cemetery fee, no notice in the official record. Why is dying official business? There is nothing more private. The ground was rocky, one foot of dirt then glacial till. Men would wear rain slickers around the grave—women and babies, umbrellas. The potatoes filled five burlap sacks. They would last through April.

She hated the outhouse from the beginning. The bed was secondhand and noisy, their pots and pans from garage sales. Her mother sent money for a new couch, but they found a perfectly good one at the dump. They dragged the couch to the car, lifted it onto the roof rack. Eric threw Iris a bungee.

Iris kicked the couch when they brought it in. "I just wanted a goddamned new one."

"You want goddamned water too," Eric said. "A well is twenty-five dollars per foot."

She threw a pillow. They set the couch under the large photo of the polar bear that had stalked his unit six years ago while on maneuvers near Deadhorse.

"Arctic training," he said when new friends came by.

"Get your feet off my table," Iris said to his friends.

"The bear was about to charge," Eric said. "Thirty miles per hour."

The friends stared. The bear looked so alive in its frame, panting pigeon-toed toward the lens, mouth open.

"But why kill him?" Iris said, passing out beers. "Why not shoot high? Just scare him off?"

"Survival of the fittest," Eric said.

"Us or him," said his friends.

"Big man," Iris said. She still wore ruffled cuffs for company. Her skirts were still very short.

"Five years in Alaska," Eric said, "and she's a self-appointed expert on bears."

"Fuck off," she said.

The friends took up the whole couch, which was plaid with ragged piping. They drank home brew until late, unfolded world maps across the plywood. They discussed broadcasts from London, Hamburg, Johannesburg. The friends, like Eric, were trim with tan faces and excellent, brotherly jawlines. The same gene pool, he knew, all the way back to Adam. They discussed at length how The End would begin: sub-Saharan overpopulation, rising oceans, AIDS, peak oil, World War III, Arabs with fusion bombs. Israelis leading the U.S. by the nose. Beware the lemmings. Beware transequatorial migrational patterns. Give us one just one small nuclear bomb: Airmail Moscow. Airmail Baghdad. Beware the rabble pouring north, even now, for oil money, for a free hot lunch: niggers, dykes, welfare mothers.

"I have kids asleep in the next room," Iris said and set her bottle on the counter.

"Lock and load," they said.

They aimed pistol fingers out the window at wetbacks, at drunk Indians.

"I don't give a shit about Mexicans," she said. "But Injun Joe was here first."

"We were stronger," they said.

She stood with a spatula over the couch. Moose roast simmered in the Crock-Pot.

"Sweetheart," Eric said. "We're just having a little fun."

She said, "Keep your voices down."

❧ —— ❧

At first, Iris called the pain in her head "the noxious weed." She asked the kids to massage her head. They pushed hard as they could with their little hands, but not hard enough.

"Squeeze," she told Eric. The kids had gone to bed. She sat on the rug between his knees, his fingers sprawled her head. He could have crushed her skull like a cantaloupe.

"Good, but you could squeeze harder," she said, "*Ich habe Kopfschmerzen.*"

"Since when do you know German?" he said.

"I forgot I knew," she said. "*Tante* spoke it. Czech too. *Bolí mě hlava.* I have a headache."

He braced his stump against her ear. His grip was awkward.

"Say something else," he said.

"Squeeze harder," she said.

❧ —— ❧

The spring health fair in Two Rivers was at the library.

"I smell shit all the time," Iris said, "as if shit's always on my shoe. Follows me."

"Are your kids still in diapers?" the nurse said.

"Not just human shit," Iris said. "Dog shit. Horse shit. Cow shit. Elephant shit."

The nurse wrote a doctor's name on a prescription pad. His office was in Fairbanks. Iris washed her hands in the sink. Outside, Iris blocked the sun with her palm. The kids were high in the tree above the dumpster. "No, no!" Iris called. "Don't go higher!"

"Let them climb," Eric said. "Let them have fun."

He cleaned the dash of the F-350 he'd always wanted, bought on credit, with a grill like teeth and an aerodynamic topper.

The kids climbed farther, chattered higher. Birds pecked seeds in the slushy mud. Eric drove to find a ladder. The kids waved.

Iris sat against the tree's trunk and chewed aspirin. The kids bombed her with pine cones, which rattled around her. She pressed her head against the skin of the tree, rough and wrinkled, old, cool. The kids squealed like gigantic baby birds.

"Quiet!" she called. "I can't stand it!"

"Silly Mommy!" They waved when the ladder appeared. The truck parked grill to dumpster.

"Hold on!" Iris called upward.

❧ —— ☙

When Iris woke blind in one eye, they packed the car again. The woman from the glacier said she'd feed the dogs. Fairbanks was ninety-seven miles. The hospital wards were white and steel. Ophthalmologists peered in. Radiologists injected dyes, studied scans, teleconferenced Anchorage.

"I have children," she told everyone, nurses, doctors. "I have two of them."

They set a pen in Iris's hand to sign papers.

Eric locked the motel door, slipped the chain into place. He made the beds in the morning, smooth and tight, showed the kids how to bounce the quarters. They all ate food from the cooler to save cash. The motel was across a bridge under construction. Small boats floated on the river under backed-up traffic. The cars moved slowly. Iris told the kids stories with her eyes shut: "I thought the thing in my head was a weed, but now I know better. He's a little man in a shabby brown suit with wide stripes and suspenders to hold his pants up. He sat down on my earlobe once. He just planned to take a little snooze."

"When did he come?" said the girl. A motorcycle passed on the shoulder.

"Long ago," Iris said. "The little man thought my ear was a cave. He climbed in. He carried a tent and poles. He's small and well-trained by the best professionals. He likes dark places. He dragged in his old armchair and a folding footstool and an old-fashioned lamp with a pull cord. He likes to play cards by himself. When he smokes a cigar it clouds my eyeballs, fills my nose with puff, puff."

"Will the doctors get him?" said the boy.

"The doctors will get him," Iris said.

"But your mom," Eric said, "has to help the doctors."

"This is the last of it," Iris said. "It's happy happy all the way now."

"I could have bled to death in the war," Eric said. "I didn't allow it."

So they begged her. "Please, Mom. Don't allow it."

After surgery, the doctors were hopeful. Iris went home without an eye patch. Fall was yellow all over and lasted two weeks. She sat in the window and watched the trees. Some days the boy would sit on the metal roof above her, cross-legged, she knew, in the leaves. The steel rivets ran past him in perfect lines. Below, in the yard, the girl played with the dogs, touching this nose, then that scruff. If Eric arrived, he'd yell at the girl, "Get those dogs on chains. Loose dogs kill people's chickens. Where's your brother? Where's your mom?" The girl had a small face with a dark circle under each eye.

But the chickens were miles away, safe in coops. The window was cool. Iris could feel the boy overhead, very still, watching birds, watching a moose cow, her calf curled in weeds. The cow flicked her ears when the boy moved to a cool spot. The cow chewed slowly. A dog ran off toward the highway. The girl called out. The moose rose at the commotion. The calf's legs were impossible, tall and thin, bent at angles for winter locomotion. The girl waded into brush after the dog. The moose trotted off, not looking back.

No one could see the boy on the roof. No one in the world knew his location.

When the girl gave up, she stood in the yard again. Someday she would be taller than her brother. She was almost taller now. Someday, she would tell her brother what to do. When the girl stood on the porch, she called at the door. Then she banged the door, tried the knob.

⚓ —— ⚓

Iris always preferred scalding water. Their bathtub was shallow, secondhand from a hotel gone under and dismantled. She submerged anyway, blew out ripples.

"Look," she said, holding her head. "They scalped me."

Eric sat on the toilet lid. "That head of yours is getting expensive."

He tried to remember that first night, but her face was missing from the scene, though her dress was intact and her legs and her hand on his skin, though the barstool spun just right, though the punk band sweated and mouthed words, between the lyrics, only to each other. What was the whispering about? What was the big secret? The boy resembled her. The girl had her sideways glances. If Thor arrived, he'd sniff the bar soap at the sink. His golden costume would fill the small bathroom. His headpiece would bump the light bulb in the ceiling. Instant darkness.

Eric said, "You've got to try harder."

She spat pink water. "Why wouldn't I try? Life is so wonderful."

Her nose was bleeding. She held her nostrils for the next dip under. Great-Aunt Iris had drowned baby rabbits as a girl before the Second Great War. A barrel, a bucket, and a long wooden spoon—all that kicking, fussing, and overflowing.

"Never trust doctors," Great-Aunt Iris often said. "Many doctors at Auschwitz."

Iris counted the seconds underwater. Twenty, thirty, fifty.

She focused on the little man. A tidal wave would surely drown him, would flood every orifice, prevent his advance across the landscape with clever maneuvers, strategic crossings, access to overlooks and tunnel entrances, shacks set aflame, bread from babies, horses slaughtered for roasting. She could stay under longer, until the armchairs rode up in waves, tumbled with footstools, solitaire cards floated like fish with maps of troop movements, generals' wish lists, love letters signed in blood by aging countesses back home, balled up, some partly burned during late-night horseplay.

"This has nothing to do with doctors," he said as she resurfaced. Her head was just a small balloon. He said, "Concentrate."

She dipped away again.

Did you never want children, Tante?

Qviet now, my best girl. I dislike your complaining.

Her nose bubbled the waterline. Eric pressed her stubbled head.

∝ —— ℘

Winter came. Summer. Fall again.

The nosebleeds, the doctors said, had brought on the anemia. The anemia in turn produced the fainting spells, the blow to the head against the porch step, during which the little man was planting rancid onions, and others dipped along the forest fringes—warriors, lean, crouched in feathers. She found an arrowhead, tasted the tip.

Three days of vomiting followed the concussion, aspiration leading to a lung infection. Fever. Anchorage was eight hours driving, ninety dollars in gas. Her bare legs dangled from the high metal table. The gown was tied behind her back.

"I know exactly where he is," Iris said, as her fingers pinched like tweezers at her temple. "If I could only get my hand in, I'd rip him out."

"If it's spreading," the doctors said, "there may be other symptoms."

Eric stood by the clock with a shuddering minute hand that never moved forward. He followed the doctors out.

"What symptoms?" he said. "What's possible?"

The doctors talked like TV people. Their coats were just cotton smocks, their necks weak, never in the sun. Double chins in their early forties. Eric had been trained to kill with one hand. A rope. A rock. Rubber tubes hung from their collars.

"*Vaše hodiny jsou rozbité!*" she called after them. "Your clock is broken."

They were all talking in the hall.

"*Vaše hodiny jsou rozbité! Vaše hodiny jsou rozbité!*"

A nurse came with a sedative.

❦ —— ❧

The next winter, Eric attended men's meetings in North Pole at the middle school put on by an affiliate of the VFW. Sometimes he was gone all night.

The men held hands in circles. The chairs were plastic, round tables with pads of paper and pens in four colors. He was familiar, he told them, with casualties of many kinds. By bullet or trip wire, a knife in the back, friendly fire, land mine, IED under the tire, rubber as weapon. He'd read all the literature on death, pain, and phantom limbs. The men nodded. Some wore ill-fitting uniforms. Some were thin and limped. They agreed war casualties seemed accidental, indiscriminate, that specific intent was lacking in war.

"She was tall at first, a willow," he told them. His love could not be described. When a man said, "I know the feeling," Eric wanted to crack his teeth.

"She's become strange," Eric said. "Lavish."

The men murmured.

He told them about Seattle, the mother, her checkbook, envelopes with twenty-dollar bills.

"Spoiled," said one of them. The men shifted positions in their chairs.

He talked about the hippie camp down at the creek, Reiki and drumming circles, Iris smelling of liquor and weed.

"Some are predisposed to suffering," they agreed in general. "Some give into it."

"Sickness is a form of tyranny," they nodded. "Some people can't stick with name, rank, serial number."

"Most people are cowards."

"Right."

"Think of the gas chambers," they said. "The Nazis. Those Jews walked right in. What kind of people would walk right in?"

"Sheep."

"Hitler got a few things right," they said.

Eric shook his head, as if waking up.

"Wait a minute," some said.

"Humans are sons of bitches," Eric said, and they agreed heartily.

"Man, let's think bigger," they said. "Let's try to *understand* all this."

"Assassinations are cleansing."

"Jefferson said: Revolution every ten years."

They discussed ambush and sacrifice and the most expressive targets: the Pipeline, the Valdez Terminal, the Space Needle.

"Talk, talk, talk," Eric said.

He showed them his missing hand, told them how he'd bled out in a slow puddle from stretcher to airlift to the Gulf to sick bay to Frankfurt, then undergone sequential truncations to the elbow. They went around the circle showing scars.

They wrote *What's Needed Is Conviction* on the chalkboard, more each week:

> Are YOU still Evolving?
> Fuck, yeah, I'm Evolving.
> Beware the Lazy. Beware the Conquered.
> Kiss My Fat White American Ass!
> Ha! Ha! Amen brothers!
> Axes. Deserts. Capillary action.
> Death of Darwin = Death of God.
> So few truly SEE. So few truly LOVE.
> I can SEE. I can LOVE.
> Build The Ark. Build it soon.
> Pitchforks,
> Spears.

Hand-to-hand.

The chaplain came to clean the chalkboard. They built fires by the swing set after.

They gripped the chains in calloused hands.

"Higher! Higher!" Eric called.

He breathed in smoke and willow leaves unfolding.

When her arm went limp, Anchorage called the Mayo Clinic.

Summer again.

Eric called a friend who wanted twenty acres. "I hate to see one inch of it go."

They shook hands over beer at the lodge. The friend also bought the little blue car.

Sycamores arched over Minnesota. Crickets sang. Bats swooped, ate bugs until their bellies filled. Fireflies glowed but were outshined by the heliport. They sat on benches with gold plaques. A helicopter angled in. The wind made talking impossible. The spotlight wagged across the lawn, its fresh-cut scent mixing with ambulance exhalations. Screaming sirens, billboards for fast-food discounts, hedge clippings.

Iris's mouth said, "I love the smell of it."

Eric's mouth said, "I still love you too, of course."

They sold more land to pay the bills, first seventeen acres along the rock wall, then three wet acres to some hippies, then ten more, including the butte, to a lawyer and his pregnant wife. The doctors gave Iris a thumbs-up and said, "Most likely remission." Two years went like that.

They got married finally at the courthouse in Delta. Eric got a contract with a road crew, union wages. He showed the kids maps of the world, told them about the Founding Fathers and building railroads and riding trains in the Great Depression, breadlines and the CCC, big dams and bootstraps, oil fields and rags to riches. Shackleton. Apollo. Desert Storm.

"You choose who you are," he said. "Bear or mouse."

He told stories of King Odin and his wife Frigg, daughter of the earth. How Tyr's hand was bitten off by Loki's son, the crafty wolf.

"Why?" said the boy, who watched his mother chewing like a rabbit.

"This wolf was always making trouble," Eric said. "So the gods tied him with a magic chain made of strange materials: footfall of cat, beards of women, roots of stones, breath of fishes, feelings of bears, and spittle of birds."

The girl sometimes wore her brother's clothes, baggy with rolled-up sleeves. "I'd kick the wolf in the teeth," said the girl. "I'd cut his tail off."

"Finish your dinners," Iris said. "Stop chewing like that," she said to the boy.

The boy crouched in the top bunk. The girl took her father's maps to bed with a flashlight. Eric came. He sat on his daughter's mattress with the maps. The nations outlined themselves in the continents, scissored along in lines. Africa could shove Spain into Lithuania if he wished it. His fist could ball up all of South America with Antarctica, the penguins tossed over Russia, past China and Guam, losing speed as the ocean cooled near Anchorage, where a tsunami might hit and wash all the paper to Vancouver Island, or New York City, or Sydney.

"I hate war," Eric told them. He folded the map, and the boy dropped down. "But evil marches on." Handouts. Bloodsucking majorities. He rocked them until they wiggled free.

Eric talked on about the Blitz, the lessons of Hiroshima, Vietnam, facts from their nearly complete Britannica. Sarin gas in unsuspecting subways, he said. Letter bombs, shoe bombs as reported on the ham radio. "Jets," he said. "Women and children," he told them. "The whole earth on the edge of collapse. Just a few safe places. We still own thirty acres."

He paced the tiny room. "Your mom is better. We won't have to leave here."

The kids on the couch or porch step, eating cookies or legs of meat, telling their dad that it would be OK.

The neighbors brought caribou in freezer paper. Iris fed it to the dogs. The hippie camp pulled up stakes, moved south with their guitars and looms. She cleaned school bathrooms for extra cash, took toilet paper home in her coat, blue sloshing antiseptic cleaners, wire brushes, bleach in jugs.

Were we rich when you lived in Prague? she sometimes asked on her knees to a toilet.

Ja. Ja. Very rich.

What kind of car? to the sinks, to the rusted pipes. *A chauffeur?*

A Bugatti. Papa owned half of Prague vhen they took him.

Iris shoveled dog shit into the wheelbarrow, dumped the pile in the trees. Some days were hot. She could smell the pile from the lodge. She went to see people. To read the Anchorage paper, the back pages. Items for sale. Items wanted:

> (1) Pallet king crab WANTED. Fresh only. Need Sat.
>   for BIG wedding.
> Circus tickets (4) WANTED.
> Firewood. Firewood.

Did we eat caviar? Veal?

Vhy eat fish eggs?

Both Irises laughed with open mouths.

Iris plucked aphids from tomatoes in the kitchen window. The faucet was leaking. She rolled their fragile bodies between thumb and finger.

But what about me? to the faucet. *What about me, is what I want to know.*

But for Herr Hitler, said the faucet. *You are very rich foreign lady.*

What else?

But for Herr Hitler, fancy hats, fine clothes, best cafés in all of Prague.

What else?

But for Herr Hitler. Clap your hands, vaiters come running. Filet mignon, dipped in garlic butter. Palačinke with jam. Duck à l'orange.

Iris smelled opal brooches and first-class berths on ocean liners, Persian rugs up grand stairways toward twenty-foot ceilings with frescoes painted by old, bent peasants who arrived through the servants' entrance.

She hated the generator fumes always in the kitchen.

"Can't you smell it? Diesel."

"We can't smell it," Eric said. "We don't smell anything."

A mask made no difference. Nor did bandannas or cross-ventilation.

Iris walked up a butte behind their house for better breathing and the overlook. She left the kids with the satellite TV clicker. "Don't burn the house down," she said, and slung a jacket on, the dogs yelping on their chains. She walked slowly up. She knew the trail, where pasqueflowers popped up in May, where ferns unwound at tree line, where the chocolate lilies appeared each August by heat of soil, by angle of sun, by urgency to *get it done*, to rise from the bulb, to bloom for the feet of bees—bulbs that had been boiled like rice in pots by Athabaskan women on their knees, over fires, behind rocks on windy overlooks. She rested at the top. The beholder owns all of it. Mine. Mine. Mine. Where did the women disappear to? Where do all the gone-people go?

When Iris called her mother, she said, "Can I come home?"

She'd tried the PO clerk, who wore spicy cologne. He slid parcels sly across the counter. He was a cautious lover with a skinny cock, was transferred to Kodiak. She tried other men while the kids were at school: the tribal judge, the telephone man, the Mormon boy with all those books.

Eric found a letter from the clerk. He picked up the mail after that.

He signed for heavy wooden crates from Blessed Be Ammo of Coeur d'Alene, from Don't Tread on Me, Inc., of Billings. He stacked the crates in the shed along with large spools of wire, clock parts, a Taurus revolver in a black case, a Kevlar vest. Eric walked the perimeter of his land with the dogs. At that time, he made small bombs only: PVC pipe, nails, and gunpowder, tested on the rock wall by the road. His hair grew long, and he tied it back. He invited his friends for food and fires, enormous flames between the trees.

"Want to know why I did it?" Iris said in bed one night.

"I don't," Eric said. He opened a book on submarines.

"I still like your cock," she said and torpedoed down to it.

"Stop it," he said, and his elbow deflected her. "I'm tired."

"If it wasn't for your cock," she said, "I'd take the kids and go to Europe. I'd go to my homeland, go on the dole."

"You'd never go on the dole," he said.

"White chocolate," she said. "Chandeliers."

When she thought of the little brown-suited man, he stood alone on a mound in the woods. The forest had surrounded him somehow. The woods were dark and terrible, enemies of low grasses, of high trees. They made great sounds in their wooden language. The forest crawled forward on dirty elbows.

They dug a garden. Everyone dug one.

"I hate dirt," she said, digging.

They caught red salmon in dip nets in the Copper River as the Athabaskan had, but zipped into reflective life vests. They tied up with ropes to sturdy trees, scrambled down to back eddies and submerged the nets. They knocked the fish between the eyes with sawed-off pipes, slit the bellies from the anus, strung the gills still breathing. The mountains were mounds of dumb purple. The sky was pale and cool, the sun somewhere too low to see. She squatted with the pole between her legs. Her rope to the tree was taut and sticky.

"I hate salmon," she said. "I hate the smell of it."

Eric hauled in his dip net hand over hand. He scrambled up the rocks and stood at the tree. He cleaned the knife with a glove. He looked down on her at the river. Her pole was bowed by pulling water. Whole huge trees seesawed by. She wore rubber waders, a hat, a too-big sweater. She might have been a small sad man, he thought. Her rope to the tree knotted at his hip. If the rope failed, he knew, she'd be swept away quickly. Such cases made headlines each year. Her waders would fill. She'd sink fast, glacial silt clotting in the boots. Her body would be found by the bird dogs of Cordova, or by the fry of the delta, sunning themselves in the brackish pools, or by big fish out at sea, jack kings, halibut down deep, or sleeper sharks wagging at the surface, swimming toward her dispersing molecules. From how far could a shark find her? He didn't know. One mile? Ten?

The wind picked up and took her hat.

"Come eat," he called. "The fish will be ready."

He slipped the knife into its leather.

⁂ — ⁂

She got thinner and bluer again. She stayed inside, lost track of most seasons. Winter nights showed every nebula. The dogs barked at every sound. Why bother trying to sleep?

Were you really a communist? Iris asked at night to a shadow at the window.

She'd been reading Karl Marx in bed. She weighed a hundred and ten. They'd sold the truck but still had payments, hitch and winch, trailer, canoe. She rolled joints for nausea, snuffed stubs in a teacup on the bedside table.

Vhy not communist? Everyone eats. Everyone shares.

A Red? A real Pinko?

Tante Iris rolled her sleeve, stuck her arm in the window. Iris examined the tattooed numbers.

Eric rolled over.

What else? Iris said.

But for Herr Hitler, you vas never born in this country.

What else?

But for Herr Hitler, you speak many languages.

What else?

But for Herr Hitler, you never meet that man there. Never become barbarian.

What else?
No children.
What else?
No sickness.
What else?
You know vat else.

◆ — ◆

They ordered a wheelchair when her legs quit. She retched in a bucket beside Karl Marx. Her eyebrows disappeared, lashes, pubic hair.

"I vant to sail by steamship to Prague," she said on the toilet.

"Stop it," Eric said, covering his ears.

Irisitis. Irisoma. Iritosis.

In the last autumn, he took a job pouring concrete in Delta, bought posts and wire at cost. The ground was still soft enough for digging. He cut the signs from scrap plywood. The kids painted NO TRESPASSING on every one, with black trim too. He nailed the signs up, but people don't like to obey. When a four-wheeler skidded up the road, Eric stepped in the center to block its path.

"Can I help you, sir?"

"This your place?" The stranger lifted his visor. He popped pink peppermint gum.

"Yes, mine," Eric said, leaning on the posthole digger.

"Sixty? Hundred?" the stranger said. "I'm looking."

The sun drifted into a cloud.

The visor snapped down. The engine revved. The rig shifted to reverse.

The stranger will be back, Eric thought as the exhaust dissipated. But first he'll rocket straight to the lodge for a beer. *Who's that son of a bitch on the hill?* he'll say. *Some kind of claw for a hand.*

He has a hook too, the owner of the lodge will say. *Your tax dollars working.*

The little man in the corner will look familiar, the wide collar and suspenders. The stranger will eat peanuts.

A skeleton wife, the barmaid will say. *Screwed every guy in town and then some. Talks a little Kraut now.*

The little man will buy drinks all around. *Raise your glasses to a fire sale.*

Eric stepped off the driveway, back to his fence. A bird sat on a post he'd been working on.

"Shoo," he said and javelined a hoe.

The bird sat, white and black and smaller than an apple.

He tore off his claw and flung it at the bird.

"Get out of here!"

❦ —— ❦

"How'd he come back?" the boy said. He locked the door and stood at the window. The house was small now that the kids were bigger. The couch was torn on all three cushions. The bear was dusty in afternoon sun. The girl wore the new blonde wig, passed it to the boy.

"A seed?" said the girl.

Iris nodded. She wore her daughter's feather boa and a plastic tiara.

"*Knoflík mu upadl z bundy když ho vytáhli*," Iris said, tugging a sweater button.

"A button popped off his coat?" said the girl. "As they pulled him out? Surgery?"

Iris nodded.

"Don't lie," said the boy, now wearing the wig.

"My head is full of shit," Iris said, holding it. "All our heads are full of shit."

"Don't lie," the boy said.

"Give me the wig," said the girl, trying to snatch it.

"Don't talk like that," Eric said as he stood over boiling noodles.

They ate slowly. They did not eat.

"Sometimes I wish it was you," she said, looking around her.

The boy set his fork down. Eric stood. The girl stabbed a noodle, dragged it.

The boy would count massacres. The girl would be taller than anyone. She would tell them all what to do.

"If it was us," Eric said, "it would be all different."

"Don't lie," the boy said.

"Give me the wig," said the girl, but he slapped her hand.

That night Iris burned the cookbooks. She stirred pills in his tea in the morning. Eric drank it and slept all day. The concrete boss fired him. She unplugged the clock by the bed.

He filed for unemployment. He went to the toilet after, saw his father's shoes in one of the stalls.

He knew in olden times they'd have summoned a healer to their thatched hut. They'd have paid the hag a ducat or traded a chicken and received a potion: *Drink this, my pet, and I promise you many long years yet.* In olden times the warriors would have marched off the ship and charged ashore, outnumbered and outmaneuvered. Death was quick and good: a short, fast run across the cow pasture, lance in hand. Call out! Pound the chest! Draw the attention of a well-aimed arrow!

Great-Aunt Iris once had a dog. The dog had an ear infection. She cooked garlic for a cure in an iron pan, dabbed the garlic in the ear with a swab. The dog suffered on. It was old. She found her stash of pills in an old canvas shoulder holster. She wrapped a pill in fine French cheese. The dog sniffed. The dog ate. Forest circled in. But now dark and comfortable. His fire on the mound was only glowing. The mound was just a pile of dirt.

But aren't you sad, Tante?

My family, of course. I never found them.

But the beautiful closets?

But I'm alive. Iris gave Iris a truffle. *Herr Hitler, he could not kill me.*

›—‹

The bills arrived at the PO. The property was sold in increments of five and ten. The house was sold by an agent. Loose change was collected at the lodge in pickle jars: HELP A NEIGHBOR with Iris's picture.

The last yard sale was muddy with flurries, early summer. People came anyway. Bunk beds, wheelbarrow, Crock-Pot. A girl bought Iris's red rubber boots. The chainsaw and dogs were priced to move. Eric made change on the step. If Thor arrived, he'd crush the house with a boot. Burn it. From a tree the boy counted rivets on the roof. His arm was broken from a fall. The girl played chase with the dogs until a kennel truck came, ran after the truck until it drove out of view, dust up her bare legs. Iris napped on the couch with a price sticker in her wig.

Eric packed the boxes into her mother's car. Iris rode in the back seat, a new old woman. The polar bear stood on its head beside her, both buckled in, the kids in front.

One wooden crate was buried in the trunk. He left the others with a friend.

"We'll see the Space Needle," said the girl. She wore the Kevlar vest.

"Yes," said Eric.

They splashed south.

Once Tante Iris caught the FBI in her yard, a little man in brown.

She shook her pistol at him. She said, "Strip down to undershorts."

She took his pants, coat, and shirt. She burned them in the rabbit barrel, stirred the fire with an old paddle. The man stood shivering, early spring, very damp, now smoky. The sky was blue, friendly.

"I have a wife and family like anyone," he said. "This is just a job."

She was not in a rush. She told him about Prague. Still a nice city, a very good old bridge with musicians playing the rims of goblets. Hymns and show tunes.

"Painters making tourist pictures," she said. "Friendly beggars." Buildings spared from Allied bombing. "Thank Gott," she said. "But alvays summer in America."

The man coughed.

She said, once, after the war, she'd returned to her father's block in Prague. Smoke billowed from the stacks above the curlicued rooflines, locked doors, feathered heads in her father's windows, some kind of powwow.

She'd paced the sidewalk with a sign for the residents: THIS IS MINE! EVERYONE OUT!

"But no one goes," she said to the little man. "Everyone stays."

Her garden was only tiny fingerlings. Breeze tossed them, merciless. She bent over, weeding, swinging her body between rows. Even the tiniest weeds stood no chance.

"I don't want to be a pest," the little man said. "But I'd like to go home."

"Ja, Ja," she said. "I get blanket now."

She wrapped him in a musty blanket. He walked out the gate with edges dragging.

She waved. "Goodbye, goodbye, goodbye!"

PTERODACTYL

The plan was to meet Larry at baggage claim. But Larry sent a stand-in, some nephew, or that was the story, with sideburns too long and a belt buckle too gold, looking borderline, like a wanted poster. At the baggage carousel, he turned his back on Pete, huddled to his ancient phone, whispered into it, didn't offer to take Pete's duffel, asked for a twenty at the parking exit gate. Pete peeled a bill from his wallet.

They drove around a bit, the freeway, got gas. Pete filled the tank with his credit card. The nephew talked to friends under the flat roof of the diesel island. It never rained here. Sand swirled on the concrete. A neon cactus blinked an ALL NIGHT sign.

"Pay you back," said the nephew. He smoked by the pumps, offered Pete a puff.

"Where's Larry?" Pete said. A gecko blocked the security camera lens.

"Soon," said the nephew. "Very soon."

They stopped for milk and bread.

"You don't look a thing like Larry," said Pete.

"Ha ha," said the nephew. "Neither do you."

The apartment was on the first floor. A metal stairway wound up to the same places forever. The nephew offered Pete cola and toast. He took a shower while Pete searched the cabinets, pawed the drawers under the TV console for any trace of Larry, any proof, one of his fly rods, for example, or one of the very flies Pete had tied himself—the woolly booger in olive, irresistible to rainbows, that Larry had stolen on the Madison in '86—or Larry's brand of Scotch, or any scrap on Department letterhead, or a pair of Charlotte's socks or frilly underthings. When he found a Ziploc of white powder stuffed under the kitchen sink, he dialed Larry, hung up without awaiting an answer, then made another call. When the cops kicked the door in, he'd not taken his coat off. He stood behind the sliding glass on the balcony, watched them tackle the nephew in a towel, crushing the coffee table.

He climbed over the railing into the bushes, ran fast away, an anonymous informant. He rested behind a dumpster on the open field behind the apartment. Vegas was famous for such petty crime, a major stop in the artery of ugliness flowing north from Mexico to all down-and-out USA. Headlines were of course the tip of the iceberg and petty civilians must occasionally transact with the evil. Macro meets micro. Tough love was tough. If the nephew was legit Larry would bail him out in the morning. He'd be late, as usual, for conference registration at the Luxor.

Cops have no interest in walkers. He took off walking, enjoying the night air.

The grasses were really weeds but he thought of the High Plains where he and Larry had done their best digging, before Charlotte, the toe joint of the Camarasaurus, an entire intact Hypsilophodon. He stumbled over a bag of trash, but ouch, it was just a stray cactus. He kicked the cactus away. This was what people did now. The cops flashed their Maglites from the balcony into the grasses, lithium, he guessed, since the beams turned the grasses blue. Pete crouched low and listened to the walkie-talkies talk fingerprints. His duffel sat in the nephew's trunk, his conference packet, his shaving kit. He felt for his wallet.

He ran when the Maglites swung away. He crossed a street into an enormous parking lot. Cars filled it with cheers smeared on back windows: GO GIANTS. GO GOPHERS. He huddled behind a van, then walked quickly to join a boys' soccer team herding through the aisles with families in tow. The athletes were still sweating from their game. He looked like any uncle or a coach in street clothes. Their bus idled with door open and lights on and the group aimed for it. He spoke to the nearest kids about their victory and they went on about the final goal.

"Nice passing tonight," Pete said to a kid at his elbow.

"Thanks, man," said the kid. "I was on fire. All Hollywood."

The group slowed for the police lights, blue and red across the street and open lot. *Drug bust . . . Desperate people . . . Let's go see . . . Not if you want to eat tonight.* But to Pete, from here, the lights looked like inconsequential sparks and the open lot looked scrappy and much less vast. Pete peeled off from the team just before the bus. One kid followed, the Hollywood passer. The bus pulled away without them. When a cop car sirened by, the two dropped to the ground beside a wheel well.

"Hey man," the kid said. "What are we doing?"

The kid was skinny with a buzz cut. In headlights his lips were the color of cherry candy. Very thin. Very dirty. Jeans. Flannel. Boots.

"A little payback," Pete said, eyeing him. "A little fun."

They walked for a while, Pete turning corners and the kid turning too, following.

"Cops after us?" said the kid after several blocks.

"Not even on their radar," Pete said.

"I'm all in," said the kid. "Devotion forever."

They walked flat sandy right angles, cut the hypotenuse through more vacant lots, right angles again, a few playgrounds. The houses were ranches with windows like faces, flat roofs, lawn art, and solar panels. Boulders were painted like turtles and ladybugs and Pete said, "Why can't they leave rocks alone?"

"I could use a fizzy drink," the kid said, sitting on a happy face.

They stopped at a diner on a corner. The place was stucco and brick with big glass roll-up windows, had at some time been a filling station.

"Got money?" said the kid.

Pete slapped his back pocket. "What do you think?"

He was happy. Larry would have to think hard about always being late—flights, fishing, friendship—and now he could help a needy person. He liked contact with the younger generation. This kid would be a son's age. They sat at a booth by the window. The salt and pepper were in packets and the kid tore them open and poured from the corners. He gobbled fried eggs with his face near the plate. He poured sugar direct to his tongue.

"Hungry," said Pete and sipped beer, spectating.

"Extremely," said the kid. When his plate was clean, he went for a platter abandoned on the lunch counter, crusts of grilled cheese, only the centers eaten out, a pile of fries zigzagged with ketchup, and half a sausage patty. He added salt.

"Where are your soccer clothes?" said Pete. "Where are your cleats?"

"I need to get to New York," said the kid.

"I was supposed to meet this friend at the airport."

"A pilot?"

"Punctuality is a choice."

"Can he get me to New York?"

"Larry screwed me over more than once."

"Screw Larry then," said the kid.

The kid started in on grilled cheese, dipped the crusts into tiny jars of jam, arranged the different flavors around his plate. He dropped the extra jars in his pockets.

"Maybe Larry's sick," Pete said.

"He's not sick," said the kid.

"I could call him up, I guess. See what happened."

"Yeah, call the dick up."

The kid ate French fries slowly, one at a time, licked his fingers between each, put his head down on the table to rest once, almost slept, sat up groggy, looked around for the waitress, sipped his drink. He straightened up and got alert for the story Pete was telling about a fishing trip with Larry, the stolen fly on the Madison, then a mistaken slice with the fillet knife, which woke the kid up a hundred percent. A finger. A clinic in Three Forks.

"There are no mistakes. I learned that in reform school. Just kidding."

"Do you play soccer at all?"

"I play all the time."

"Where are your parents?"

"I just need you, *Dad*, to spot me some money."

"The system doesn't work like that."

"Why not? A hundred bucks?"

"When you beg," Pete said, "you hand them power over everything."

"Them?"

"Everyone but you."

"Fine. Let them have it."

"You can't get to New York on a hundred bucks."

"Two hundred then. Perfect."

"I want things too," said Pete. "I don't just get them."

"Why the hell not?" the kid said. Pete didn't have an answer to that one.

"I'm a hypnotist," said the kid, swinging his fork back and forth in front of Pete's face. "Spot the nice boy some cash. Be good to him."

Pete ordered chocolate cake and the kid gave a thumbs-up.

"I see you have a hollow leg," Pete said.

The kid lifted one leg high above the table. "Hollow everything." He lifted the second leg and the two legs can-canned together around overhead until the waitress yelled cut it out from the register. The boots were worn and cracked at the soles, no socks. The kid seemed drunk with food, a runt, delirious with calories and the fluorescent lights shining on his skin. The kid devoured the last of the sausage, dove into the cake when it arrived.

"You can also be a hypnotist," the kid said and ticktocked the fork in front of his own nose. "If you hate Larry. I hate Larry."

"I don't hate Larry, but I don't say no to a little revenge."

"I hear you."

"Larry's always late, bossing people on the job. Like someone made him king. Cheating in small ways."

"Who doesn't?"

"He stole my girl, that's all," Pete said. "I don't hate him in the least for doing that."

"I love Larry then," the kid said, licking the fork, cross-eyed. "I would suck Larry's dick if he was here right now."

Pete ordered another beer. The kid ordered a refill.

"I could give you a ten," said Pete when his foam settled.

"Not enough," said the kid. "I'll go find Larry or some guy like him."

"Can we get off this broken record?" said Pete.

The kid saluted. "Anything for you, captain."

"Here's the thing, if you want to understand about Larry," Pete said.

"Tell me the thing."

"He got the girl, Charlotte. I told you."

"A love triangle," the kid said.

"But he used my sudden situational disadvantage to his advantage."

"Oh please," said the kid. "Tell me another one. I haven't heard such a good one in a long while."

"Do you want to understand the thing or not?" Pete said, and the kid waved him on. Once when Larry and he were younger people, they were on a Department project in New Mexico and he was in a sour mood and he had walked up a sandy hill near the work site, leaving this new girl, Charlotte, back at camp with Larry and the rest of the Department. He'd walked up a trail to this hilltop, a 360° view to cool off at the summit—something Larry had said about his carbon dating estimates, his calculations—and this camp pet had tagged along with him up the switchbacks. It lived in a mound just off the kitchen tent, a semiwild rodent that followed the scientists around, no dogs allowed, so people missed their dogs, kind of a stand-in, a symbiotic relationship with the camp, a marmot hybrid of some kind, domesticated, with a name like Mack or Joe, now forgotten, but noted in the camp log by a succession of teams working there for years.

"Camp rat?" said the kid, sitting up. "I know this one."

"The death was a red flag for Charlotte, I'm sure of it. Picked Larry instead of me."

"Charlotte picked Larry because of natural selection in the desert?"

"On my watch. But worse than that. Astounding."

"Mr. Wonderful."

"There's nothing wrong with me," Pete said.

The kid continued with the cake, asked color and size of the rat, how it died, rolled his eyes, said, "You of course had carried your big stick with you. Your weapon for protecting small defenseless friends."

"It's the desert," Pete said. "There aren't sticks just lying around."

"Sticks are everywhere."

Pete sipped his beer, watched the kid, a new animation.

"As are giant lizards," said the kid. "Coyotes. Cougars."

"It came from the sky. A huge winged thing. The rest is not table talk."

"Come on, man. Finish it."

"Another broken record."

"A hawk? An eagle?"

"I don't know why I started this with you," said Pete.

"Tell me about the huge winged thing," said the kid, leaning in. "Condor?"

"Bigger."

"Great horned owl?"

"Bigger."

"Vulture."

"Bigger."

"Is this story really true?" the kid said.

"Of course it's true," Pete said and the beer sloshed and Pete mopped the slosh with his cuff by the button, licked the cuff. "I know exactly what it was."

"What's bigger than a vulture?" said the kid. He was really thinking.

"I dig them up," Pete said. "Impossible that it was what it was."

"Concrete fact?" the kid said.

"I deal only in facts," Pete said. "Bones. Impressions. Data."

"Tell me," the kid said with his fists on the table.

How could Pete tell this kid? That on the hill he had walked and thought *Charlotte*, and taken the switchbacks back and forth to both heat and cool the thought, to hold and study the thought, *Charlotte*, to turn *Charlotte* over in his hand, the rodent following, trusting, thinking whatever rodents think, while Pete observed the shape of her neck, which had impressed itself so clearly in his mind, the clavicles' exquisite articulation, the damp T-shirt. He made plans without Larry in them, uphill steady, forward only, the rodent never tiring either, though it stopped to consider blades of grass, every succulent, sniffing Pete's leg when the chance came. He stopped to study the tents below, discerned the path of their movements in the sand as patterns, indications of possible futures. He pushed his hand down his shorts, pleasured himself while watching the tents, rocking joyful back and forth on his still-young toes, ankles, knees, and hips, and at this vulnerable moment precisely, the rodent's sniff transformed into a lick, the small tongue no doubt searching for salt deposits in the hollow, the desert dehydrates after all, wreaks havoc with elementals, the back of his knee, cold rough rude proboscis, lapping his tendons and fragile regions behind the ball and socket's joining, which rocked and rocked as the rodent probed. Pete kicked the rodent. It tumbled off. A shadow passed over, very high at first, soaring in updraft, but the crest of the skull was huge and distinctive as was the graceful arch of the wing, which had evolved for flight from an extended thumb, translucent from below. It soared, dove. The talons took Pete by the scruff, circling up with him dangling, wings pumping hard, boots dangling high on the corkscrew thermal, soaring there, beautiful desert below, tents nothing, Charlotte, Larry nothing, *fine fine*, he thought, *king of the world now, now and that's it, time and me together, and who cares what happens next?* Then the big head turned, descended. The thing had evolved only to a soft pulp skull, he knew, just a prehistoric brain. The talons released him. Pete fell hard onto sand at the top of the hill. The thing flew up again, dove again, but for the rodent.

"Picked the rodent," the kid said.

"He made love to her in his tent that very night," Pete said.

Under the table, the kid set his boots on Pete's knees. "Made love."

"Larry and her," said Pete and pushed the kid's boots off.

"Give me the money and your luck will change."

"What's happening here?"

"It's the beer," said the kid. "Loosening your inhibitions, sliding you closer to resolving the unresolved traumas of your unremarkable past."

"It wasn't fair."

"It wasn't fair. So you will give me the money."

"I won't."

"I'm tired of you already," said the kid.

The kid pushed the cake to Pete's side of the table. He slurped to the bottom of his glass, the straw searching the bottom emptiness.

"No one gets a free ride," Pete said.

"Look, man. I'm in trouble," said the kid. "What do I need to do for the money?"

"It will only perpetuate the pattern."

"I'm coming over there."

The kid slid out from his seat and was next to Pete now, very close, his face turned into Pete's shoulder as if he might wipe a snotty nose on his shirt.

"What happened," said the kid, quietly, "to the rat?"

"You are not getting my money."

"OK. Consolation prize. Who did it? What was it?"

Baby's breath on Pete's cheek, skin too young to truly stink yet.

"The future is as important to the present as the past," Pete said, dizzy.

"The strike. A bat of some kind?"

"You wouldn't believe in it."

"I believe in everything."

"I was afraid."

"Shut up for one minute," said the kid. "Listen."

But there were no words now, no sound, only, at all. Only a hand on Pete's leg, only on his crotch, only a tongue slipping in his only ear, private. *I could help you and you could help me*, but not in those exact words, but some other form of mentioning, thoughts breaking and entering. *Help me. Help me.*

Pete pushed the hand away. "New York does not exist."

"It does," the kid whispered. "Give me money."

The hand was back. It felt wonderful to have the hand there, rubbing him, exploring the zipper, the underneath, saying, *what can I do for you?* and Pete saying back, "there is nothing," but holding the hand there, pressing the head down to the hand where the mouth joined in, friends in a pile of pumping parts, *you, I will, you, please you, please*, the waitress backing away, turned her back on *it, Yes, it's working*, Pete said, little creature working so hard, *let it try, don't discourage it, let it spread its wings and fly a while*, hot pleasure down the legs and up, *Yes, please*, the hand said. *Go on, I'll beg for it*, up skylines past sky-scrapers scraping, *don't drop me*, his head tossed back, a grunt from below, the little spit.

The kid returned to his side of the booth, finished the cake in silence. Pete waved for the check. The kid set down the straw, watched the cars and trucks drive by. He looked tired but also sure and energized somehow, ready to dig a well in the desert with a broken shovel. It was a busy road, very near the interstate. A man rode by on a horse and the kid sat up and Pete saw the kid forget about Pete.

"Maybe we should call your mommy," said Pete. "Your new career."

The kid was standing on the seat now, his face and fingers to the glass.

"I'll have to rub your snot off that window," said the waitress.

"So you care about snot now?" the kid said. "Snot's your special area of interest?"

"This is a shit place," said the waitress.

"I need to get to New York," he said.

"I've seen all that shit times fifty," she said.

"Can you help me out," he said, "or not?"

The kid jumped off the seat, jeans and a too-big T-shirt. He threw a twenty down from Pete's wallet, stuffed the wallet in his pocket, walked out of the diner. A bell tinkled as the door shut.

Pete watched the horse with lighted halter and reins, some stunt for a casino.

When he staggered outside, the road was a mile wide. The kid was far down the sidewalk already, following the horse.

"Where are you going?" Pete called.

The kid stepped out into the first lane, stood, looked both ways.

Pete was on the edge of the road himself, and now the kid was in the second lane aimed for an arcade across the street, kid stuff, games, the kid now dashing to the median, then off the median toward the other side, and the car came out of nowhere, screeched to a stop, the kid slipped by it, pounded the hood with his fists, kept going, no way to keep tabs on a kid like that, no way he would make it on his own. The desert was a dangerous place. On the other side, the kid scratched his shoulder, turned against traffic, stuck his thumb out.

Pete was on the median now. A truck flashed its brights and slowed for the kid.

"Hey! You can keep the wallet!"

The truck stopped beyond the kid and the kid ran to meet it.

"Hey!" Pete called. "This is a first for me!"

The kid climbed up into the cab and slammed the door.

"May you never run out of prey!" Pete yelled.

The truck pulled away.

Pete waved both arms, kept running down the median, but the taillights were soon lost in traffic. He should get in shape. He stepped back toward the sidewalk. Cars swerved away from him. He looked for the Luxor sign in the sky, the shape of a great black pyramid, waved down a cab, explained his money situation. The front desk paid the fare on the Department's tab.

"Have a good night," said the driver, some college kid, at the Luxor drive-up.

"What do you mean by that?" said Pete.

The driver shrugged, drove off.

From his bed, he thought of the kid in the truck, hand on knee, whose on whose?

From his bed, he clicked and the news jumped on. From his bed, he clicked again and a plane took off on cue out the window. From his bed, he replaced the duffel with a click and food was brought to his door on a tray. From his bed, he said to the plane *lean up over the desert, fly onward, plane*, and it did, seemed to do exactly as he'd commanded, mountains encircling, full of rows and rows of believers.

But still there was doubt.

He watched the plane blink away.

The plane was fine.

The pilot, a believer also, knew his business—levered the controls up, marshaled the curve of wings and air together as his team, summoned lift via pressure differential = the miracle of flight. From his bed the pterodactyl would rise far higher than any God-made mound the earth could offer as a hurdle, would reach nearly zero friction at invisible altitudes, would soar on and on there.

GET 'EM YOUNG, TREAT 'EM TOUGH, TELL 'EM NOTHING

The night guard was getting sloppy again. Another bottle, empty and bottom-up, between the tundra moss and perimeter wall. The sun had just cracked the edge of day. Contrails crisscrossed over the little canyon.

Private Martin, the day guard, had stopped his march at the bottle, stood fresh and ready, adjusted his rifle strap. It was a pint, a message stuffed down the throat as usual, soggy but clear, FaREWell in pencil. He toed the bottle with his boot. The compound had been abuzz for days, which always got the night guard drinking, flinging bottles willy-nilly, crushing cinquefoil and dwarf azaleas, as if these tough little flowers, shrunk by cold and evolution, were just a bunch of petals and nothing.

Private Martin looked back at the guardhouse.

He stood straight as any soldier. The years, he was sure, had not yet bent him. A perfect record. He would be on the first flight out at evacuation, someplace warm. His back blocked the guardhouse's view of the bottle. The plebes were always watching. But everyone drank "on compound," a minor offense, a code violation, evacuation was near, and friends were friends.

And after all the overlapping tours, he wondered, all the redeployments, families abandoned back home, why must they watch us too? Why can't Command trust its own men? Wasn't drinking on duty a legitimate expression of complaint? Action becoming Free Speech? Of all the arguments in the night guard's favor, this last, he knew, was weakest, since two wrongs did not make a right.

You'll make a fine lawyer, she had written whenever he got carried away. *A fine man someday.*

I'm going to be a botanist, he'd reminded her. *A botanist, mark my word.*

Shrubs don't raise a family, she'd written. *Paychecks do.*

No wind yet.

The new day at the compound was flat and cold, vehicles at the sally port, diesel fumes and buzz of planes. His breath was silver in the first morning sun. The land was flat and blue on both sides of the canyon, a modest but important line on every strategic map he'd seen. His canyon. Their canyon. Its edge opened up not twenty meters from his boots. If he lay in the tundra, tucked his arms, he'd roll right down off the edge.

You would never consider such a thing, she'd written of such ideas. *Suicide.*

Are you intentionally misinterpreting, he'd written back.

Morning bugle interrupted, sang out over everything Private Martin could not see over the wall. It was the northernmost outpost on the Northwest Front. He had always been fortunate, always a day guard.

You make your own luck, his wife had written. *My mother warned me*, erased though still visible.

He'd wondered privately: What was the feeling of the wall in darkness? Maybe he'd drink on night duty also. Maybe rant, stomp, and break bottles.

What about mercy for invisible suffering? he'd written.

I suffer, she in her simple cursive. *Others quit after one tour.* Then a paragraph about the kids' teeth: one lost, one grown in. Then their shoes, then their marks in school.

A squadron banked and he aimed for fun. He kicked the bottle, and it jumped the path. It skittered down the spongy slope toward the canyon lip, which was smooth from wind, then tumbled over, free and flying, a long flight down.

Private Martin slung his rifle over his shoulder, got to walking his day shift.

✦ —— ✦

Their section of the wall faced west, four thousand paces from corner to corner, give or take. Seven hundred seventy-five seconds each way, give or take, depending on stride, age, and ambition. An old rope bridge swayed from rim to rim across the canyon, built by nimble, primitive people with herbal cures for vertigo: two ropes for hands, one for feet, now reinforced with steel—so they said in the mess. The compound's scouts sprung across it, skulked deep and invisible into enemy tundra, now green and gold as the sun rolled across it. The scouts made jokes in the middle, spit in the chasm. They might not return. His knife was sharp, in keeping with evacuation orders.

Private Martin walked until warm then slowed.

Hemp? she'd written. *Scouts? In this day and age?*

Small elite units can damage runways.

Cowboys and Indians. Give me your commander's name.

The bottles were the least of the night guard's antics. Once he'd stomped into the fragile plant life the outline of a giant middle finger extended at the end of the runway. The flyboys were impressed. And once before the President's visit, the man's profile in the tundra with horns and fangs added. "Boys will be boys," the President had said. "Leaders need a sense of humor."

But he worried about the tundra. The plant life was puny and sluggish already, at such disadvantage. One cook claimed revival within decades, the marks erased in a century. War was hard on the men. Damage to the field was to be expected.

Private Martin about-faced at the south corner and marched back north. He heard a convoy rumble in the sally port. The guardhouse light changed from green to yellow. When the siren sounded, he knelt—as per protocol—among harebells, asters, and Labrador tea. He sighted in across the rope bridge, which bounced a little on windy days, though this day was calm, just the sirens and convoy flurry. Through his rifle he scanned enemy tundra. Nothing. His knees did not tire for a very long time.

Once he wrote to his wife, *Not one normal-sized tree for 300 miles.*

She wrote back, *How do you know that for a fact?*

He listed the texts he was reading as proof: *Arctic Ecology* and *Barrenland Beauties: Showy Plants of the North.*

And the sun doesn't behave, he'd reported. *Hardly down in summer, hardly up in winter.* She'd written back about the hedge dispute with the neighbor.

But he understood misunderstanding. For example, the tundra was printed on the maps in simple swatches expressing *cold* and *flat* and *nothing is here.* He knew better. On his hands and knees, the tundra was a wonderland. The tundra was teeming. The plants were small, even tiny, yes, but bursting in color—yellows, pinks, and deep purples—as if the roots knew time was short, said, *so let's get going*, and did, throwing stems up overnight, leaves uncurling, gorgeous mini-pistils and microstamens.

He kept marching when the siren died, about-faced at the north corner, stopped at the guardhouse for coffee.

"What's up with the convoy?" he said.

"No clue," said the plebe. "I'm really hungover. Evacuation hullabaloo."

He liked this plebe. He took the coffee and sipped south with the cup. When the siren sounded, the cup tumbled away as he knelt and aimed. The siren stopped and, marching again, he passed all manner of night-guard graffiti that had withstood the years and elements. After all this time, he hardly noticed them. ~~RUN FOR YouR LIFE YOU SHITheAD~~, one said, the letters four feet tall between gutters. ~~STICkS & STONE HURT MOrE IF YOU DO IT RIGHT~~, a line he thought never flowed well. ~~ROSES ARE DEAD~~ was in cursive in orange spray paint from the loading dock.

There was no telling with the night guard, who sometimes only used green "ink"—though from what natural green source was that durable? moss? ferns?—crossing out with a single line. ~~STUPID LIARS~~ was a favorite from their first year on the wall together. ~~THINK AGAIN YoU IdIOT~~ was the third year's mood. ~~ONLY DEAD FISH GO WITH THE FLOW~~ was typical of the fifth, with lighter meditations and wildlife jokes. ~~A RoPE BRIDGE IS UsEFUL~~ was scrawled the sixth, but friends could agree to disagree. The rope bridge looked mostly useless to Private Martin. Their scouts had never learned much on missions to the west.

CONSIDER ROPE
YOUR FRIEND

appeared near the guardhouse several years ago and cemented their unusual bond. The words gave Private Martin pep in his step for ten thousand paces at least, signed as it was "your friend," which touched him deeply, since true friendship was rare for him even in wartime—sad-ish, mysterious, energizing—yet surely liable to form when two men walk the very same path for endless seasons in each other's boot prints, one by night, one by day. The words were scrawled in some putrid putty. Private Martin never wrote back. Never scrawled:

CONSIDER ROPE FOR WHAT?
YOUR FRIEND

No copycat cross-out since he was his own man and there was room on the west wall for only one sign-painting maverick.

He sounds insane, she'd written.

Private Martin saluted the guardhouse each pass. The roof was tin, low-pitched with no overhang—a poor shield from wind, no good at all for rain or snow or the burning sun. Last night, during the evacuation hubbub, the night guard had shifted moods, scrawling:

OH I AM A LiLY NOW

Private Martin marched past several times before he noticed. The words were too big to be seen at first—five paces per letter—some spiritual crescendo, spelled out in tar for the tarmacs. He didn't like the sentiment, too peacenik, something. He smeared the tar with his handkerchief, marched to the south latrine, burned the handkerchief in the igniter as a jet took off, as the rope bridge swayed in the wake. Across the canyon the tundra specks were musk ox. They stomped lupine and dwarf juniper. They grazed and mated.

The cargo plane dropped from a cloud and landed. Sirens still.

At lunch Private Martin ate his sandwich slowly and listened to chatter in the guardhouse: evacuation seemed certain, enemy on the east road. Of baloney and cheese, he thought, this might be the last. Fill your belly. Wait for our scouts. Clock off at shift change. He was happy for mustard. He licked crumbs from his fingers. Afternoon was lively. Maybe they would send him for further training, poisonous plants, biological agents. The equator. South America. A tremendous amount of air traffic, incoming, outgoing, truck convoys, jitters in the guardhouse.

He tapped at the guardhouse, shrugged his question.

"Something's up," said the plebe behind the frosted glass. "But no one's saying."

The sun climbed over the canyon then down again.

Private Martin felt no fatigue—shift change was coming. Once off duty, he'd go straight to the tarmac, step up a ramp and strap in, find a corner in the cargo hold, wave to the saps guiding the plane out. Good luck, he'd salute, the flight lifting over enemy tundra. It was all the same from the sky. They'd refuel south. He'd call their shady street, rope swings from sturdy branches. He'd bring her a pinhead pine cone. A peace offering.

Vast latitudes, he'd tell her about the flight. *Whole forests, tiny like bonsai.*

I'm so glad. Do you remember how to take the trash out?

He would reenlist in a month.

A small fighter took off while a tanker angled, landing. They crossed in an X. So it would be with the evening bugle, shift change, he and the night guard on opposite sides of the guardhouse—each in and out different doors, never exchanging a word, separate clipboards and check marks, too dim in the rush to note the face, to recognize it again at another post, even elbow-to-elbow buttering rolls or tearing meat from bone like brothers.

At dusk, the evening bugle sounded. The shift change light blinked.

"Where's the night guard?" said Private Martin.

"Don't know," said the plebe.

"He sick?"

"Don't know," said the plebe.

The plebe shuffled papers. He made a call. A jet roared and they waited for it to go. The plebe hung up, adjusted his cap and sash.

"I don't know where the night guard is," the plebe said. "But someone's got to march the post."

"I've been on all day," said Private Martin.

The plebe tapped a keyboard, checked the monitor.

"All this commotion," said the plebe. "I'll look into it."

The plebe waved him on.

These plebes were all very small men, nearly dwarfs. They'd been chosen, he suspected, by their diminished stature for particular work that suited them. No shame in that, no shame. He forgave the order, the imposition. What could a soldier do? The siren sounded and he knelt by the wall, which his nose told him had been splattered by the night guard's urine. ~~NOT EVEN DOGS PiSS oN THEIR OWN~~ was written in brown boot polish. The monkshood were dead. The poppies too.

The siren died.

Behind the latrine at the electric fence, he watched the jets jockey to line up. Cargo planes glided in, light as balloons. They skidded to stops then dropped their ramps. Trucks backed up, honked, drove on.

The plebe looked more exhausted with each pass, his sash more wrinkled. Monitors tinted him an underwater color.

"When do we evacuate?" said Private Martin.

"It's wild in here," said the plebe. "Doing my best, pal."

"Where could he be?" said Private Martin. "He's never this late."

"Right now," the plebe said, "consider yourself the night guard."

The compound hummed with streaks and flares. At the north corner he unlocked the first aid locker and checked the checklist against the contents of the kit. The night guard had scribbled on the inside lid:

~~YES To PiLLs~~

The checklist listed several:

(50) TABLETS (aspirin)
(14) TABLETS (cephalexin)
(27) TABLETS (quinine)
(20) TABLETS (antihistamine)
(7) TABLETS (morphine)
(1) TABLETS (potassium cyanide)

The morphine was gone. And the rope and bowie knife, the shells, wrong caliber anyway. The flares. The aluminum blanket.

Once the night guard had tied a noose. What a joker. He'd hung it in the north corner latrine at the perfect height for a man to try while, with nothing better to do, he waited for his bowels to move. Private Martin had, of course, taken the noose down. Should have reported it as per mental health protocol. But what if the man had a good wife, had children? Since nooses tended to embarrass. Since Command was sure to KILL The MESSENGER, to ignore the night guard's sly sense of humor. Since the noose was a clear symbol of political protest, a call of the homesick, the frightened, THE DAILY DrEAD of those marching corner to corner, living lives daily unlived. Wives waited while presidents convened mountain summits with cognac and cheeses. No mercy, these men. They showed no mercy.

For weeks, the back-and-forth with the noose had continued, hanging the noose, taking it down. No words. No voices. It was an unambiguous conversation of gesture, as with musk oxen in the rut, pawing the lichen at thirty paces, tossing their huge heads and curling horns before running at each other at top speed with rock-hard skulls three inches thick, designed through eons for just this purpose: the boom of union. Its echoes carried for miles over all that flatness while the dizzy oxen stood and shook.

Night duty: in flares, the canyon rims were silver then faded gray then gone.

A new plebe sat duty at midnight, pimple-faced. He jumped when Private Martin stepped up.

"Where's my relief?" Private Martin said, saluting. "I want my ticket for one of those planes."

"The compound's on orange," the new plebe said.

"I've been on for eighteen hours," said Private Martin.

"Can't switch on orange," the new plebe said. "Pay attention to the rules."

"My mistake," said Private Martin.

The new plebe pointed over Private Martin's shoulder. "Cut the bridge when our scouts get back." As if this most essential of unsaid essential standing orders—handed down from all high commands to all rear guards across history—needed repeating now by this tiny man. *Cut the bridge when our scouts get back.* What else was the rear guard for but to cut the bridge after the scouts returned? Private Martin had eyes, sharp ones. He knew his job and that high command and the rear guard were equally important in the end.

The little man continued, "I have no time for your small potatoes."

⚜ —— ⚜

Private Martin marched the wall until 03:00, corner to corner, his legs still strong. He could march this path for a hundred years, until the war was over everywhere, on every battlefield.

Until the cotton grass all grew back, the fireweed and monks-hood. *Of course I trust the night guard. He's my friend, my comrade.* A plebe could never walk this far. A plebe could never stand this long. A plebe would never step off the path. A plebe would never try the rope bridge.

A flare, then darkness. The rim rock was slick when he got there, stepped carefully. All clear. All quiet until the next jet, the growing flames behind the wall on the tarmac. He looked down over the edge. He'd seen the scouts do it a thousand times, but he'd never seen the river before. The river all on its own down there, all silver. From the rope bridge, the guardhouse was a tropical tank with a fish in a sash. The rope bridge took his weight hardly bouncing. He tightroped out onto it, one meter at first, ropes in his armpits, then three more meters, still not dizzy, nothing but the river below to catch him, heel to toe, heel to toe, forward, onward.

I need help here, she'd written. *Where's your loyalty? Where's your devotion?*

I don't have a legal mind. My mind's more expansive. Don't smirk like that.

One glove dropped away. He held tight, the rope burning his palms. He might have crossed all the way to enemy tundra but for the signal lights. They flashed first north, then south—long quick, quick long—some code. He sat down and dangled, tried to memorize their pattern. Scouts of some kind, friends or enemies? He knew what to do, turned with new courage, headed back across the rope bridge, step by bouncing step, up the slope. He told the plebe what he'd seen. The little man got a lieutenant on the line.

"Congratulations," said the plebe. "Important news."

"I have sharp eyes," said Private Martin. "Commitment."

He asked for food. Cold soup arrived. He drank it.

"Seems the night guard's really taking advantage," Private Martin said. "But each man must live with his own conscience."

Morning bugle sounded. When the night guard was a no-show at morning shift change, the new plebe studied the clipboard. Private Martin leaned. When the new plebe smiled in comprehension, Private Martin smiled too.

"Well here," the new plebe said, tapping. "Says you're to serve out a double shift. Some infraction with a bottle. That's why he's a no-show."

He set down the clipboard.

"I did my double shift," said Private Martin. "One day, one night, twenty-four hours. What's this about a bottle?"

"Don't bite my head off," said the new plebe. "It's your infraction."

"There's been a mistake," said Private Martin. "There's no infraction."

"So now you're changing your story?" said the new plebe, swept his hair aside.

"You're new," said Private Martin. "This is not your fault. Let me explain."

The new plebe closed the window and waved him on, as planes ringed the sky and peeled off to land. He turned up his collar and pulled up his socks. He marched north, turned down his collar.

Each pass, he tapped the window. "It was not my bottle. It was not me drinking."

"Whose then?" the new plebe called after him, stepping out of the guardhouse to yell it. "Says there they have an airtight case against you!"

At lunchtime more cold soup. He slung the soup onto the tundra. The new plebe saw and wrote something on the clipboard.

"What are you writing?" Private Martin said, stepping to the window.

"Not guilty?" said the new plebe. "Isn't that what you're claiming?"

"Not guilty," said Private Martin. "A false accusation. I've served a double duty for someone else's crime."

"Whose bottle then?" said the new plebe. "There's a witness who says different."

"A witness?" Private Martin said. He rattled the window. "Impossible. It was not my bottle. There can't be a witness."

"Sworn and signed." The new plebe waved the clipboard. "Right on this paper."

"I dispute it," said Private Martin. "I have a witness myself. He'll back me."

He heard a plane take off. Planes were only flying out now, heavy and full.

The new plebe bent over the clipboard. "All right. Who's your witness?"

"My witness regarding the bottle is the very best witness," Private Martin said. "But I can't say why without incrimination."

The new plebe dabbed his tongue with the pen. "I need a name. I don't know your whole roster."

"I don't know his name," Private Martin said. "My witness is the night guard."

⋘ —— ⋙

That afternoon he sat in a bush and ate old berries. Shots and calls and wails behind the wall. An explosion or two, then many. Smoke billowed high in the west. The ground shook with each plane exploding or taking off. East was clear, almost serene. No scouts.

"Holy smoke," said the new plebe.

Private Martin asked to speak to the Captain, gave his ID number.

"His whole platoon is gone," said the new plebe. "You should've asked sooner."

The new plebe did not refuse to call a general. He dialed a keypad.

"Who's their witness?" said Private Martin, pounding on glass. "Because mine is an unshakable witness. If I could just get the message to him."

"I can't guarantee much," said the new plebe.

"You are not my commander," said Private Martin. "You are just a plebe."

"I have commands from your commander," said the new plebe.

"I'm going," said Private Martin. "I'm getting a plane like anyone. I've served."

"The MPs told me to expect this, of course," said the new plebe. He pulled a drawer open. He lifted out a sidearm and set it by the monitor. "Those shots you hear are deserters. Cowards crawling onto planes. AWOL. The same as you're suggesting now. You could die that way too. In dishonor."

"Who's saying AWOL?" Private Martin said, backing away. "I know what I signed up for." He repeated the denial all day, each time he passed the guardhouse. Sometimes sweetly like a boy. Sometimes deep in his throat like a man. Sometimes raspy or snappish under his breath. "I could twist your head off." The new plebe nodded as if Private Martin had been calculated with pencils, maps, and protractors.

Near dusk, Private Martin lingered near the guardhouse. He urinated in a shrub the color of soup. Sirens wailed without rest so he rested. Intercoms droned through the brick. He tried to climb to a window. ~~ThROWN UNDER The BUS~~, but which bus? There were only open-backed trucks with canopies flapping, filling with men, filling planes taking off. When this business of the bottle was cleared up, he and the night guard would share a huge clear bottle. Wine or port in comfortable chairs with a pass to the officers' lounge. They would exchange names. Clap arms around the other's shoulder, his hands very near the night guard's neck: explain yourself.

Perhaps you shouldn't trust the night guard as completely as you do. She'd written it more than once. He sat in the south latrine to prepare the rebuttal on toilet paper: *Who else is there to trust here?* Sometimes mail took a week to and from Nebraska. She had not written for a while, not even a drawing of the dog by his daughter. He could have divorced her by mail. Papers only. He knew he should try harder, should have.

At evening shift change, the new plebe was gone. Another had appeared on duty, very old, with uneven shoulders.

"When do I evacuate?" said Private Martin. He'd eaten half a ration, so kept his temper.

"Those in the brig are last to evacuate," said the old plebe.

"I'm not in the brig," said Private Martin.

"Those serving out infractions are last to evacuate," said the old plebe.

"Where's the night guard?" said Private Martin. "I need him."

A scuffle was heard in the back room of the guardhouse. The old plebe turned, then the scuffle went silent. The old plebe's chin was shaking.

"Most likely," the old plebe said, "any night guards shipped out this morning. Packed their duffels after their shifts."

"This morning?" said Private Martin.

The old plebe's fingers shook. He rechecked the clipboard. "Says here."

He held the clipboard to the window to show a signature.

"I'm sorry," said the old plebe.

"Stupid liar," Private Martin said.

"Walk," said the old plebe, as a mother might, as if to say *This is for your own good.*

Night fell. The compound was noisy just over the wall, screams and burning, blasts and blasts, but the brick was thick, could take this and more. He marched slowly, looked for the lights of scouts. He tried to remember all the night guard's slogans. Could remember only ~~WE'vE BEEN HAD~~.

He walked in the blasts to the first aid locker. The door was blown off, the pills strewn. Once a general had shaken hands with him, called him "son" at a training scenario. The new guards were ordered to defend an old-fashioned rope bridge.

"This is old-school," said the general. "Keep your eyes peeled."

"I see no one on the rope bridge," Private Martin said, squinting. He wasn't sure how far to go with the simulation.

The general squinted also. "My God. I see thousands. The bridge is swarming."

"How many did our scout report?" Private Martin said, doubtfully.

"The scout was taken," said the general. "We fear the worst."

"The enemy," said Private Martin. "Masters of manipulation."

"Flags."

"I see them."

"Prepare our boys for single file," said the general. "Hand-to-hand with savages."

"Seems primitive," said Private Martin, shy now. "An intellectual absurdity."

"Yes, son, of course," the general said, taking his arm. "Give them rifles. Give them caps." Then he whispered the secret: "Get 'em young, treat 'em tough, tell 'em nothin'."

At 04:00 the guardhouse was empty. The fever pitch had petered. A few shots from time to time, a call, a door slam, a set of propellers, then at last a long quiet.

Private Martin woke with his face in the greenery. Ice had formed on his cap. He rubbed his arms, blinked at a rosy bud. The air was full of smoke and he breathed it, stared at the bud through it. The tundra was not one dumb thing, but billions! The tiniest stupidities knitted together. Doltish leaves, small like mouse ears, forking foolishly from dimwit twigs overlapping endlessly with same, blending together only in the eyes of thickskulled watchmen and other hoofed mammals. A continental moronic collage.

He jumped up. He reclipped his belt over the strap to prevent the rifle flapping on his climb over the electric fence. He climbed. His skin did not tingle.

He marched around to the runways. The sky was quiet for the first time in years. No planes in the sky, though the runways were black and burning. The compound billowed. The remaining planes lacked wings and wheels. Men lay about dead everywhere, scattered, lonesome. Tall men and small men were hard to distinguish on the tarmac, legs and arms splayed, faces bloodied or missing or seized in expressions of surprise. He sat by a pile of men and parachutes. They watched for rescue planes.

Years ago, on his wedding night, his wife had played a memorable prank on him. A country inn. He'd carried her over the threshold, baby's breath in his buttonhole. The room was quaint and small. Her body was almost nothing in his arms. He'd spun her on the braided rug, between identical twin beds. The moon shown on his shiny shoes. She'd laughed at his expression. "Twin beds!" She'd called ahead to the inn to make sure of the prank. She'd laughed as he spun her. "I got you. I really got you."

⁊ —— ⁊

It would be hard to find a reliable jury.

He found a truck still running. He drove it around barracks with the doors chained shut and boxes and linens thrown out the windows. The truck drove round the munitions fire, the PX and sick bay. The truck circled the dump, searching, selecting, shifting, backing. He chose twelve intelligent-looking plebes, still sashed, all shot in the head. He pried their eyes open when possible. Most were still at least lukewarm since a jury needs to be on the ball.

For the judge he found a maintenance man, still in his hard hat, one eye missing, but who otherwise looked very much like his wife.

For the night guard he found a yellow-haired man in a private's uniform, though he always imagined the night guard as dark. No matter. This man would do. The man had been hanged with several others from I beams off the control tower. They turned slowly by their necks with heads bowed. Private Martin cut this man down, flopped him in the truck with the others. His face was familiar, perhaps from volleyball in August or perhaps he was the man who had once borrowed tweezers. A friendly face, a good face.

The trial took place outside the depot at noon. The roof still smoked. Birds and fox sunned themselves on the runways, eating. The jurors were seated against the liquid hydrogen tank, which made them seem smaller and much more careful. The old plebe was foreman. He sat on the end of the jury with a clipboard. The judge presided from the truck bed. A spent flare was his gavel, which Private Martin borrowed to open his case.

The new blond night guard looked bewildered but angelic. He dangled from a goosenecked light post among drums of radiator fluid and heating oil. Private Martin skated over the concrete slab around puddles of jet fuel as the judge read out the charges. In answer he did not sneer or smirk at the allegations against the defendant:

(1) AWOL. Pernicious Desertion of Comrades. He began with Love and Loyalty, the Golden Rule of Impossibility.

"How could he?" he said. "Since if he deserted me, it would kill me, in fact and in spirit. I've done it myself. I know desertion."

That issue dispatched. Next,

(2) Perjury. Demolished with clever maneuvers of logic.

"But did he lie about the bottle? Stab me in the back?" he said. "Where's the proof? Some paper with his signature as witness about the bottle? I scoff. I write lies all the time to my wife. I love you, etc. Does it make me a liar in general?"

The jurors nodded. He was on a roll and he knew it. The judge was impressed for once.

"And a rat, you say?" he said. "The generals fumigate weekly, do they not?"

Some laughed at the joke. The night guard looked pleased, swaying on his rope with every puff, his hair shining, ruffling.

"She was always wrong for me. Children!"

The bees were loud now, this unexpected turn. The buzz emitted from a cloud.

The jury was nearly on its feet.

"Quiet down now," he said. "I'm finishing."

Not even enemy landing gear could tear their attention from his final argument.

"Do you, comrades, for one moment, believe that I don't know a good man from a bad man? That I cannot tell coward from hero? Friends from enemies? Black from white? Because, if I don't know what I know I know, why would I still be here? Why not fly off with the generals and cigars? Or lie in bed with my wife nipping her neck?"

The old plebe was nodding off. "You didn't want to love her much."

"Why choose such bad news?" said the judge, sneering again.

The night guard was beginning to slump. Private Martin straightened him, touched the bruises on the man's neck.

"Of course," he said, waving at a fox. "We are the most animal of animals. Why belabor it? And I never answered one of his many messages. Who can blame *him* for bitterness? I told him nothing. I'm the one."

He tore the man's coat open—brass buttons popping, collar and shirt.

"Look close and see," he said. "Yes, the guilty must pay or the world goes to pieces." He stabbed the gavel at the nipple. "But you'll find no black heart here."

Handshakes all around. Now the buzz seemed a cheer, the esprit de corps everyone knew about. The judge apologized for ever doubting him.

"We just want to live!" he called. "Just leave us be!"

The jury and court officers took their time in going, enjoyed each other as people do at happy partings, though an enemy plane was taxiing. The plane spun to a stop at the dump and turned toward the depot.

Private Martin drove the night guard to their old wall, carried his partner on his back, and set him on their rock rim. The swarm might soon press to the rope bridge.

"You married?" Arm-in-arm they watched, legs dangling. "Me neither."

"I always knew about you."

"I never doubted."

"What would it be if we doubted?"

The sun dropped. It flashed on the eyelets of boots and badges or silver rope and bayonets or sweat on lips, mica pulverized or nameless crystals, all pomp and pretty, the compound changing hands, with some justice, "Let's hope," thorns and buttercups.

He laid his head on the night guard's shoulder.

He petted the beautiful golden feathery hair.

They watched the sun. It blinded west, waited for the swarm to swarm invisible behind his back, to fill the compound, to take every post everywhere, at the corners, to circle the two slumped guards on the rim with no weapons. They'd been flung away.

They held each other steady on the rock cracked open by nearly full-sized daisies, which bobbed so free on the edge, as always hinting, urging: Why not just go? Why heed anyone?

TRUE CARNIVORES

Theo stood on his tiptoes on a chair facing the fridge. His chubby arm disappeared up to one striped shoulder, hunting inside the up-top freezer for Cherry Pops or Chocolate Twisters. He wore a tricornered hat with a chin strap. The counter was spotless but for a stack of sparklers and matches for later. Theo's hand explored deep internal regions, over ice cubes forming and crusted walls. Fog poured down his too-tight shorts, sank across his scraped-up knees, and pooled on his toes.

Auntie watched him from the breakfast nook. She was tucked behind the half curtains, which were flowered, tied back with sashes by her sister, Theo's mother.

Sun soaked the kitchen windows, cast the breakfast nook in shadow: the table, Auntie's father's papers from the lawyer, her father in the urn by the wooden fruit bowl, the envelope with Auntie's plane ticket.

Sometimes Theo stopped, hugged the freezer door and listened for his mother, who was sucking up the living room with the vacuum, inhaling around couches, devouring at the feet of table legs, gulping pennies and game chips and plastic men too broken to bend for.

Auntie bit an orange to begin peeling it. She signed papers one by one. They'd stacked up for six months since the funeral, accounts consolidated, deeds transferred, the will all sorted out. She'd slept in the guest room. His estate was far larger than expected.

Citrus sprayed and Theo stopped to sniff. He stacked clam cakes in the bend of his arm, then bins marked chowder and frosty bags of lobster claws. He nibbled an edge of foil, then spat the foil out. The dog wagged and licked it up. Theo's fat belly was showing. He was a beautiful boy, so like his mother, so like herself.

You feed him too much, Auntie said at the funeral.

Her sister answered, *We'll miss you so much when you go.*

Auntie set the pen down. She pushed the papers to the urn.

If she squinted hard, Theo at the fridge might be a one-armed boy: victim of shark bite or amputation on doctor's orders. Who knows, she thought, where arms go when the mind wanders, when the retina is asked to stretch its object, to squeeze new options from rods and cones, to make suggestions to the optic nerve. If she squinted harder, he was the black-and-white boy in her father's baby pictures. Same nose, same eyes, same set of mouth.

Theo's face red with cold and failure.

Auntie licked her citrus fingers.

Out the window, the day was blue and fine, cooling finally. Birds ate at the feeder. Big ones chased the little ones off. Go away, little nothings. Find your own! They hopped on the lawn for the next best answer. Telephone lines cut through the branches. Birds clustered head-to-head or sat alone.

Then the chair teetered. Theo's tower leaned. The chair legs tipped out from under.

"Watch out!" Auntie called, but too late.

He held an ice cream sandwich aloft as he fell. His mother was too far off to hear the crash, the vacuum too loud. He lay on the tile. His eyes filled with tears as the mother-shape swooped in. He blinked them back when the shape was just Auntie.

"Don't tell," he said.

"I wouldn't," she said. She set the tricornered hat back on his head.

He ripped the wrapper. They sat on the floor and leaned against the fridge together. The vacuum roared up the front hall. Auntie yanked down his shirt to cover his belly. The gap in his teeth fit the ice cream at an angle. She'd tried to advise her sister. Theo must learn to fold his clothes, he must eat his peas, he must work harder at spelling.

You should make him brush better, she'd said once at the bathroom door.

They're only baby teeth, her sister had said, hand on the doorknob.

Theo had brushed in the mirror as they'd talked, then stripped for his bath, danced on the bath mat shivering. Bubbles and water filled the tub.

I hate to see bad habits forming, she'd said, but the door had shut, locked.

What would we do without you! her sister had called over all that splashing. *These lawyers are such a handful! And you with your training!*

Let me in, Auntie said. She rapped on the wood. *Let me in.*

The fridge clicked and hummed against their backs.

"You look sad," Theo said, and she said, "Why would I be?"

The vacuum was on the front stairs now, thumping up each carpeted runner, cord pulled to its limit, when the doorbell rang and the dog barked and ran to the door. The vacuum died. Bare feet thumped from the landing. "Thank you, I'll take it," her sister's voice said to yet another deliveryman, though the old house was so full already, closets, attics, mirrors, chairs. Her husband blown to bits in his third foreign tour. Still, her sister had too much money.

Do you need so much? Auntie had said. *Aren't there better lessons to teach him?*

It's not a question of need, her sister said. *I'm a person who likes nice things.*

The vacuum resumed, a wand to the highest corners, gulping spiders and webs rebuilt since last time. Apologies mean nothing, prescribed, polite, and forgotten quickly. The ice cream sandwich lay melting. The cat licked it fast. The dog arrived and thumped his tail.

"I'm bored," Theo said. "Let's do something fun. Let's run or something."

She stood and stretched. The slightest scent of toast lingered from the morning. She slid the toaster aside and found one fat crumb. She licked her finger, stabbed the crumb, then set the crumb on her tongue. She turned a circle as the crumb dissolved. As a girl this had been her kitchen too.

At the nook she tore up her plane ticket.

Once, when the sisters had been nine and ten, they'd wrestled over a locket on their mother's guest bed. *It's mine. No, it's mine. She gave it to me,* but who can say with so many years intervening, so many objects lost in linty corners, between mattress and box spring, drowned in the elbows of drains. Found is found. Possession being nine-tenths of the law, she'd learned. The locket was pewter. Her sister was taller and stronger, but was therefore too sure, therefore lacked imagination, therefore was less ready for the quicker hands from under the bed, from behind the door, for a patient will. She had won the locket on the guest bed, but cried. Since fingernails cut. Since to gouge is startling. She had run then too, down the front stairway.

Get a backbone! her sister had called down the banister, her face screwed up, leaning out too far over: *You nasty little thief!*

Then the fall. Both legs broken. Father kneeling on the Persian runner. Blood.

Is she dead?

Not dead, her father said. *But I hope we've all learned a valuable lesson.*

The locket was given to her sister, compensation for months of convalescence.

It's not fair.

What's not fair is life, he'd said, kissing her sister's cheek. *Just look at history.*

He was a lawyer himself and an amateur historian of early American pottery, shards and jugs, and a furniture restorer: spindle-backed chairs and wicker, which he viewed as the most marvelous of all the cottage crafts. *Think of the miracle,* he'd said at auctions. *Wicker starts as humble swamp grass. Soak the cane. Bend it. Shape it. Well-cared-for wicker will last for centuries.*

Now, the vacuum was directly overhead, in the master bedroom, searching out specks. The cat cleaned its face with tongue and paw. The dog stood waiting.

Theo showed Auntie his bleeding elbow. She knew any mother would kiss it.

"Let's go, Theo," Auntie said. "Let's go for a little ride."

Her sister's bank was the Marblehead branch. The drive-through had closed early, but the lobby was open late. Theo ran around the lobby, dirtied the windows with sticky fingers as he stared out at the lobster boats, which bobbed in the harbor and docked, at the hands on board that threw ropes to hands onshore, at the hats and beards above those hands, at the pink sky, at gulls that tipped and balanced over boiling wakes. When he'd had enough of the view, Theo crawled between Auntie's legs. He punched calculator keys in the center island.

The teller examined Auntie's paperwork, her sister's ID and account information, then excused herself to a supervisor.

The branch vice president emerged from a cubicle. "Closing your account?" he said from the teller's window.

"Every one of them," said Auntie. "One cashier's check is fine."

She sold her sister's minivan in Dover.

She traded for another, paid cash for the extra.

"I want green," Theo said, and she pulled the thumb out of his mouth.

The newish green car had Alabama plates. It was the Fourth of July all the way to Pittsfield, chrysanthemum bombs and peony explosions. Roman candles ignited from front porches. Sulfur smoke drifted across the winding road.

"Can we call Mom?" he said, pointing at a rocket out the window.

Auntie dialed and handed the phone back. He said, "It's ringing and ringing."

The mountains were only low hills lit up in waxy blasts.

"The mountains get bigger." She passed him a grinder wrapped in white paper.

"Great," he said. "I can't wait to see everything."

He slept till Albany, which still fizzed and popped after midnight. Speed bumps woke Theo. Marble columns were red, white, and blue. She parked at the port-a-potties.

"There're fifty states, each with a capitol," she said. "Big decisions are hard."

Theo said, "I know all about that. Mom told me."

The car steered by bunting-clad buildings and tricolored fountains, past capital guards in glass-bubble booths, around roundabouts with bronze horses rearing, to horseshoe drives to spotlit mansions, then surged up ramps, through tolls, lanes merging. When sirens blasted, the car pulled over. An ambulance passed, then a squad car.

"Where are they going?" Theo said.

"To save someone," Auntie said.

"A heart attack?"

"Probably just a broken leg."

"Or robbers in ski masks robbing the bank?" He made a gun with his fingers. "Stick 'em up, Auntie!"

She stuck her hands up, said, "You watch too much TV."

"I do!" He squealed, laughed and laughed.

The city went dark in the rearview mirror. It was much too late for robbing banks. More likely a fire, she thought. A stray bottle rocket. Or just one last cigarette in bed, the whole building going up like tinder, *Help us!* they are calling, good people with infants in upper windows, still believing real help is coming, not just sirens and expandable ladders. *Hold on, good people. We're almost there!*

They stopped for crepes in Columbus.

"Are we going to your house?" he said with strawberry syrup on his face.

She licked her thumb and rubbed the syrup. "I sold my house."

"Oh," he said. "Can we call home again?"

She dialed and handed the phone across the table.

Theo listened. "I think her phone's broken."

＊ —— ＊

They found a Y in Fort Wayne that was air-conditioned. At Starved Rock the grasshoppers were thick and spitting. Theo hopped behind them with a paper bag.

"Just one more, Auntie!" he said, and she said, "Don't be greedy."

He lost his first tooth the next day in a burger in Joliet. He dropped it in a baggie.

The roads toward St. Louis cut straight through fields that were flat and plowed east to westward. Towns announced themselves with stop signs and corn museums. The green was bigger than any blue bay, no lobster boats or buoys bobbing. They snuggled at night in the queen-sized beds. She let him hold the clicker till 8:30. The pillowcases were musty but soft. He read the signs from county to county, MACON, TAZEWELL, his pronunciation perfect. Theo preferred the windows down past farms and tractors. Train tracks strung silos together. Deer twitched tails, ran and jumped wire fences, then stood under big black trees. They sang *Mississippi* across the river, aimed at the Gateway Arch, which stood graceful and silver in the blue morning.

"What time did Mom say she'd meet us at the Arch?" Theo said on the off-ramp.

"She might already be up there."

She glanced at her watch. He waved up at the tiny windows. They locked the car in a ten-dollar lot. They ran swinging hands along the river, past the brewery and the stadium. The north leg shot up from concrete like a miracle. Bulky and clean-cornered, it thinned as it rose, then reached for the south leg at the crotch, became it, then descended.

Theo ran with his baggie. "I can't wait to show her."

"Chop-chop! Auntie!" he called from the ticket window.

The guard let Theo push the elevator button. The capsule ticked sideways then upright as it rose. The observation deck was a tunnel of windows with seats for kneeling and looking out. He skated up the slippery floor. He examined every face.

"Where's Mom?"

"Has she ever let you down?" Auntie said.

He sat by the elevator. He'd already done the tour in the underground museum, studied the animatronic Indigenous people. A school arrived for the morning History Talk, "Lewis and Clark: The Preparations." "St. Louis," staff said. "Where the captains found thirty hardy men and dropped boats in the river on President Jefferson's orders."

The kids clapped and nodded. One asked for the bathroom. The next group came pouring out of the elevator.

"Dragging boats over mountains," staff said. "Eating dog and parsnips . . . Clark and York, his slave, did not see eye-to-eye . . . Mosquitoes . . . Sacagawea and her papoose were minted on the modern quarter . . . Terrible bouts of diarrhea."

Kids grimaced. Staff handed out sew-on patches. The elevator doors were polished steel. Older kids came in the afternoon, high school. "Syphilis," staff said. "Lewis only shot himself later . . . was out of his element in the city . . . Melancholia."

"Suicide," some kid said.

"What's parsnips," said a girl in braids.

"It was like a thousand years ago," said another.

Sometimes it was quiet, sometimes swaying in big gusts. Theo picked cheese off his sandwich. Mustard smeared his face. Auntie did not touch it. The river lay fat and brown. The elevator opened often. More schoolkids. He smoothed his hair every time.

"You look fine," Auntie said. "She'll think you look very handsome."

Each time she dialed and he listened, he said, "We have the wrong number."

Get a backbone, little girl, she thought. Stiffen your spine.

Late afternoon, the sun dropped behind the tallest buildings. Auntie looked out one side, then the other. Illinois was flat and dull, belching smoke, the fields too far to see. Missouri was exactly the same but taller, prettier, made with better blueprints, glass and steel. Flags ringed the whole stadium. Wind caught the flags and flung them around. Below, people left work early. Walked dogs. Turned cartwheels. Kissed. Waved.

"I think I see Grandma!" called a girl who ran to the elevator.

Theo covered his ears for the last of Napoleon and Seward's Folly, maps, star charts, and frontier medicine: purging pills to open bowels, lancets, forceps, gonorrheal syringes; Peruvian bark, laudanum; trinkets for the Indian Question; ammunition for thirty thousand, dinner, muskets, swivel cannons. *To our inexpressible joy,* staff said, "Clark's words at seeing the Pacific . . . Smoked salmon all winter and Chinook squaws."

Auntie ate when she could wait no longer, the bliss of the very hungry. The ham from the cooler was sweet and salty on buttered rye. Tomato seeds dripped in her lap.

Theo dropped pennies down the south-leg stairwell. He listened for clanging.

"You can't drop stuff down there," staff said from behind him.

Theo dropped a nickel. Staff stepped away.

"We'll be closing soon," staff said to Auntie. The city was dark.

Often Father had set them on the front steps for punishment. *Face to face*, he'd said. *Hold hands.* Knees touching, he'd told them exactly what to say:

I love you, one had said to get it over with.

I love you more, the other had said, picking her nose.

Again, he'd said. He drank from a sweaty glass delivered by mother.

I love you so much I could kiss your face off.

I love you so much I could eat you alive.

Try again, my dumplings. Do it right.

It's enough, Mother had said. *Let them stop.*

They need to learn a lesson. Right makes might.

Mother had died soon after. They'd lived on in the house, inherited by Father from his father, the second of five, who'd got the house when the eldest was lost at sea, some storm, the land purchased from a Quaker before that, who drank cider since wells could not be trusted, who had thirteen children since half died, farmwork, maize and oats, offspring of a whaling captain when lamps burned blubber, these mammals dragged port and starboard around Capes, Horn or Good Hope, back to Nantucket five years later, to repair leaks with tar, to start fires with flint, to teach the natives to pray, who knew his rights, who brought suit if a coop encroached on his tobacco.

Why does my sister get the house? she'd once asked him in the hospital.

Don't overthink it, he said. *She's got a kid. Rules are rules. Keep it in the family.*

In the elevator ticking down the leg of the Arch, staff gave Theo a lapel pin.

They walked by the stadium. The sky glowed above it but all else was black. A cheer rose up at some home run.

Theo ran.

"I want to see buffalo!" he called into the night sky.

⚜ —— ⚜

They went to story time at small libraries. They filled out patron questionnaires. They passed fences made of tires, wagon wheels, pallets turned upright. Wicker mannequins naked in dusty windows. Bikes in a mountain at a dried-up gas station, joints rusted black from rain, SALE TODAY = FREE. "Should we take one?" Theo said, but there was so little room in the car. Water towers stood guard over every town, potbellied and swan-necked. Amish girls sweated over cheeses in low, shady roadside stands. They wore bonnets, aprons, and sneakers. Mastless sailboats lay in cactus fields. Wicker chaise longues. Wicker rockers. Wind socks sucked north, south, east, west.

"Where are we going?" Theo said, leaning out the window.

"Everywhere," she said. "There are no rules for us."

The continent was juniper, maple, and cottonwood. Cattle in every color. She baked birthday cakes in kitchenettes, folded in laundromats. He cried all night sometimes. He dropped each tooth into the baggie. "Dear Tooth Fairy. Please don't take these yet." When he was nine, they finally made it to Yellowstone. At Old Faithful, buffalo mingled between geysers. The rangers announced next eruptions. The earth was dry and cracked but burped and boiled.

"You'd cook in there in fractions of seconds!" Theo said.

He'd grown taller. He was getting very good at math. He wore a feathered headdress from the gift shop. The feathers danced in the sulfur updraft.

"But I'd catch you," Auntie said, gripping the loop of his backpack.

"I said *you'd* cook. Not me."

"I thought that was a figure of speech. *You'd cook* meaning *I'd cook.*"

"And if I was," Theo said, "what if you didn't?"

"The ranger would come," she said. "Pull you back just from the pool just in time."

"But if the ranger didn't?" he said. "My skin would melt."

"They would fix all that in the hospital," she said. "Skin grafts."

"What's a skin graft?" he said.

"Patches of skin from someone else," she said.

"My mom's skin?"

"Or mine."

"What if the hospitals ran out of skin," he said. "Some bad guy stole it."

"The doctor would give his own skin," Auntie said. "That's what doctors do."

The pathways were wide enough for wheelchairs. He yelled every sign to practice his reading: "Stay on path!" "Noxious

gases!" "These animals may appear tame but they will gore you!"
A wolf chased three bears in a meadow. Tourists surrounded
a porcupine. They soaked in the Boiling River in shorts near
naked college girls giggling. Theo watched them roll in an eddy.
A ranger came. He stood on the bank looking down at the girls.
He called out through his hands: bear on a kill just upriver.
They all had to go. The college girls stood, dripping. The ranger
supervised departure, helped the girls to their towels.

"Was there really a bear?" said Theo.

"Rangers don't lie."

"Are you sure?"

"Yes."

⁂

Fourth of Julys cracked their eardrums every year: Niagara. The
North Rim. He sat on the laps of Santas and Easter Bunnies.
He trick-or-treated in safe-looking neighborhoods. She kept a
sewing machine in the trunk for costumes, a panda, a zebra, a
lobster with red mitten claws. Fences made of stacked-up cars,
smashed, rusted. Coyotes skewered on barbed wire. Sandlands,
grasslands, salty seashores. She bought a new phone. They saw
a cancan show in Virginia City, bought cowboy hats and boots,
which Theo quickly grew out of. When he was ten, Auntie
could borrow his biggest T-shirts.

"You'll be as tall as your dad," she said. "I knew him first, you
know, your dad." She wore his sweatshirts on cold mornings
while the car warmed up, sniffed the dirty collars. "We need
to find a laundromat."

"I don't remember him."

They camped at Bannock and toured the old courthouse. She explained horse thieves and capital punishment, lynchings and Robin Hood. He could hardly believe it. Jupiter was low in the sky. They drank hot chocolate. They sent a card to his mother from the Little Bighorn, where warriors had crouched behind rocks with arrows. Theo studied the address, dropped the card in the slot.

"Are we bankers or something?" he said, since they did business at banks in various states. She explained safe deposit boxes, hedge funds, offshore accounts, white-collar crime. She kept cash in a sack beneath the spare in the trunk. She kept the car keys no matter how he begged to hold them. They drove up into mountains. They turned in at every Lewis and Clark pullout, where the Corps of Discovery had almost starved, where the Corps of Discovery had gone without water, where the Corps of Discovery had trudged through chest-deep snow behind their Shoshone guide, Old Toby.

"How could they really trust him?" Theo said on a sandy bank. He kicked a charred log from some old fire. "They roasted the horses one by one."

He got back in the car.

They camped on the Lolo. Trees drowned out highway noises. The ridges stood steep and dark. The fire was warm and good. Wind moved only the top branches.

"Sacagawea saved them, yes," Auntie said. "But she was kidnapped as a girl."

"I know," Theo said. "We're kidnappers. Smallpox spreaders."

Theo cooked a hot dog on a stick.

"When you were little," Theo said, "who was the faster? You or Mom?"

"I was faster."

"But," he said, "she broke both legs once."

"Yes. But I was faster even before that."

The trees were black and close over the tent. The moon tipped on the east ridge.

"My mom's tuna casserole's really good."

"My tuna casserole's excellent too. I'll make it at the next motel."

The fire snapped with Theo's grease.

"My mom's tuna casserole is the best," he said. "No one can beat it."

A rabbit appeared in the firelight, big ears turning.

"Do we have enough money?" he said.

"Your mother made sure we had plenty."

"What if the bank with our money caught fire?"

"It's in a computer," she said. "Not a building."

"What if the computer got a virus?"

"They'd fix it."

"What if the tech guys caught the Plague?" he said. "Spitting up blood. Arms falling off." Bats banked and dipped around the smoke.

"Tech guys would come from the next town over."

His hot dog had split down the side. He pried it onto the bun.

"What if every town got the Plague," he said. "All America. Corpses all over."

"They'd fly helicopters in from Canada," she said. "Full of tech guys."

"What if the whole world got the Plague?"

He ate. Coyotes yipped. The moon hoisted over the ridge and stood there.

"What's that weird pot in the trunk?" he said. "Under all those papers?"

"It's an urn, not a pot," she said. "Don't touch it."

Wicker lampstands at yard sales. Wicker baskets at farmer's markets brimmed with tomatoes, onions, piles of beans. "The cane is hand-twisted," she explained, tricolored, her father's favorite, some empty, or holey, or eaten, or crushed, or burned. Fences were made of license plates or skies nailed to split rail. Grassy Knolls, Trails of Tears, bison and missile ranges, golden roller coasters in the desert. He saved his allowance in a sock. She peeked out a steel restroom door to watch him hide the sock in the trunk, beneath the sack of cash, beneath the spare, smoky breath at his mouth. He hogged the covers every night, stacked all the pillows behind him. He thinned and ate and grew in sudden growth spurts. He paid close attention to the dials and pedals, sat behind the steering wheel when Auntie pumped gas. He learned to pump gas. He learned to use the jack, fit the lug wrench, change a tire. When he was twelve, they began to shop in men's sections. His voice was cracking. She bought him deodorant.

"I use deodorant too," she said. "We have a lot in common."

He dropped the drugstore bag on the bed. He peeled his T-shirt off in the motel mirror. His shoulders had widened. Muscles were forming. He snapped off the deodorant cap, set it on the TV, raised his elbow to his ear, rolled the deodorant stick across his armpit, crushing and re-crushing each crinkled hair. She lay back on the bed, looked up his beautiful spine, the low spots between his ribs, the golden fuzz still on his nape.

"What else do we have in common?" he said. "I can't think of anything."

The letters to Santa finally stopped. He brushed his teeth with the door shut. One New Year's Eve, they watched fireworks in Anchorage: dandelions bursting up and gone in the jet stream. They'd taken the ferry from Bellingham to avoid customs, driven up the ramp and parked on the car deck. They slept on the upper deck under heaters. "Fun?" she said, and he said, "Fun," as the ferry slipped up past Canada, fish camps, and trawlers. Mountains spiraled to glaciers hanging, clouds swirling round highest peaks. In Fairbanks the motel pool was glassed in. He carried her around the no-running area. She kicked in his arms, "Theo! Theo!" before he tossed her in the deep end. She floated by the drain, let chlorine soak into her. She had had no idea such joy existed.

At the Grand Canyon he said, "I want to see Thomas Jefferson."

They camped at Mount Rushmore, but that wasn't good enough. In North Dakota, they were stopped at a roadblock. The trooper flashed a flashlight in the window.

"Where are you from?" said the trooper.

"Bangor, Ohio," Auntie said. "What's going on, officer?"

"I can't give details," said the trooper. "Just tell your son not to stare."

Theo blinked in the flashlight.

"She's not my mother," Theo said, but the trooper was already at the next car.

⚜ — ⚜

He slept with the TV clicker. Animal shows looped all night. Experts murmured as insects swarmed. Every gazelle ran for its life. He lay on bath mats, clicked from station to station, chewed vitamins slowly. "I'm big enough for my own bed." She said she'd think hard about it. Reporters appeared in every country, diseased frogs in disputed areas, elephants killed for ivory trinkets. Turtles got inoculations, fish needed decontamination. Storms rolled around the globe on all-night weather, balled up in polar and equatorial regions. El Niños, nor'easters, typhoons. Ships bobbed then capsized. Penguins were marooned on desert islands. He watched with the sound off as seals were tossed and smashed by flukes. Dictators shot parliamentarians. Lions and orcas always won.

"I love you more than anyone," she said in a sleeping bag.

"Could we go to a movie?" Theo said. "Or bowling?"

VACANCY flashed in green or pink. "We're from Boston, Minnesota," she told a waitress. "Portland, Kentucky," she told another. "Sisters, Texas." "York, Arizona." "You always get it wrong," he said. He chewed saltwater taffy, pulled it from between his teeth. Pig roasts, salmon derbies, Six Flags, chocolate factories, dairy farms, abandoned ski jumps, mansions passed over by Sherman, log cabins, volcanoes. Once, she saw Theo's picture on a milk carton, then in a post office in Louisville, then on *LateNite FBI*, but the photos were unrecognizable now, a much younger boy, a different mood. Her own face, set at the bottom of the screen, had been smooth-skinned then, the beginnings of the lopsided smile. They stayed west and south, steered clear of the north Atlantic. It was so easy, so much empty space. She nipped at night from a flask. Her skin grew dry, not enough aloe in all the world. And her back.

He walked on her spine, her face in the motel carpets, but only if she begged him, then later only if she let him drive.

"But you're only thirteen."

"Almost fourteen."

She slept with the keys at night. In St. Paul she lost him at a disco skate, found him with a girl in slush and fog, the Zamboni driver. They found old phone booths all over, favorites in Abilene and at Devil's Tower. He parked and lay on the minivan roof. She pulled the glass doors shut behind her. He rolled his eyes to the stars, cold steel on his back. A satellite flew over and he watched it watching everything everywhere.

"What is love anyway?" he said. "What does *love* mean?"

She pointed at her ear, mouthed, *Can't hear you.* Handsets were sliced away, phone books ripped up for toilet paper, but dials still spun easy on the finger everywhere.

"I should look it up," he said. "My nice dictionary in the back seat."

She fumbled to dial.

"What will you say if she ever answers?" He echoed off cliffs and billboards.

She didn't say what she would say: "I win, I win, I win."

◆ — ◆

At Monticello they arrived for a small FIRST EVER! festival, strolled a pop-up street called Mulberry Row, tents and booths of weavers, spinners, and pewter-pourers. They stood at velvet cords that said DO NOT ENTER. They watched ponies drink at hollowed logs. She tried raccoon caps from a man in buckskin. Theo was too old for them now. The smith showed him how to swing the hammer, how gravity must take the weight so as not to overtax the wrist and shoulder, since a smith must swing it for many long years, he said, to feed his family, an entire lifetime shoeing horses, outfitting soldiers in case the nation, at any moment, should be called to war.

"How can that rock be burning?" Theo said, staring at the coal.

"It just does," the smith said, chewing gum.

"Are you supposed to be a slave?" Theo said.

"Well," said the smith. A little man walked in in velvet, a red wig, a powdery face.

"Fine day," said the wigged man in a British accent.

The smith bowed. "Good day, sir."

Theo said, "You're supposed to be Jefferson?"

"That I am," said the man. "And you must be a young patriot."

"I learned all about you in the visitor center."

"Very fine," said the man. "A boy who loves his country."

"And what you did to Sally." Theo stepped forward very tall. "I saw the video."

"Knowledge is good," said the man, backing out. "Power is complicated."

The man strolled up the Row waving at the craftspeople in leather aprons on their porches. Theo followed, then Auntie. The man slid through a staff-only door.

"Is there no one who is not polluted?" said Theo on the way to Appomattox. "I want to go to Canada!"

They bought a blue convertible in Las Vegas to cheer him up. Traded for yellow in Valley Forge, then a pickup with a topper in Silver City, a stick shift.

"I guess I'm back to pilot again," she said. "Since you don't know the clutch yet."

Theo took the keys from the salesman and headed for the truck.

"Watch me."

◈ —— ◈

They joined a funeral motorcade in Provo. The graveyard was on a red rock hill with a picket fence. People held black umbrellas. They parked. Someone waved them over.

"Thanks for coming," one woman said.

"Such a loss," Auntie said. "I'm so sorry."

They declined the invitation to the wake. With the family gone, they sat in the front row. The backhoe stood ready in the distance. Afternoon cooled.

"We don't belong here," Theo said. "Mormons."

"People are people," she said. "Try to be open-minded."

Prairie dogs burrowed between graves. RATTLESNAKE signs hung on the fence.

"John F. Kennedy cheated on his wife," he said. "The lunar landing was a fake."

"They couldn't fake a thing as big as that," she said.

"Wake up, sister!" he said. "Hollywood! Moon rocks made from Styrofoam."

"Don't call me sister," she said. "And where's my urn, by the way."

"You get the urn," he said, "when I get the address."

"This is puberty," she said. "That urn's my property."

He stood at the grave.

"What if she wonders how tall I am?" he said. "What if she wonders if I learned to read right? If I'm happy. If I'm good at all."

"You see how soft you are?" she said.

"Was it Maine? Rhode Island?" he said. "I see boats. A harbor. It's gotten foggy."

"I'm worried about you," she said.

He kicked some roses in the hole.

"I know where the money is," he said. "I know how to get it."

"You may think you know."

"I want the address."

"It's no use discussing locations," Auntie said. "Your mother's dead."

Theo dropped out of sight. His sneakers gonged the coffin.

The flashlight died that night. She made a tent of some chairs and a blanket. She threw a coat down. He threw it back. The air was full of dirt and salt. She coughed and sneezed. She was getting stiff, arthritis. The stars spun around.

"Let's do something fun," she said. "Blue whales? Redwoods? Dinosaur fossils?"

⚓ —— ⚓

She bought passports in an alley in Salt Lake City. He didn't speak for two thousand miles.

The CBC played ragtime all through Saskatchewan: Saskatoon, Prince Albert, Flin Flon. Going north, the land turned from brown to green to red to white. They left the pickup at Split Lake and chartered a plane, small and bumpy, that landed in Churchill. They stood in a line. She bought polar bear tickets for the next morning.

At the restaurant he ordered lobster, small and red on a very large plate. Its claws were pinned with wedges, arms enclosing a crock of hot butter. He ripped an arm out. When he twisted the thumb from its sheave, the cartilage stood out naked and translucent. He ripped the other arm. Silty juice flowed down his wrist. He licked it. He cracked the shell with his teeth, dug in fissures with his fingers, smashed the shell with the small hammer provided. Pried, twisted, hacked, then slurped. He chewed with his mouth wide open, molars crushing muscle, tongue sliding in and out.

She set her fork down. "Stop it," she said and he said, "Stop it."

He ripped the spider legs out, one to ten, then two antennae, then plucked the eyes, and set them both beady on her plate. He tore the lobster in half. An orange pile fell from the ragged sinew of the tail. He spooned the pile and gobbled orange.

"You're grotesque," she said. "This is not how I raised you."

"*You're grotesque,*" he said.

He cut the tail open with the scissors provided, then folded back the ribbed skin. How many times had it molted? Zipped down the front to wriggle out. How many shells lay just offshore and empty? Under lighthouse beams in circles for decades, skidding thoughtless over waves, over matings and hatchings. Theo set down the scissors. The whole restaurant was eating. No one was watching. The tail meat curled in his hand, bashful, shy, ready to pump up and down and swim away.

"A bottom dweller," he said. "A carrion eater."

He turned the tail over. A green vein ran the length of the underside. He inserted his finger, ripped the vein out, dangled it high over his open mouth. Dropped the vein in.

                                     ✧ —— ✧

Morning, the hall was long and dark to the lobby, past the coffee maker. A ten-foot bear stood opposite the brochure rack. Theo wore a bandanna on his head. He pushed by the bear and out the door into the night-black northern morning.

The Polar Stalker was a glass-roofed vehicle with extra-wide tracks designed for snow. They shivered and breathed diesel as they stood in line with tickets, then climbed the stairs through the narrow door. Heaters blasted at the boot line. The guide had pimples, said he'd never been out of Manitoba. Theo sat by a window. She slid in behind him. She offered a muffin. He snapped the window latch, flung the muffin.

"Don't feed the wildlife," said the guide, but grinned.

It was a nine-mile loop to Hudson Bay. The Polar Stalker rolled and bucked over tundra. The sun lay stubborn below the horizon.

"Churchill has more polar bears than anywhere," droned the guide as the lights of town grew smaller. "We are on a migrational path." The sky was full of stars. The Bay was the nothing in the distance. The Stalker rumbled toward it. Clusters of light bobbed and wagged toward the Stalker. "Kids on the way to school," said the guide, as the snowmobiles raced by in packs of threes or fours behind headlights, kids bundled behind the drivers, coats and scarves whipping and snapping in the last efforts of the moon. Auntie slept. When she woke the land had ended and the Bay begun. The sun was starting gold on the water. Birds bobbed. Seal heads appeared and disappeared.

"You see 'bears' all over," said the guide. "Yellowstone. Jasper. Everywhere, like mice, in those low-latitude places." The Stalker rolled on along the shore. "But what you see there are just grizzlies and black bears. Omnivores. Meaning they'll eat anything: berries, roots, trash. Like dogs or goats, what have you, OK, but that's not a real bear."

Theo's face was so young, listening. She set her eyes on the side of it, her mitten on his shoulder. He swatted her hand away.

"The polar bear is a real bear, the King of Bears," said the guide. "He stalks you. Eats meat only. Will drag your kid off. A true carnivore."

Theo sat up, searched the tundra.

"Where are all the bears?" someone said in the back.

"Polar bear sightings are not guaranteed," the guide said, monotonous and calm.

The Stalker rolled along the shore. Woodpiles littered the beach. Rocks lay in lines pinned with icy webbing. The Stalker idled near promising air holes, trundled on. When town reappeared, the Stalker aimed toward a gift shop.

"I'm sorry," she said over his shoulder. "I wish we'd seen at least one bear."

"There are no bears."

"We just hit an off day."

"The ice is melting," he said.

"We'll retake the tour."

"They all sank."

"But there are islands," she said. "There are Greenpeace ships."

The Polar Stalker parked, passengers disembarked.

"The bears drowned," he said. "They're all dead."

At the Stalker office, Theo whispered with the guide at the reservations counter. Auntie found the restrooms. When she came out, Theo and the guide were gone. She headed back through the town toward the motel, past houses crouched on tiny lots, facing any way they wanted, plywood, plastic flowers sprouting in the snow, each with dogs on chains. The urn might be anywhere.

She passed groups of trick-or-treating families. "I'd forgotten," she told a mother with a very small soldier. "Halloween." She merged with the crowd door-to-door. Kids ran ahead with their candy sacks open. Moms hustled behind. Men stood with rifles at street ends in the glow of flares at the edge of the tundra, the town's perimeter. They wore camouflage parkas, spoke into walkie-talkies. She stared out at the land behind the flares.

"Bears," a man called to her.

She nodded, looked around at the families.

"Where's your kid?" said a mom.

"I'm going to find him now."

"What's his name?"

When Auntie said it, the woman turned quick, called "Theo!" between her gloves.

They all stopped and called out. The women in booming voices. The kids in costume dropped their candy, screaming it. The men in flares yelled it, then searched through binoculars, jumped on snow machines ready to ride.

"Theo! Theo! Theo!" they called.

Like a mother should.

Her face burned. Her mittens covered her exposed ears. Where had her hat gone? No trees, no road signs, no road. She thought of home, the Atlantic, where trees were giants leaning deep into well-paved streets. Leaves were red this time of year, had only just begun to fall and rot. Phone lines tunneled through limbs, union men trimmed them. Squirrels ran the tightropes, leaped from branch to knot of fungus growing, fought for nuts to stuff in nests. If a dead one fell and lay in the street, kids called other kids over to poke the skull with sticks, to grimace at seepage, to jump back if the dead thing moved.

She waved them on. "He's at the motel." The families kept on calling as she ran.

The snow was stiff and noisy underfoot. Dusk, the far-out flat was still visible. Nothing. White reflected any star. Hudson Bay was just a gray line forever. Snow machines raced out in search of the missing boy, the motors eaten by the wind.

The motel was all lit up. She did not unzip in the lobby. She turned a circle by the bear that seemed to watch the TV across the room. A cooking show, some casserole. When Theo appeared down the hall, he was taller now than the vending machine, peanuts and cookies.

"Theo," she said. He didn't turn. He pounded the machine with his fist. He kicked the machine then searched the slot at the bottom, stuffed a packet in his coat, someone else's, green with a stripe down the arm. He disappeared down the hall, toward the service entrance.

She sat with the bear. Its shaggy head touched the ceiling, bullet-shaped, pure white. She could see no bullet hole. Dead, yes, but with front paws sprawled as if for embrace, web-footed, claws taller than her thumbs. A slick black tongue lolled between incisors, yellowing. The eyes were not bad eyes. Hungry. Surprised by sudden death.

She borrowed a flashlight from the night clerk. She slid the truck keys across the counter. "Please give these keys to that boy I'm with."

The fluorescent bulb blinked on the fax machine.

"To your son?" The clerk swept the keys into a drawer.

"Just the boy," said Auntie. "He's someone else's son."

She wrote an address on a motel pad. The night clerk leaned to see it, some upside-down place way down south.

"This too," Auntie said, almost passed it over, pulled the pad back only when the night clerk reached. She ripped the top page off, balled it up and took it with her as she headed for the door.

"Be careful," said the night clerk. "Don't walk too far. Bears are out."

But she wanted to walk far, to meet a bear ten feet tall, a living one, shake hands.

Auntie stepped into the window-lit town and out of it. Not one fence for a million miles. She pulled her mittens off, unzipped her coat, unwound her scarf and dropped it. Maybe it would reunite with the hat. She tottered out into the tundra, followed some snow machine tracks. They were still calling out. She should tell them to stop.

She walked. It had been so long since she'd just gone walking. The Bay was not so far.

BIG BLACK MAN

Night on Fern: an old brick street paved over smooth half a century back, when asphalt first came into vogue in America.

Danny turned the key in his mother's side door lock. *Milk,* she'd asked: *One gallon. Skim only.* Found a five in her change purse. *1% if you must,* she'd said. *There's a sweetheart.*

He turned the dead bolt also, since his world required dead bolts, since a big hand might emerge from anywhere and the two hands might separate shoulder from clavicle, just the beginning of *limb-from-limb,* a dream, a retreat from the civilized. Danny had given up the Episcopalians after college three years ago, moved to St. Louis just last year to really experience how the unfortunate lived. He served pie in a soup kitchen on Thanksgiving. He joined the NAACP, attended meetings, endured his mother's homecoming greetings, gin and tonics and Brooks Brothers gift cards.

Danny stuffed his mother's keys in his pants pocket. *Hurry,* she'd said, but who hurries for skim?

He walked slowly, strolled. He carried her dog under his arm, football-style, down her long driveway, like the tall boys in high school. When the dog licked his skin, he held its tiny snout shut.

"I'm sorry, li'l prick," he said to the dog. "But I can't let you do that."

The yards on Fern were enormous, well-tended by gardeners, perched on the edge of the Bluff, just above all those poor people down in the South End, the swath of small sagging roofs that filled the flat between the Bluff and the river. Fern had been the grandest street in Peoria once, still had the best views of the river and the bridge, since the new gated communities out north had no views at all. *The doctors and lawyers are all moving out there*, Danny's mother reported on his Christmas visit. *Since the South Enders are swarming up here*, she'd warned him at Easter. *Snapping up the cheaper places off Fern—Button Ball Acres and Cooper Court.*

I'm installing a security system, she'd said just this morning over eggs Benedict. He was home for the Fourth of July.

My mother, he'd said. *Terrified of People of Color. Classic racist.*

Call names if you want to, she'd said. *But our property values will never recover.*

This is America, he'd said. *Land of Upward Mobility.*

You inherit all this, she'd said, waving her fork. *You'll care someday.*

I'll earn my own way, he'd said, dropping his napkin on the dirty plate. *Unlike you, I've evolved as a human being.*

She had smiled sweetly at this last bit: *Evolution.* As he walked down her driveway, he could feel that smile working its way through his brain, digesting his cortex, his reasoning lobes, his junctions and synapses.

At the sidewalk, he set the dog down between his mother's brick pillars. The dog was white, four pounds, black-marble eyes, the tail clipped off. Danny tugged the leash. They headed toward Stanley's In-N-Out, the only convenience store open at that hour, just a glow, blocks away at Fern and Henderson.

He wished he had more friends to talk to, a tribe: hunting, gathering, sacrifice of captives on top of some butte, smoke and drums, a powwow. His classmates were all trying for Wall Street, had moved to the coasts, finishing law school, *more proof of the Exodus*, his mother said often. *They'll be rich, marry pretty women.* He had studied anthropology in college, for now worked in a copy shop. *Poor you*, he would have said to the enemy boy. *The world, for you, is truly unjust.*

The trees on Fern leaned over, tall, thick-limbed, a polite aging jungle.

A car approached slowly from behind and passed, an older model, dented and boxy, wide and low to the ground, growling, blue or some light gray color. Exhaust belched as it passed by. One taillight was out. Danny trained his eyes on the dog as the car went by, since eye contact invited interaction, as with stray dogs and drunk beggars on St. Louis street corners. The dog barked at the car, high-pitched and ridiculous. The car slowed and Danny slowed. He considered his cell phone, considered 911, considered the Mace in his canvas shopping bag. Mother had insisted on it ever since last year, *Danny's Mugging Down on the Tennis Court*, as she called it to her friends, or *The End of Danny's Interest in Tennis*, though privately Danny called it *The Awakening*, the moment he learned he understood nothing yet of his frightened inner man.

He watched the car roll all the way to the corner of Fern and Henderson, where it turned with the green and disappeared.

He walked on. If the dog got ahead, he pulled the leash back. If it fell behind, he pulled it forward. Sometimes they walked side by side, but rarely. The night had been stormy, was still dripping. When the dog lifted its leg at a storm-broken branch, Danny tugged and the dog hopped along, dribbling. It drank at puddles at the end of driveways, rain mixed with toxic runoff, herbicide against the recent dandelion infestation. He'd heard all about it from his mother. Danny let the leash fall slack. He listened to the tiny tongue lapping. He listened for car wrecks, break-ins, armed robberies. "The Cacophony of Poverty," he'd once titled a college paper, which he had asked his mother to read very carefully, so she might comprehend his new, broader thinking. "Creatures suffer due to the Age they are born in," he'd written in his conclusion. It was not *right*, he knew, it just *was*: cows in India vs. cows in Texas proved that *fairness* and *logic* were silly words, though professors made careers mining these contradictions.

His mother, he was sure, had never read it. She wanted med school.

I'm applying to graduate schools, he'd warned. *African American Studies.*

Don't be silly, she'd said.

For now, he was biding his time in printing, the front desk of the copy shop near the St. Louis Arch, where he made copies, reports with graphs, gladly, for people of every shade.

The boxy car returned head-on from the corner, seemed to hesitate as if looking Danny over, as if Danny was important to the occupant of the car for some reason. But then it jumped, sped up Fern, turned left on Button Ball Street.

He told the dog to *gitty up*. He wiped drops of damp from his face with his forearm. He avoided cracks in the sidewalk.

More and more brick pillars stood under graceful iron streetlights casting umbrellas of light on edges of huge yards, marked out a century back by Midwestern tycoons. These men understood their own value, planted shade trees by seed for great-grandkids' swings, built back entrances for servants, commissioned cast iron figurines for out front, with iron loops raised high for hitching teams of horses. They were ambitious men who'd paid well for this breathing room.

At the Hartleys' house, Danny saw two black girls hiding behind a hedge. *Just girls*, Danny rethought.

The dog was barking like crazy. The girls glowed for a moment in the light of their cell phone through the newly trimmed leaves, a big girl and a slim one, then the phone went dark.

"OK, I see you there," Danny said. "Is that your yard?"

He leaned for a better look in the shadow of the hedge.

"You think it's my yard?" said the slim girl. "You think we like sitting here on our behinds? A car is tailing us. He's been after us for blocks. Our phone just died. You got a cell phone?"

Are you listening, Mother? That thesis won highest honors.

She'd smiled. *I'm very proud of you, of course.*

He'd showed the thesis, a little tattered at the edges now, to a Mexican kid at the copy shop recently. The kid said, *What do you know about that stuff anyway?* Danny had asked the kid to a Cardinals game. Mother had sent him tickets. He went to the game alone. The kid said he did not follow baseball.

"Are you undercover or something?" said the slim girl. "Where's your badge?"

A van passed, followed by a taxi, followed by a city truck with a logo on the side for the Sewer Authority. The pipes and cisterns were overflowing from the storm.

In the headlights, Danny turned for a better look at the girls. The bigger girl might have been pregnant, or just had baby fat in the midsection, a slight case of lack of control. The slim girl looked stunted, twelve at first glance, but more shapely than the other girl, with a face more serious than sixteen, though poverty could age you. They wore very tight jeans even in this summer humidity. No sweat on their foreheads, thanks to eons in Africa, cruel climates in the American South.

He thought of the Mexican kid bent, filling a paper tray.

"I sympathize," he said in the light of a motorcycle passing. "I'm on your side."

"Thanks," she said. "How did we ever survive without you. Got a phone? I can ring my mom up."

Danny laughed. "Ring her up?"

"That means *call*," the girl said.

"I know what it means," he said.

An electric company cherry picker came and went.

"I live on this street," he said. "I grew up here. I'm just visiting now."

"My mom's employed on Western," she said. "She could arrive in the vicinity in five minutes flat."

He said, "*Vicinity?* Just speak normally."

"I read the dictionary each night before slumber," she said.

At this declaration the bigger girl laughed, as a bus lit them up through the hedge. The slim girl poked the big girl in the gut, and they instantly entered into what he could see was a private joke. They whispered back and forth.

Danny watched, excluded, leaned over the hedge to catch a word.

"I'm not moronic," the slim girl said to her friend, eyeing him. "He's harmless, most likely, but I've got him under observation."

It was dark again. The rain fell, then stopped, could not make up its mind.

"You should not be in that yard," Danny said too loudly. "The owners are nervous old people."

"We need this hedge only until the car gives up," said the slim one. "Goes off to pursue someone else."

"Pursue . . ." he said. "No."

"Stalk, track, harry, hunt," she said.

"Where are you going, anyway?" he said.

"We don't divulge our business to strangers," she said. "It's against our policy."

"I'm on your team," he said. "I'm a good guy."

"We don't need a team," she said.

"I *want* to help," he said, unable to stop himself.

"Could you restrain your dog?" she said. "Could you muzzle it? Phone? Yes or no?"

He stuffed his hands into his pockets. "I saw your phone working a minute ago," he said. He had heard about scams involving borrowed cell phones. They could be working with the car.

"Speak of the devil," she said, as she peeked over the hedge down Fern.

The headlights turned onto Fern from Button Ball, sweeping across lawns, tree trunks, front doors, flashing back from leaded windows, Danny and the dog, a loop of leash between them, first low beams then high beams. Danny stared. The girls ducked.

"Can you and your dog just move along?" the slim girl whispered from the darkness.

"It's not my dog," Danny said, blocking the light with a fist.

"Go," she said. "Go."

The car drove nearer and Danny decided, obeyed, walked with the dog to the end of the hedge, decided again, waited there, bent as if to tie a sneaker, then the other, as the car cruised along the hedge very slowly. He looped the laces around his shaking fingers as the car sidled up, stopped, idled.

Then it passed Danny by again and turned left.

Danny returned down the hedge, stood across from the girls.

"He's gone," he said.

"He'll return," said the slim one.

He looked for sky through the branches, where was it? He wished he had some gum to offer the girl, anything, to stuff her mouth with a wad of it.

"So why stay?" he said. "You need to move on. What's so funny?"

"She thinks everything's humorous," said the slim one.

"I'm not being humorous," he said.

"She gets to decide what's humorous," said the slim one. "This is America."

"I know what you mean," said Danny.

"That's great news," she said. "But he will wonder who you're talking to. Get it?"

"No, I don't."

"See, we're hiding from him back here in these shrubs. So if you're talking to invisible people, well, that's a clue that might blow our cover."

"I can help," he said. "If you let me. I'm your biggest advocate."

"I don't need you," she said. "I'm going to be a lawyer. Breaking out. Busting through the glass ceiling."

"Statistically unlikely," he said. "I hate to tell you."

"They said the same to Abe Lincoln," she said. "That's my trajectory."

He laughed. They'd been bused to a replica of Abe's little cabin every year in middle school: Springfield, the tallest boys ducking under the rough-cut doorjamb, taking swings at plastic hams hanging above the hearth, whacking the DO NOT TOUCH signs while the docent was busy with a group of gray-haired strangers: *Abe's life was full of early failures*, said the docent. *But Abe kept going despite each setback.* The boys rolled like puppies over Abe's parents' fragile quilt—kicked the spindle-legged table over. "Stop!" Danny had called at the boys leaping for the wax arm that drooped down from the loft, the arm, of course, meant to signify Abe, the boy, everyone's hero, who had dozed off while reading some precious volume, the book borrowed from a neighbor, a ten-mile walk to return it, the future Emancipator's head far too near the tallow flame, though Danny had never climbed the ladder, never saw what was *really* up there.

The boys left. The docent was still listing pioneer mishaps: scorched books, drownings, lost elections.

Danny had sat on the hooked rug. The cabin was filled by the sound of gentle snoring, a hidden sound system. Were these humble beginnings *necessary* to save the nation? Was a shack *required* for the hero's character? To change the shape of history, *the trajectory*? *What can I be?* he'd thought. He knew the answer even then. He'd smuggled Abe's arm onto the bus, flung it from row to row with the boys.

"Abe Lincoln's my hero," Danny said.

"No one loves Abe Lincoln better than me," the slim girl said.

"I've read three biographies," he said.

"The next Abe Lincoln is going to be a black girl."

The bigger girl laughed.

"Who is it in the car?" he said.

"Some *debaucher*," she said. "Some *perverted deviant*."

"Why's he following you anyway?" he said.

"Gee, let's see," she said. "*Fellatio. Cunnilingus.* Use your imagination, Mister."

She could say whatever she wanted, since she was slim, attractive, and behind a hedge; since he was less than average height for a Western man, pale and unintimidating. He ground his teeth. The dog reared to Danny's knees on its small back legs like a stallion. *Take NoNo with you*, his mother had said, had handed over the leash and the Mace together.

"You have quite a vocabulary," Danny said. He shoved the dog off his knees.

"I'm a product of my environment," she said.

"Why doesn't your friend talk?" he said. "Is she pregnant or something?"

The girls both laughed and laughed and then Danny laughed too, and the muscles relaxed in his neck, face, and shoulders. He felt as though he hadn't been so happy in years. Perhaps the copy shop job would soon be behind him. He could hand his uniform to someone like this girl in the hedge, ambitious but oblivious, on the verge of big disappointment.

And what would his mother say, he wondered, if she saw him at this moment in conversation with two shapely black girls. A waterfall of joy.

He took in the girls' two midriffs in passing headlights, *danger*, belly buttons on display, both with small fake-gold crucifixes dangling between sweet round breasts, which made him dizzy with happiness and sadness, lust and loneliness. Their lips. The hedge was recently trimmed. The scent was the green of sliced leaves.

"Something happened to me on my mother's tennis court," he said.

"No time," she said.

"What's your name?" he said, when the street was quiet again.

"Mary Lou," she said. "My companion here is Sally Mae."

"You don't trust me," he said. "Sad, but I understand."

"Here he comes again," she said. "Duck behind a tree or something."

He hated ducking behind a tree on her orders. But the dog barked and barked at the car and the bark could be heard blocks away. He hauled the dog in, hand over hand with the leash, picked it up, held its muzzle shut.

"It's your job, I know," he whispered to the dog. "But they don't want heroes."

The boxy car rolled down Fern, taking up both lanes toward the In-and-Out, which must be closed by now. Rain glittered in front of its headlights. He would buy no milk for his mother tonight.

Last summer, before he moved away from home, he'd encountered a big black man on his mother's tennis court, at night, alone. He'd been hitting forehands on his mother's backboard. His mother's court had just been resurfaced, spotlights installed on the corner fence posts for nighttime practice. Fern was a pleasure then, life too, but how does one say such a thing to strangers? Or that he'd never thought of moving away from home before that night. That he had immediately preferred nighttime tennis practice, the swing of the arm with no one watching, so many more imagined eyes than real ones. The pleasure of concussion with the ball, the pleasure of air escaping lungs, the pleasure of sweat cooling on his young skin.

The car came back.

The driver had rolled down a window and Danny found himself squeezing the dog and the dog was whining, squirming, and he squeezed it harder till the dog realized it must quiet down, and it did. The enormous black man who had been standing watching at his mother's net, an electrifying revelation, branches and leaves astir, behind the fence, everywhere. He did not know when the man had arrived, his intentions, his views on people in big houses.

He could still feel him.

The driver of the car had swung the door open. A foot with a boot slid onto the asphalt, a white boot, pointed toe. Danny had always wanted a pair, a secret, go to Montana, help out on the reservations, ride off into the range herding cows.

Then the second boot dropped out.

Danny was dizzy waiting for the driver of the car to make his decision, just as he had waited for the big black man at the net to decide, to either go away or to do *something else* entirely, though the big black man had walked away, melted through the fence, had closed the gate behind him, had turned up toward Fern, never to be seen again.

Danny heard a siren coming. The boots retreated. The door slammed. The boxy car rolled on, just as Danny had driven away that night after the tennis court, to the middle of the bridge, after the black man's departure, to the river, had flung his old cell phone over the railing first, then wallet, then racket, then Grandfather's watch, stripped down to briefs, flung all to freedom, had then lifted himself over the railing, teenagers whistling as their cars flew by.

"Jump!" they'd called. "Do you want to die?"

"Yes!" he'd called back, though no way they heard him.

He jumped, fell a hundred feet, a ten-story building, the equivalent, far enough to snap a neck, knock a brain unconscious of the big frightening world, unlink the Chain of Events called *Danny*.

Instead he splashed, plunged, surfaced, floated in the river—a young man turned to driftwood, fish food, pollution, trash. He watched himself bob away on the river's surface, past the factories, barges, sports bars flashing on the waterfront, his body floating past the riverboat casino, toward the locks, sucked in by the doors and levers, up and down, sure they would crush him. The bridge was so graceful on the other side in the sky as he floated in it. When Mother saw the bruises, when he told her about the big black man instead of the bridge—the missing racket, cash, and watch—she drank coffee with the officers at the police lineups, and later she stood by him for the sentencing of the much shorter black man, a man with a much different face and girth from the original, the one and only big black man.

The Scapegoat had worn a jumpsuit to the trial, "Innocent! Innocent!" he kept calling. The guard had unlocked his cuffs before the jury's arrival through the small back door. He had glanced back at three children, one boy of middle school age and two girls with braces. The family lived just below his mother's house in the South End, within "easy walking distance" of her tennis court, the DA had said. He had often glanced back at his wife, who'd looked tired, who'd brought peanuts in Ziploc bags, passed nuts to the kids when the judge wasn't looking, when he was whispering with lawyers, or drinking water the bailiff poured, or instructing the jury about reasonable doubt. The DA had talked and pointed. "The defendant lay in wait, hid himself in the shrubs."

Three months with time served. Mother had thrown a garden party, invited the Jumers and the Oakfords, but not the Haverhalls, since what Mr. H had done with his babysitter's sister. The Scapegoat had glared at Danny.

Behind the tree, Danny caught rain on his tongue, swallowed it.

Abe Lincoln rode to trials on his horse, thinking and riding, a depressed man also, melancholia. Everyone knew this. Abe Lincoln let his kids run wild in the White House, did not believe in corporal punishment. When little Willie Lincoln died in the White House, his father never recovered. "My poor boy, he was too good for this earth. God has called him home." Abe Lincoln was ten feet tall. Abe Lincoln forgave the South for everything, welcomed the Rebels back into the Union with open arms, since hate pulls a body apart.

"What are you doing to that dog?" she called out from the hedge.

The dog whimpered and an ambulance sped by, then a station wagon, then a taco truck, and the slim girl dashed out to it, running into the street, waving her arms.

"Stop!" she called after the truck. "Help! Come back, Mister José! Miguel!"

"He's gone," Danny said.

He watched her stand in the street. She stretched her arms after the taco truck, followed it a little along the dashed centerline. He followed her to the curb, stopped in the edge of a streetlight's halo. She was out of breath, her chest heaving up and down. Her jeans were rolled up at the ankles. She had lost one sandal in chase.

"I need to tell you something," he said.

"That's it," she said and retreated from Fern. She swept past Danny on the curb toward the sidewalk.

"We're departing," she said, heading toward the hedge up the sidewalk. "He knows our position. What's wrong with that dog?"

The scent of sweat rose from Danny's shirt, mixed with the sweat off the skin of the girls, salty fear, leaf trimmings.

He followed her. A decision. He pulled out the Mace. Another decision.

"Stay where you are," he said.

He heard the bigger girl laughing, running, almost to the Hartleys' brick pillar already. Headlights turned onto Fern from Button Ball.

"Oh, brother," said the slim girl, turning, stopping, hands on hips at the hedge. "One lunatic per night. That's our quota."

"Who's in that car?" he said, waving the can. "Do you know him?'

"Are you deaf, Mister?" she said.

"I don't like your tone," he said.

"We're shoving off," she said. "Toodle-oo."

The bigger girl was running fast down the sidewalk, getting smaller, and the slim one was also picking up speed, Danny following with the Mace aimed at her back.

"What's your name?" he said. "What's your real name?"

"No one cares about your little spray can," she said.

She was a very fast runner.

"I have to tell you what I did," he said after her.

"No one cares about your stupid story," she yelled over her shoulder.

The girl had a role, a purpose after all. He ran after them past several driveways. The can of Mace led the way.

"You don't know me at all!" he called after them.

"Oh, we know," she yelled back.

He stopped at a puddle when out of breath. Abe Lincoln wanted to save the Union, that's all he aimed for, nothing more noble.

The girls were just tiny footsteps running.

He knew they did know. He'd always known. The big black man knew.

But the Scapegoat knew everything.

He knew Danny's mother was standing at her side entrance waiting, searching the night for her boy, though in time she'd give up looking, pull the curtains closed. Why didn't the judge listen to the Scapegoat? Why didn't he slam his gavel? *Order, enough is enough!* Or if not, why didn't the bailiff put the judge in chains, walk the judge across the Savanna to a ship at port, load him in? Or the daughter with braces. *Where is my life? I get mine too!* Stand up on the bench, stomp, cry out, point a finger at Danny, take him out in the jumpsuit. Since we are all alone anyway, inside and outside the windows and doors shut tight and locked, the key swallowed by the gentleman of the house or the lady in the frilly cap, or buried in the rose garden out back with a golden trowel. *Dig as long as you want. You will never find the key,* they say. The Scapegoat knew this best. *You will wander dark dripping streets forever,* they drone on, the savannas and cotton fields, with stained hands reaching for another stained hand, *Hello, please, let me in from this rain.*

Until this ends, Danny thought. When will it end?

Perhaps tonight, the boxy car would drive up his mother's driveway. A man in white boots would stoop at the door, fiddle for a while to pick the dead bolt, since it always stuck even with the key, slip into the kitchen, check the fridge, spin the hat on the counter, before heading out to other parts of the house.

JUDAS CRADLE

The old lady lay by her bike on the cobblestones. Her basket was bent. Her loaf of bread was crushed. Her skirts twisted in her chicken-bone legs. Black birds hopped near.

The hotel van idled over the bike as if waiting for an apology.

Ronnalee sat in the middle seat and snapped a picture. She opened the guidebook.

"You people," said the tourist in the far back seat, the only other rider.

The driver rolled down his window. The old lady sat up, her legs sprawling before her, shook her fist at the hotel van, then sucked the fist where the street had skinned it. The driver growled something in the foreign language. The black birds pecked at muddy crumbs. The street was a canyon, the steep stone of the Bibliotek on one side and slouching public houses on the other—split-timbered, leaning, and postcard-charming.

Ronnalee snapped a picture of small faces in the small arched doorways, so low she'd have to duck in if invited, and of curtains peeled back from second-story windows, lacy, yellowed, gathered by gnarled fingers. The shutter clicked. Sharp chins pointed down through watery glass, through sashes first painted five centuries back, through spectacles at the ends of foreign noses. This city was full of unattractive people. When the old lady shook her fist at the windows, the curtains dropped. The shutter clicked again then again.

"She's certainly feisty," Ronnalee said.

The castle sprawled on the hill above the city between spires and domes and wires from poles. It looked down on all the ruckus at the Bibliotek entrance: traffic snarled on either side of the van. The crowd in the street held phones to ears under umbrellas. Ronnalee snapped a picture of the Bibliotek's famous doors, which were twenty feet high, bronze and locked, first carved in wax by some young guildsman long dead, page 38, The Bibliotek: Important Features. A line of people wound down a ramp to a human-sized door propped open by a ticket taker. No sirens came.

She dog-eared Bibliotek, a "must-see-later," then Appendix A: Torture Chamber.

"We're nearly late for the castle tour," Ronnalee said.

The crowd sat astride pink stone lions. They filled the Bibliotek steps to the cobblestone street. They crowded the van, the old lady, the bike. The spokes spun on but barely wobbled. The old lady's mouth was red, which cut her face open or shut as she squawked at the driver, whose shoulder hung out the window. He bellowed. The old lady growled. Ronnalee snapped another picture. *Fighting like bears*, she would say back home explaining the photo. When the driver spit a bird flew up. When the old lady spit her mouth worked saliva forward first. *Behind the teeth*, Ronnalee would say. *I rolled my window up*, and her guests would laugh before the next picture.

The day was gray as was the case two hundred days per year in the region, page vii, Introduction: What to Expect.

"Her bike seems uninjured," Ronnalee said. "We meet our guide at the funicular in nine minutes."

"You people," said the tourist in the back seat. "Always panties in wad lusting for castles."

"I beg your pardon," Ronnalee said over her shoulder.

She had tried to forget him since the breakfast buffet. He had not bathed, though the tub down the hall was available to every hotel guest. They had stood in line with towels and soap.

"No, I don't pardon you," said the tourist.

She would have corrected him, but the old lady was now crawling toward the van, the fur of her coat, old fox or beaver, dragging through puddles.

"What a creature!" said Ronnalee.

"Yes, a creature," he said, leaning over the backrest, close to Ronnalee's face.

Ronnalee pressed the lens of her camera to glass: hand over hand, knee over knee, *a lizard licking.* A student bent and stood the bike up but the old lady kicked it over in a puddle. She kicked the student too and he hopped away and the crowd laughed and curtains dropped against second-story windows.

"How ungrateful," Ronnalee said.

"Perhaps that student planned to rob her," said the tourist. "Perhaps he only pretends to be a student."

"That's a dismal outlook for one so young," she said. This tourist was putrid, thin, pale and beardless, putrid in putrid layers of coats on jackets that might have belonged to five different people. A lunch sat in his lap. The bag had been used more than once, crumpled, torn.

"Perhaps he follows her home," he said. "Perhaps rapes that poor old lady in her bed. Perhaps cracks her skull like melon. Don't find her for weeks. No one misses her."

Ronnalee dug in her handbag. She handed coins over the driver's shoulder. "For her bread," she said and checked her watch. "We really need to hurry," and when the driver dropped the coins in his pocket, she tapped his shoulder. "That money is for that poor old lady," she said slow and loud. "To compensate for damage."

"That driver," said the putrid tourist. "He don't understand one word of you. To him you are gibberish."

By now, the old lady had climbed the tire. She stood bowlegged partway up the bumper. Then she dropped out of view.

"Where's she gone now?" Ronnalee said. "Give her the money."

The crowd drank beer from steins and sucked chocolate on sticks. Took pictures in groups and exchanged cameras. They crouched and pointed under the van.

"Absurd," Ronnalee said. "Can we get around her?"

"Always drooling for crowns and silken beds," the putrid tourist said.

"You don't know me from Adam," she said, tossed her head.

"I know you," he said. "You want the Rack, the Thumbscrews and Judas Cradle. You want baskets where heads drop in." He rubbed her shoulder with a sticky hand.

"I'll get my money's worth," she said. "But I'm here for the Queen's Gardens."

"Bah," he said. "The Queen's Gardens."

"My cousin Joan's a gardener," Ronnalee said. "I'm here for her."

She opened the guidebook to the Queen's Gardens, page 79, then flipped back to Bibliotek, page 36, oldest on the continent, where the finest books had once been stolen by the pope, the vellum and the illuminated, the monk-made masterpieces. She turned the page. The best books were wrapped in oilcloth and carted to Rome. A treacherous journey, a theft over mountains, such misery for mules falling left and right off snowy cliffs. She set her thumb in the crease to mark the page.

"What's she doing now?" Ronnalee said.

The old lady had reappeared at Ronnalee's window. She pressed her tongue to Ronnalee's glass.

"We barely brushed her," Ronnalee said and unclicked the seat belt. She slid away from the tongue and across the middle seat. The putrid tourist sipped Coke from a straw. The van idled. The old lady's tongue spread gray and flat, turned circles on its tip then figure eights. Old teeth and gums crushed lips and cheek.

"What's wrong with her?" Ronnalee said. The crowd now blurry, backing away.

Ronnalee returned to the guidebook, page 38, where the best books were being carted back from Rome by yet another pope one hundred years later. New mules and servants, but the very same mountains. It began to rain a little. Little rivers ran between the cobblestones. Puddles pooled over iron grates.

"Four minutes," Ronnalee said to the driver. "Funicular."

"I tell you," he said. "Your words are stew. Try to believe your newest friend."

"All right," said Ronnalee. "You tell him then."

The putrid tourist said something to the driver in the foreign language. The old lady stepped back bowlegged. She waved a crooked finger at Ronnalee.

"She once electrified a boy with that finger," said the putrid tourist.

"Ridiculous," said Ronnalee.

"Burnt off his skin," he said. "Cooked him quick. Only jaw left in ashes. His parents swept him up."

"You know her?" said Ronnalee. He waved a meat sandwich.

When the old lady's hands gripped her crotch, the crowd backed off further, the smallest behind the tallest. Her skirts hiked up over her knees, crotch thrusting back and forth, eyes rolling then staring hard at Ronnalee. The pumpkin mouth opened and closed, lustful and avid, with animal sounds heard through the driver's open window.

The two men laughed. Windows slammed on second stories.

Ronnalee dropped her camera.

It had not happened in years: Ronnalee's privates dilated and burned and cream leaked out of her, the monster waiting behind the door. She gasped a little and shuddered. She crossed her legs after. The seat under was wet. She pawed the handbag for a tissue. She sat on her raincoat.

"Drive. Drive. Drive," she said.

The van honked. The crowd parted. The van lurched on. Nothing was better for forgetting than making plans: in the hotel that night, for example, she intended to write on the castle postcard in her tiny and distinctive script, edge to edge, to somehow make it fit: *Joanie: I made it. Towers struck by lightning TWICE apparently. Pelted by stones, uncountable, from below the moat. A moat! The timbers of bridge burned, replaced, ramrodded, often missiled by burning balls of tar from lines of archers, hundreds of years, diseased livestock set afire, bellowed in slingshot (yes). Trebuchet, brainchild of best French engineers, taller than castle walls, rolled in from foreign borders, enemies, propelled by peasants running in spokes of wheels. Thank goodness for the USA. I'm on the hotel coverlets right now. Bathroom light across*

my legs. The Bibliotek, what a door, bronze. We're told the enemy
had no trouble slipping into this city. Small boats at night up the
river. Through tunnels and gutters, mixed in streets under hoods
with the population, alien jawlines, bumps on noses, infected limps,
etc. Joan. The hills round the city are low and worn. We're told the
King worked hard to rebuff invaders, but these hills! These streets!
They fold in and over narrower passages made for fine dead horses
shod by blacksmiths beating anvils ringing over church domes and
stupendous arches built on the new king's orders, "He wants a fine
arch, by God, He'll have one. Praise be." True Adventure. Wish
you were here. xo R.

The van turned at a grand hotel, passed vendors with trinkets, painters dabbing outlines of the castle, which stood
now between a steeple and a last protected grove of trees. The
shopping district was big smooth glass, perfume shops, and
ladies in furs.

"Perhaps they'll take us at the noon tour," Ronnalee said.

"Perhaps," the tourist said.

The van jerked right at a T-shirt shop toward an arrow to
the CASTLE CAR PARK. The castle disappeared behind a
cathedral, reappeared from a billboard, was sliced by a radio
station's space needle. The van stopped for local children with
runny noses.

"The castle seems to be moving," Ronnalee said.

"The castle goes nowhere," said the putrid tourist. And he
offered Ronnalee his sandwich.

"I could not possibly eat it."

He offered the empty lunch bag then. "For vomit," he said.
"Sour stomach."

"Just a little lightheaded," she said. "Travel is the best cure."

She fanned her face with the guidebook. The castle, 71–95: World's Largest Wooden Wine Cask; Gallows on Castle Square—true-size reproduction; Prison Complex & Torture Chamber (lower level); Cannon Walk on the Parapet; Armory and Diorama; Prince's Brothel; Queen's Gardens by the Forecourt; Reflection Pool; Memorial Tablet; Harness Room/ Apothecary; Royal Brazier (rebuilt after 1672 lighting strike); Palatinate Costumary (original furnishings); Grand Stairs to Upper Wall (best views of famous wine region); state-of-the-art Conference Center; award-winning Cask Café (lunch daily/ dinner on weekends, call for reservations). Don't miss newly renovated Servants' Dormitory (a thousand hammocks!) and Invisible Hall (firing squad/WWI). Fireworks on New Year's Eve and Liberation Day. Gift Shop with audio tours and collectibles behind Ticket Kiosk.

The van stalled at a traffic light. When the engine caught, the light was red again.

"Don't be anxious," said the putrid tourist when the van rolled on.

"Why would I be anxious?" she said. They were passing the Opera.

"Perhaps you hate this city now," he said. "Hate that old lady."

"How could I hate a total stranger?" she said.

Her loved ones back home would gasp at the story: *How I Almost Missed My Castle Tour.* Joan and Bill and other friends. They would lean in around her Shaker table, would turn over the photographs, would ask, *What had gotten into that old lady? To carry on like that?* And *That young man in the far back seat? Why so rude and scruffy?* And Bill would add, *Why so angry?*

That's the heart of it. Why can't people be grateful? And Ronnalee would clarify: *Putrid,* she'd say and they'd laugh hard at the word, together like a tribe, and Joan would say *God made us all so different.* Bill would add *Yes, but nothing in the world is worse than rudeness,* a perennial argument between the pair, Ronnalee not taking sides, while Bill cut the cheese brought by Pat, some English cheddar with herbs, and Joan would roll her eyes at her husband and rub Ronnalee's back at the sink, and with the hand in place just so, Ronnalee would enter the subject of fear. *I was afraid,* she would tell them. *Almost got out of the van at the wax museum. No,* they would say. *And miss the castle? Well,* and then she'd admit part of it. *The fright. I truly nearly wet my pants.* They would laugh and debate over crackers and cheese and Ronnalee would swim near the monster again. *The place looked evil: black doorways and tiny cold faces. Black birds galore. Gargoyles on every roof.* She would bring schnapps from her carry-on. She'd have boiled potatoes and cut the bread. The fondue would be bubbling, the pot bought duty-free at the airport before the flight home. Her guests would follow rules to the letter: kiss your neighbor if the bread drops in. She would sit next to Joan. Bill would sit at the other end at his place card. Pat would say he'd never left the Keystone State. *You're so brave,* Joan's fingers under the table. The monster.

Wipers whipped the window. The van turned onto the Car Park ramp, which sloped down through an old stone archway and disappeared beneath the castle. Traffic sped across the top of the archway, a bridge to the rest of the city. Tourists walked across and smiled for pictures with gulls as background. The gulls fluttered when black birds landed. Their brains were pea-sized. Easily frightened. Easily frazzled.

"I could get out. I could walk to the castle," Ronnalee said. "People are walking."

"Free country," said the putrid tourist.

Other cars followed and pinned the van in the line. At the bottom of the ramp, the entrance gate chopped up and down under the archway, perhaps built by Romans. She checked the Introduction: Early Settlements. The castle disappeared from view as the ramp dropped away. A dog ran from the Car Park entrance looking over its shoulder.

The putrid tourist pulled his boots off with all the delay. His toes were gray and soft, crossed on the backrest. The van was nearly up to American standards with seat belts only across the lap, tinted glass along the top of the windshield, a handheld radio with a coiled cord. The windows were locked by a button somewhere. The putrid tourist used no seat belt. He sat among a mountain of luggage: suitcases, totes, duffels. A sty swelled one eyelid shut. She hadn't noticed the sty at the breakfast buffet. Epsom salts would bring it down. He scratched his neck, pink and scaly, under a bandanna with pirate print fabric.

The van rolled to the gate and stopped. The Car Park entrance was tall and black.

"Good things come to those who wait," Ronnalee said.

"I disagree with you," said the putrid tourist.

The gate snapped open. The van drove through. The Car Park entrance was a lofty chamber dividing into three smaller archways. The leftmost was blocked by an orange cone. A car stood uncertain in the center entrance, taillights blinking. A man stood with a chain in the rightmost archway. He dropped the chain when the van approached. The driver saluted as the van rolled through. The man picked up the chain in the rear window.

The dark was sudden. Ronnalee blinked, wide and blind. Her mouth went dry.

The van drove down and down, swaying, rocking. She'd once been seasick on a lobster boat. Maine. Black rock shore. Sun. Her insides spewed to the sea, to lobsters in traps where electric eels whipped by, claws chopping at them, ineffectual. The boat bobbed on waves above. The van drove deeper. Headlights corkscrewed across the rock. She sought a horizon just as the captain had instructed.

"You speak English well," she said after a right, a left, then she lost track of the turns.

"I studied in your United States," said the putrid tourist.

"I live in Pittsburgh," she said. "There are no castles in Pennsylvania."

"I studied all America," he said. "Several years of you."

"You know Pittsburgh?" she said.

"I know your bombs, your drones," he said. "Your CEOs all murdering babies and the invisible people everywhere."

The driver turned the wipers off. He said something to the putrid tourist. The tunnel had fancy electric torches sometimes, and small faded posters and billboards at junctions: a circus coming, a taxi company, an unreadable candidate.

"I'm a Democrat," she said.

"You burn babies as slaves in your faraway factories," he said and yawned.

"No one ever means to kill a child," she said.

"Instead of your cotton plantations," he said, "your slaves are in Bangladesh and China. Very small hands for very small work. Very small flat faces, brown or yellow is the color now for your computer chips and fancy pants. You reap without whips."

"I love babies," she said. "I give to charity, women's causes and cleft lips."

The putrid tourist picked his teeth with his nail.

"I don't have babies myself," she said.

"If that old lady likes you," he said, "she won't fry you maybe like that boy."

"No one can electrocute a boy with one human finger," she said.

"Of course, yes, of course," he said. "My grandpap saw the electrocution himself. Everyone old here remembers it." He was leaning over the middle seat. "That old lady, she was wearing all white. She took this boy into room full with toys—my grandpap peeping at window, standing on barrel to see. 'She wasn't even ugly yet. Very beautiful once.'" He stabbed his crooked finger at Ronnalee's head. "She was taller then, and thin, dark like tree over crying boy. Her arm flies up like so. Finger like this. Electric volts."

"I don't care," Ronnalee said as he climbed into the middle seat.

"Stupid boy," he said. "This boy glowed like your hospital X-ray, his bones flickering black and white. This boy's face was mask, face of horse. Very painful."

"I don't believe you," Ronnalee said.

"That boy was weak," he said. "Groveled at her feet. He should never grovel."

"See there," Ronnalee said. "We agree on something."

Ronnalee turned and stared into the red of taillights. The tunnel was empty but for an occasional doorway and piles of fur or charred wood. Her crotch was cold. She recrossed her legs. Sometimes the tunnel nearly scraped the roof. The van sped, then turned, then slowed, then sped ahead again. One hand shook. She held it in the other.

"I think we're driving in circles," Ronnalee said. "Where are all the other cars?"

She tried the door handle, which was locked and useless, then she explained everything: "As you know, my nation is a very large one. I don't know our president at all. A person like me can't get anywhere near him. We don't have his ear. I can't just tell him what to do to make the world a better place."

"You think ignorance absolves you," he said.

This man was so hard. There was no getting at him. Bill was easier. She'd buy Bill a chocolate hammer at the castle gift shop. Bill was so handy with tools. He'd been depressed. He would enjoy the hammer, and Joan would be grateful. She tapped the driver's shoulder and pointed. "A little heat?" she said and hugged herself to show her meaning, but these people were not intuitive or good at understanding body language.

The radio crackled. The cord drooped as the driver spoke into it.

"I did want a baby," said Ronnalee, turning her knees. "But my husband left me for a younger woman. She's almost a girl, much prettier. Her name is Whitney. I've seen her smiling at his jokes. I know I have my glitches as any human being does. There's no reason not to say it to you. You seem like a very serious person."

"Bah, beauty," he said. "There is some deeper reason he rejected you."

"I don't begrudge her," she said.

"Never lie to yourself," he said. "Lies pollute your purpose."

"I just want to go to the castle," she said.

He slid closer across the middle seat. She made room for him.

"You sound like a terrorist," she said.

"Maybe I am one," he said.

His smell was stronger in the middle seat. In Pittsburgh people bathed once a day. If a car hit a bike in downtown Pittsburgh, parties exchanged numbers. They tore paper from spiral notebooks or wrote on fast food napkins from the glove box. They borrowed pens. *Call me tomorrow*, said Pittsburgh. *We'll work out the details.* Pittsburgh shook hands over windshields, over all of Pennsylvania. Even Buffalo or Cleveland. *No sweat, my friend. Sorry for the trouble.*

She said, "Terrorists do not take castle tours."

"Very true," he said.

He flicked on the dome light. He took the guidebook from her hands. He opened to Appendix B: Famous Local Sieges. "I'll read it to you to pass the time."

"All right," she said, and he turned the page: "In the castle, the cook had spoiled the broth with some very bad fowl. This cook was taken to the cellars and strapped to the Rack. Important guests were visiting the court. Chairs were arranged for a demonstration. Ladies sat in front. Gentlemen behind. One husband kissed his wife's bare shoulder."

"How do you know that?" Ronnalee said, and he patted her hand.

"Listen," he said.

The van trundled over a very narrow bridge. "The ladies," he said, "wore white like snowflakes," and Ronnalee saw the ringlets, as if her own hair cascaded to satin feet.

"Yes," she said, "go on."

"Each limb of this cook," he said, "had an iron cuff and a gear and a soldier to crank it with. The cook did not take it well."

"Torture?" she said.

"Yes." He nodded. "First dislocation, then the cartilage and ligaments snapped. Then bones. Limbs broke free and skin ripped. One soldier wept tears to fill the moat."

"How do you know?" she said. "Where is that written down?"

The putrid tourist waved as a priest would. The van bounced and leaned.

He ran his putrid finger down the page. "The cook cried so loud, his screams were heard all over the castle, in the gardens, over the parapet, far below in the city, and echoed through tunnels where the common people hid their livestock, where they slipped away to visit lovers, to laugh at wives out of earshot."

"Like this?" she said, pointing through the window at the tunnel walls.

"Shall I go on?" he said and she said, "yes," and he explained that the cook's sister had married into an angry family, also arrogant despite their rags, also good with tools and not content with gruel, black bread, and smallpox. The men died. The mothers died. The babies died. They watched the enemy in the hills rub their blades at sunset.

Ronnalee reached and turned the page for him, as with piano lessons as a girl.

"Meanwhile, at the demonstration," she said.

"Meanwhile at the demonstration," he said, "the snowflakes spit up in spotless handkerchiefs. Men escorted the snowflakes up the stairs and strolled them by the cannons—for soothing views, for soothing countryside, for the soothing moat since peasants don't swim, for walls, for helmets with muskets, powder, and balls, for the enormous tables with wine, meat, and sweet things in pyramids."

"Plenty to eat," Ronnalee said.

"So much," he said, "as the important people enjoyed the views on the parapet, talked of liberty and order, which soothed those ladies mightily. They chatted about the Rights of Man and Revolution in America," and as he spoke, Ronnalee twirled on the parapet, one bird in the snowy flock: fluttering, puckered, joining, parting with Joan and Whitney, her ex-husband at the prison door with a diplomat. Her dress hung beautifully. The pavilion was white on such occasions. Silver trays were garnished, lemon and oysters, awaited very large beasts roasted on spits. Below, thatched roofs crouched by the river. Barges were low and patient, treading water off the docks. The city winked dull at twilight. The King's Guard sharpened swords. The peasants sharpened only sticks. "At last the castle children arrived to be fed," he said, and they flopped on Ronnalee's lacy lap, squirmed about as all children do, and Ronnalee smiled down as they wiggled between her legs, played jacks and pickup sticks under the table, popped out for escaping marbles that were batted by a three-legged cat.

"So lovely," she said, "Yes," he said, "until the rumbling began underfoot," and Ronnalee lifted her hand to feel for rain since the sky was clear that day on the parapet, not a cloud. *Where's that thunder, my darlings?* she said, and children stomped the new-cut grass, which seemed to jump and crack under them— the giant in the hill was trying to stand. *Mother*, a child said. *Methinks the thunder is inside us.*

Ronnalee flicked off the dome light. She snatched the guide-book back. Set it aside for forgetting.

The putrid tourist touched her leg. "What are you doing?" Ronnalee said.

In the dark, he used duct tape to bind her wrists.

"Is this part of the tour?" she said.

He rummaged her handbag, unzipped the hotel key. "Where's your money?"

She turned on the seat, looked out the window.

"Where's your money?" He patted her torso.

"On my leg," she said, and he unlatched her belt. He pulled off her sneakers, tugged down her pant legs, then worked the money belt down her thigh.

"I stole twenty dollars from my aunt once," she said. "So I understand you. She was sick with Lyme. In the hospital. The money was crumpled on the bedside table."

He counted the bills, licking the corners.

"Once," she said, "I kept my Scout troop's cookie money. I was their leader too, so I respect your position."

"I'm not the leader," he said.

He'd found her address book in the handbag, fanned the pages.

"Truth is important," she said. "Once I cheated on a teacher's exam."

"Passport," he said.

"I left it in the room," she said.

He flipped her over and stripped the passport from under her jog bra back strap. He threw the hotel key to the driver, who dropped it in his pocket.

"My grandfather was a farmer," she said. "He hated the

farmer by the river. He blew the dam up. Dynamite. The pond drained. Beavers started over somewhere."

"Very selfish," he said. "But clever."

"Not a bad man," she said. "Rash, yes, but everyone loved him. The flooded family went to California. They did very well in almonds there."

The driver lit a cigarette and passed it back, though a bump nearly knocked it free. The driver lit another. Water poured from the tunnel ceilings. Ronnalee elbowed the window until the bone was bruised.

"Once I shaved my cousin's pubic hair," she said. "She asked me to."

"A lesbian," he said. "Do you think that impresses me? We welcome lesbians."

"She's married now," Ronnalee said.

"The world is full of cowards," he said. He shook out her handbag on the seat.

"I'm not rich," she said.

"Camera," he said.

She pointed at the floor with a free finger. "I want to show the pictures to Joan."

He bent and plucked up the camera. Hung the cord around his neck.

"She'll pay," she said. "She and Bill."

He rummaged through cosmetics, sniffed a lipstick, tossed it away.

I was terrified, she would tell Joan and Bill over dishes. *After my escape I walked for hours in the tunnels, only me. I passed a room with a thousand hammocks, gray and limp, clotheslines with bonnets. In time I met a barefoot peasant who bowed graciously. I can't eat leather, he said. Poor thing, I said, Poverty. I told him of barn raisings and lemonade. Always be good, I warned him. He gave me directions.* Joan would drop a goblet. They'd fuss over shards, hands touching, while Bill bought Girl Scout cookies at the door.

The van passed another van. The drivers saluted.

"Joan and I were never an actual couple," she said.

"Shame," he said. "It is the favored device of repression." He fingered the sty.

"She'll leave him," she said. "I know her."

The van turned into an elegant archway, marble or porphyry, an old bunker for the avant-garde. Three makeshift structures shone in the headlights: a scrap-lumber Gallows with a pink nylon noose, a Gibbet cut from a telephone pole, and a Scaffold with a rusty pipe as a lever and a plastic bucket as the basket. Shag carpet was tacked to the priest's platform. The van drove out between disorderly pews and old recliners back to the tunnel. The air was full of the meat of her skin, the rank-sweet sweat produced at such times.

"An underground driving tour?" Ronnalee said, revived by the spectacle.

"Yes," he said. "Like your Mickey Mouse in Florida."

"We're second cousins once removed," she said.

"Yes, you are all of one blood with the Mouse."

"Not Mickey—Joan. I mean, it was nothing illegal. I kissed her once under a pear tree. I held her under the armpits first, kissed her fingers one by one."

He finished his sandwich.

"Bill could see the kids all the time," she said. "I want kids more than most do."

He set the crust on the seat between them.

"In Pennsylvania," she said. "We say, 'Speak up or be spoken for.'"

He wiped his mouth on his sleeve. He thumbed the address book in the dark.

The van wagged over pits and troubled places. The guidebook, full of Tongue Tearers and Breast Rippers, slid across the floor. Her face smashed glass. She fell in his lap. She licked blood as he leaned her upright. Her nose swelled, her head with Heretics' Forks. Scold's Bridles. The Pear was inserted into homosexuals and women who had miscarried—inside the anus, vagina, or scrotum—then the four blades expanded until recantation or confession, the power residing in psychological fear, according to the caption on page 206.

The van turned. The headlights lit a sagging table ringed by broken chairs, a map pinned with photos. More luggage piled. A bed frame was bolted to the wall. A small pyre was ready for a match. An old wooden Stocks stood alone.

"There must be," Ronnalee said, "an easier way to that castle."

"Your mind is frozen island," he said. "Frozen island in unreachable sea. No ships dock with you. No bird shits your mountain peaks. Not one fish carcass on your frozen sand. You have no sand. I was once just your way also. Before my ship came, shining white."

She tried to object, but he closed his eyes and instructed her to be quiet. "Your talk," he said, "it clogs me."

While scooping ice cream, she would say the following on the screen porch: *I did gain a new perspective on our economy.* She would begin to finish over apple crumble. The sun gone, the moon cut in half. Kids would peddle by with flashlights through fireflies. Bill would pass an ice pack to press to her nose.

The van squeaked to a stop near the table. "I will pay for the bike," she said.

"She'll be paid," he said. "I assure you."

The driver pulled the parking brake.

"Bank accounts," he said. "Passwords."

The driver walked in the headlights. A spiral notebook appeared. A pen was pressed into Ronnalee's fingers. A hand pushed hair from her eyes. "Write them carefully," he said, and she did, her wrists moving together slowly. He took the notebook.

The side door slid open.

The putrid tourist untied his bandanna. He retied the ends at the back of her head. They steered her into dark made darker by the blindfold. She tripped on her pant legs around her ankles. She kicked the pants off, shuffled on in panties. Gravel was silent under her socks. She breathed the blindfold in and out, rodent smell and creosote. Her neck was cuffed down by a wooden yoke. A hinge squeaked at her ear. She tasted egg in her teeth. The engine pinged as it cooled. Her head dropped forward.

"The police might come," she said. "Set you on that Judas spike."

"Try to concentrate," he said very close to her face. "Try to comprehend your predicament." They wrapped her ankles with duct tape. Her eyes were big inside the blindfold. The yoke was cold but she warmed it. The ankles were finished. "Your new world is old world now."

After my escape, she would tell them from the screen door, *I went back to rescue that poor woman with the blindfold.* Joan and Bill would nod in the yard, her other guests all gone home. *I passed the Armory workshops: smoky cells, vents, and cisterns.*

I was full of wonder at the Castle foundations, walls in vestibules.
Workers pumped bellows in every archway. Firing squads, muzzles
smoking, troublemakers in a heap: liars and masturbators. Handcuffs
shuffled toward barrels boiling big enough for ten to be dipped in from
hanging cages. Strong acid. Some unfaithful husband on a bench,
sawed in half, then charred, lids peeled back and cut away so the eyes
would never shut again. Your beautiful mistress hangs on the ceiling!
Look away! said the hangman, and I did. It was none of my business.
I moved on. The Judas Cradle required a room to itself, a high ceiling
to cleanse souls. The spike was tall and slender and set on a pillar. The
culprit was lowered onto it by way of a chain until the spike entered
her most precious orifice, gravity working till she fainted, then lifted
to wake her, a bucket of water administered then lowered down for
deeper in. She'd die of infection, the hooded man told me, and let me
hold the chain for a while, or of bleeding, he said, as broken bones
puncture something crucial. I walked on. There were dogs. I skirted
them. When I finally found the poor woman, I hardly knew her. The
monster stood on hind legs over her. An ugly beast: thick-limbed,
-necked, and -membered. The fur stunk from twenty paces. I snuck in
behind. My head scraped very old rock. I swung my ax. The monster
split like a melon. I kissed the poor woman for a very long time over
the monster's body. We touched each other as the children gathered.
They fingered the hems of our dresses. I ripped the locks.

She'd conclude at midnight, Joan and Bill in the driveway.
And those peasants? Of course, I see the putrid tourist's point. But
what else would all those billions do? Rice paddies? Dragons? Fortune
cookies? Peasants need kings. We all can't be lucky.

Their footsteps to the van and back. Leather-footed. Hoofed.
The yoke smelled sour-sweet. His putrid mouth was very close.
She puckered toward it.

"The castle tour, later," she said. "Your ticket is my treat."

He squeezed her head. "I take your picture now."

"All right."

She posed as best she could, difficult with ankles bound, tipped one knee across the other as her mother always said to do, *for nice lines along the thighs*, for examination years later. The flash was bright through the blindfold. X-ray light melted her skin. Then the next flash and the next.

"I'd like my lipstick."

The van clanged shut. She said lipstick on the lower lip only. She kissed herself to spread it. She sank as low as the yoke allowed.

"Take another," she said. "Please, another."

CAT

The man fished in a very small creek in the woods at the edge of town. He wore khakis and a canvas hat for ticks. His nylon line looped out to the middle of the still, muddy water, tied to a bobber. When the bobber bobbed and the line got taut, the man snapped up on the rod to set the hook. Sometimes a boy from town came by, or a girl. They stood to chat with the man about where they were off to, to dig for treasure or climb trees or write love letters. They watched the man work. Sometimes he shared hard cheese sandwiches on rye, corn chips, or orange soda from the tailgate. Sometimes it was a slim silver fish on the line and he would cut its throat and keep fishing, but often it was a fat brown fish on the line and he would cut its throat and keep fishing. This went on. The kids came and went with balls and bats, flippers and masks for the beach. The trees were thick and green.

He flung the silver fish and brown fish in separate baskets, blood on the sides.

One boy came who said he lived on the beach in a tent.

"That so?" said the man.

"Just in the summer," said the boy.

The line was slack. The water bubbled near the bobber.

"Summer is good," said the man. "Free to sleep anywhere," and the boy agreed.

"Ah," said the man, snapping his rod up.

"I think you've got a big one on," said the boy, leaning out, pointing over the water, then squatting, bracing his knees, picking his braces, his toes in the mud, no shoes. These children did not wear shoes in summer except on trips to Anacortes for school clothes, to church, to parties with elderly people.

The line tugged and the face of the man said, yes, I know I have something, but his mouth said, "I used to fish on the beach as a boy."

It was a big brownish cat on the line, green almond eyes, no blinking, "A nice one," the boy said, looking up at the man then back at the cat, beautiful despite the water dripping from its fur.

"I like sand," said the boy, blinking up at the man as the man showed him how to grip the scruff—how the cat scuffled a little, then submitted to the grip, like a mother's mouth, instinctual relaxation, the man pointed this out, and how the back feet dangled and how the tail still twitched. The cat rolled about under his fist as he peeled the hook from its spotted gums, between fang and fang, one hand and thumb holding the jaw ajar.

"I caught a starfish last month," said the boy and showed the size with his hands.

"Ah, that's wonderful," said the man and took his knife from his hip. "Dried it?"

"Three weeks," said the boy. "Brought it in for the storm."

"Ah," said the man. "Just the way I did."

The chocolate brown fur strung up along the backbone. The whiskers were brown, arching to his sleeve, sifted left, then right. The green eyes blinked.

The boy stood up and looked at the cat and the cat hissed and swatted the air and the boy stepped back, stumbled on a rock, and from his sprawl on the ground he looked at the trees.

"Easy there," said the man.

The sun flew though the leaves, speckled everything.

"I fell," said the boy, as if falling was the strangest thing.

"Careful now, friend," said the man.

The boy brushed his knees, looked at the cat.

"I hung it with a string in my tent," said the boy, as the man took a knife and cut two slices in an X across the cat's throat, not much fussing, and blood poured out.

There were leaves in the fur, speckles of them, twigs.

"The beach is both a beginning and an end," said the man.

"That's the funny thing," said the boy, watching the blood.

"Woods on one side," said the man. "Sea on the other."

"I've been thinking," said the boy. The cat drooped like a rag. "There are so many types of green in the trees," and how he wished he knew more types—not just conifers, deciduous—and the man said "Oh, you're young," and handed him the knife that the boy slipped down the waistband of his trunks, and the boy said how he knew flowers already, not all but some, and herbs since his mother had a book on them, but the trees, he loved how they leaned and whispered in storms on the edge of the sand.

The man dropped the cat in the basket with the brown fish.

"I like the beach sunset best," said the man, rebaiting the hook with a wriggling worm, and talked of orange and purple and a hint of green in between those two colors in the sky sometimes, just a line of it, so that maybe it wasn't green at all but some illusion of green created by ions, by the angle, by the necessities of physics in that border place, atoms on atoms, the rays fingering through clouds, and then the first silver stars just sneaking out, making one think of paint flecks from some artist's hand, and then the unavoidable thought that had to arise from that hand: a God at the easel, hopefully, anyway, some thoughtful entity filling everything in.

"Oh, sunsets," said the boy, leaves in his brain. "Our sunsets are best in our tent."

The boy looked around him. "I bet a jungle's no better than our very own woods."

"I can see that sunset now," said the man.

The man gave the boy the rod. The boy cast the hook and bobber. The little splash made a bull's eye of waves. Then the water was still again.

"I can see it all clear as day," said the man.

The rod snapped up. A fish followed the line, skimmed the surface. The fish's mouth opened then closed, opened then closed, speaking something clear and incomprehensible about the cat.

The man's hand was reeling, rotation slow and steady, and the fish was coming and the trees bent in and the ocean wind swayed through them, making the trees bend and toss.

The fish turned on its side in the boy's shadow. One eye stared up through the shadow to the trees.

The boy squatted, the fish at his bare toes, pulled the knife from his waistband.

As he cut the throat in an X, he imagined cutting the line instead and the fish diving away into the pool, the frayed line trailing behind it, the tail making the smallest slash with the dive, a splash, the hook in the lip for the rest of its days, the fish swimming a morning circuit of its muddy shoreline after, adjusting angle and trajectory for the hook, nibbling underwater grasses when the tour was complete. Even with the hook the grasses would taste green and wonderful. The fish would sniff the grasses first, touch nostril to tip of swaying stalk, the worm long gone, eating slowly, thoughtfully, staring at a small pink shell that lay in the mud in the very deepest part of the pool. Some child had delivered the shell there somehow. The boy would think this next. Long ago, a child found the shell on a beach with a dog. The shell had dropped from his pocket, forgotten, the child an old man now or dead in the graveyard, a cat sleeping on the stone, and a flood will enter the boy's mind next, a flood made potent by big sudden pounding rains that lifted the shell up from where the child had dropped it, washing it off the muddy shore down to the bottom of the pool, the deepest part, a new place for the shell to live now, to settle in, the shell's own small ocean, the floor of mud and sand and small tasty grasses growing, trees in miniature, private.

He thought, I must tell everyone.

He dropped the fish in the silver basket.

And how the flood then receded and the fish floated on amid the grasses, staring at the shell, the biggest shell in the Universe, the most beautiful shell the God of Shells and Fish has ever made for all to see and admire.

HOUSE FULL OF FEASTING

A bed frame and box spring were still just a dream. The mattress lay on planking, up narrow steps, but wider than the last place. Mimi kicked the covers off. Prince pulled them back. They wrestled underneath. This bedroom was larger too, better angles, but facing west, too hot for sleep. The dog panted down at their young round faces. He was big and friendly, from the pound and grateful. His tongue dripped on the pillow ruffle.

"With teeth like that, he could do some damage," Prince said. He always started the pillow talk. The dog wagged and knocked the lamp.

"But he won't," said Mimi. "He has no idea of his potential."

"He'd scare a thief," Prince said. "Bite the leg and hold on."

Mimi laughed. "Predators go for the jugular, silly. Everyone knows that."

It was true. They'd watched animal shows about it.

The dog circled and dropped on a rug. It was a blue, farm midnight: blue windows propped for a big blue breeze across acres of seedlings in all directions, counties of ankle-tall corn just getting legs, stretching arms out and out as a screen door slammed across the field.

"Doesn't that old man believe in sleep?" Mimi said.

"He's headed for the pump again," Prince said. "Irrigation eternal."

She rolled onto Prince and joined, an eight-legged animal, thumping thumping. While a siren whined in town. While the dog barked at occasional headlights at the four-way stop. While peepers sang and crickets yelled, midnight's bawling cacophony. "My God," she said as she held her ears, as she kissed his throat, thumping thumping, into this mattress, so thin and painful. Then the pump at the pond joined in the noise— *katchoom*, *katchoom*, metallic sneezes. In the dark, the pump sucked water and slime the same as frogs, the floating unseen and many-legged, Prince thought—the all and every—paramecia, algae, fish eggs and fish, beautiful life, Prince thought, beautiful death, lizards and copperheads chopped in rotors through rusty joints and pipes below, all sprayed out from the circling cannons, round and round, to thirsty seedlings.

"The last place was quieter," Mimi said and rolled off him.

"I hate when you do that," Prince said, crawling out. "Get me going, then stop."

He splashed his face without a light on. He filled the dog's bowl in the sink. A bug was swimming toward the rim, and the dog lapped it up. Prince pissed out the window as he drained a glass of water, in-one-end-and-out-the-other, a trick he'd seen on a late-night show.

"That's neat," she said, crawling off the bed. She also peed standing but over the toilet, not as well as him, but improving. She flushed. She found her panties.

"What's he need all that rent for?" Mimi said. "He's old. No kids."

"Go lie down," Prince said, but the dog didn't. They all stood in the window.

"He's got plenty of money," Mimi said. "Look at all he's got."

Headlights turning whipped their skin, whipped the old farmer's big white house across the cornfield, whipped his seedlings bent low by spray, whipped his lone tree out on the rise—the heavy trunk and lowest branches—tried to slap down the next farm beyond, so it seemed to Prince, to thrash the next state west, to lash all the wide Great Plains, to smack the Rockies flat, he thought, to pummel the Pacific, but what common headlights could flog a continent?

"We were born too late," she said. "That's all."

She was the prettiest girlfriend he'd ever had. So small and hungry he could eat her up.

Prince set the glass down. Their hands roved, and he pinched her bum.

"Old people own everything," Mimi said and kissed his wrist.

"They'll die pretty soon, I guess," he said and yawned.

Branches brushed the roof. The window was propped with old books: *Farm Ballads* and *Harrows for Beginners* and *Potato Tips for Young Farmers* and *How to Bull Fight*, all found among the mousetraps in their cottage attic, the library cards still in the inside pockets, each signed in careful cursive, *Gerald H*, all yellowed, the bindings peeled to old stitching, now all soaked and blurred from last week's storm.

"We have to work in the morning," Mimi said. She rolled down onto his side of the mattress. Prince remained at the window. He petted the dog. The animal sniffed new slime in the fields, which would dry with no trace by noon.

"You think he built this place?" Prince said.

"Like with a hammer?" Mimi said.

"I guess there's family somewhere," he said. "A brother, maybe."

"A brother. There was one," she said. "Dead on the river. The mayor told me."

Cars that late were rare. They rolled through the four-way—never stopping, hardly slowing, just music, hooting *ha ha ha*—like wild broncs and Jesse James.

"No cops out," Prince said.

"The cops don't come out this far," Mimi said, face in the pillow, mostly sleeping.

Dead on the river was a matter of opinion. The old farmer was happy to fill in "the kids" about his brother. They sat on wicker on his porch at sunset while he talked, as the flock of turkeys pecked out in the yard, as the old farmer held tight to a rope that ran taut to a pulley from a branch of a shade tree, and then down to a large steel cone inverted, like a very wide bell, over the flock. The turkeys meandered near it, almost under it.

"Gerald loved a well-roasted bird," he said.

They spooned custard into his china bowls, served a bowl to his old man's wrinkled hands.

Most of Gerald's story was undisputed: the Air Force, at the time Gerald disappeared, was getting rid of air tanks. A new design was favored. They paid cash to haul the old air tanks off. Gerald borrowed a dump truck and filled it. Back home, he welded a frame for a raft. He tied the tanks end to end, made a hut on deck from an oil tank standing. He cut the door out with an acetylene torch. A gutter drained rain to a barrel for water catchment. He sliced extra tanks at fractions, made bells to hang by the door. Town kids rang them with driftwood—*ding dong*, *ding dong*—on launch day.

"Did he build that contraption?" asked Mimi.

The cone swayed in the breeze on the rope from the pulley.

"The Cone of Silence, Gerald called it," the farmer said. "I'll have another bowl of that."

As Prince spooned out more custard, two turkeys began a squabble under the cone, pecking faces, dodging claws and flapping wings. The old farmer pulled the rope a little tighter, and the cone rose higher over the pair. Then he continued.

"At launch I was still young," he said. He'd driven all night from ag school for the raft's maiden voyage, broke grape juice on the bow with his brother. Gerald was last seen at a three-mile bend with a stringer of catfish and burn barrel blazing, twilight, just upstream of the new nuclear station, where guards stood watch on the intake gates with machine guns and walkie-talkies. This was back during the fuss over Russians. The guards claimed they never saw any raft or heard any bells.

The turkey fight was over. One bird limped away. The other stood preening under the cone. The old farmer dropped the rope. The flock turned at the sound. They pecked around the cone until the custard was gone.

"So you see," the old farmer said and licked his fingers. "Anything's possible."

◆ —— ◆

Mimi and Prince had jobs in town. The car passed farm stands and barns, swerved around kids on bikes on the centerlines. Farmers waved at them from big green tractors. Mimi preferred to drive. Prince preferred to watch the fields go by, and the road, and to feel the gears shifting somewhere down below. The road was a wagon trail paved over; the land was cut up as if by a kid having fun with a knife.

"I'll finish the mayor's report today," Mimi said.

"Good," Prince said. "Get it over with." He thumbed two books he'd brought from the attic, *How to Fix a Clock* and *The Complete History of Rome*.

"I'm so tired of all this hanging over me," Mimi said.

"Hanging over?" he said.

"I mean, is this really what life is?" she said. "These endless reports? These lists of nothings for small-town mayors? What about dreams they said to aim for? Passions?"

"We'll get married sometime," Prince said. "Have kids, I guess. Take a class."

The corn disappeared in united distance, the hills, the miles into the past and future. Mimi blew her nose.

"Your allergies," Prince said. "I'll bring something home for that."

She turned in the pharmacy parking lot. Some car was in Prince's slot. She parked in the next space over. They stood together at the employees-only entrance.

"How many acres you think he's got?" Mimi said.

"Who can say?" said Prince. "Quite a few."

They looked around the parking perimeter. They were the most attractive couple.

"I bet that farm's worth a million bucks," Mimi said.

"We deserve to be happy," Prince said.

"How hard can it be?" Mimi said. "Some seeds and a little water? People have been doing it ten thousand years." She held his arm. "I want to live up to our potential. Like the pioneers. Like the Gold Rush people. But this world's holding us back. Tying our hands."

"The pioneers had their troubles too," he said.

"Yes, exactly," she said, shaking his arm a little. "Scalpings and raids were sometimes necessary. Women and children killed by mistake. Old people too, if they tried heroics. Collateral damage."

Prince picked at a splinter in his toe.

She looked at her watch. "We have to think big."

"I want to think big," he said.

He was her most handsome boyfriend ever. Tall and slim like a sapling. She loved his name. She had very few doubts.

"I want to be supportive," Prince said. "What about the brother?"

"I found his death certificate at the courthouse," Mimi said. They leaned on the fuse box. She nibbled his ear. "Let's proceed with our plan, my darling comrade."

"Okay," said Prince.

"Like Lenin and Trotsky," Mimi said.

"Yes, all right," he said. "I'm in."

She shouldered open the door for Prince. He punched in five minutes early.

❧ —— ❧

They were careful. They did research. The seed man, for example, dropping by with samples of drought-resistant hybrids proven in Kansas. He accepted some tea. He said Gerald had been entrepreneurial, started his first venture in grammar school. He'd brought his brother in, of course, but soon every kid in town hunted worms for Gerald's outfit. Rain was best. Torrential, if possible, since any worm must surface or drown. Night crawlers sold in largest volume, then red and yellow worms, though green worms brought the highest price, since any fish in the world will bite at a green worm.

"Did they find the body?" Mimi asked and topped off the seed man's cup.

"It was fifty years ago," he said. "They didn't look as hard back then."

A dime a dozen for average worms was fair, he said. Business boomed. Mimi yawned. The brothers expanded to shiners and grubs. More kids were hired. They dabbled in tadpoles in high school. Mimi stood at the door and looked out the window. They packed the stock in tin cans. Gerald fixed old pop machines to keep the bait cool, but the big attraction was the new robotic arm that accepted coins, then retracted.

"People told Gerald, 'Son, get a patent,'" said the seed man.

"So he was clever," said Mimi. "I can see that."

"Every filling station wanted a machine. 'Worms are a durable enterprise,' Gerald said, 'Since the last man alive will have his fishing line in.'"

⚓ —— ⚓

Each first of the month they walked over to the farmer's with the rent check. They kicked off their sandals and tried out his porch swing. They glided. They shielded their eyes from the sun. "I'm in heaven," she called out over his circle drive, under his shade trees, over his old dried-up covered wagon to his fields beyond, where the tractor was rolling up the rise.

His house was two stories with dormers in the attic and lacy curtains blowing out the windows. The clapboard was white, newly painted. Daffodils sagged around the storm cellar doors. They'd finished blooming after Easter, were now surrounded by fat, budding tulips, reds, pinks, purples, and whites that ran around the brick foundation. The steps were wide and did not sag at all. The porch was cool. The screen door breathed open with the wind.

"Let's go in," Mimi said. They tied the dog to the swing.

The floorboards were wide and painted. A stool stood by the boots by the broom and dustpan. An old soft chair sat in the parlor. It faced a TV with several knobs gone and an oval frame with a wedding picture. A lamp stood over stacks of catalogs—irrigation equipment and motor parts—and samples in baggies from the seed man. Proverbs 17:1 was cross-stitched and hung in a gilt frame:

> Better is a Dry Morsel
> with Quiet
> than a House Full of Feasting
> with Strife.

The dining table had twelve chairs. The banister ran up to beds all made with tasseled spreads, to a stubborn jewelry box, to shirts folded neatly in a tidy dresser, then down the back stairs to the spotless kitchen. Their feet made prints that misted away. They drank milk from the carton in the fridge. A drip board sloped to the sink to a cup and silver spoon, clean and turned over. They washed their hands. They put the milk away.

They ran home, sandals in hand, through the rows of knee-high corn. The dirt was soft and black from recent rain, flat, no tracks from tractor tires, smooth and ready for their ankle-deep prints. Weeds were just getting strong—thistle, pigweed, lamb's quarters.

She held the spoon like a flag. It shone in the sun. They turned, glancing back between strides as if some monster might follow them—might slink out of the pond dripping froth and ferns and leeches from the cracking gape in its mailbox mouth, its tin-can eye open and rusted as it stepped or slithered between rows—but it was just the dog.

"With teeth like that, he could rip your arm off!" Mimi panted, but the dog was a lumberer, could barely keep up.

"Tear your leg off first!" Prince called. "Rupture an artery!"

They laughed and ran faster as the cottage came closer.

"Rip your face off!" She leaped. "Pull your guts out when he got you down!"

She snorted, bent and pawed the ground. She charged him through the seedlings with the spoon at her forehead as a horn. He waved an invisible cape as she passed.

"Olé!" he called.

She turned, charged again. He sliced her neck with an invisible sword. She fell, rose again, angry now, panting, ran on faster toward their waiting cottage, though she grew weak at the porch from enormous blood loss, fell, died on the top step.

He was out of breath. He would beat her home next time.

Weekdays, the dog was tied under a tree in their yard. He dug holes in dirt and lay in the cool. Birds sat on the clothesline, dirtied the towels and T-shirts. He chased the birds, made shadows on sheets—a spider, a bear—until he got tired and slept again. At first the dog had barked at the tractor. The engine was loud and the tires gigantic. But the old farmer brought bones from the butcher, meaty and fresh. They ate lunch together. He called the dog Drum and Rover, sometimes Prince by mistake. He fed the dog the last of the sandwich or meatloaf delivered kindly by Prince or Mimi the night before. Their meat was always dry, his wife would have said, but such nice kids, such a nice dog. It had been years since he had one.

Sometimes he lay on the grass near the dog. Sometimes he folded their laundry, since idle hands are the devil's playthings, since the young can learn only by example, his wife would have said. Lately, when he'd felt too tired to chew, he gave all his lunch to the dog, who wolfed it eagerly. Corn was that tiring. Everyone dies someday.

Sometimes he leaned on their picnic table with the prototype spyglass Gerald had left behind. It was fitted with a small periscope for a 360-degree view, dials and lenses borrowed from the high school science room. If Gerald came home finally, he'd appear in the eyepiece in a caravan, on the crest of their hill, wives and children in capes or turbans speaking a strange language, with dirty feet and ankles, ready for farmwork.

☙ —— ❧

"A very ugly little pond!" Mimi yelled over the pump noise one day, passing it.

"Very slimy!" Prince yelled back. "But cool." He wiped his face with his shoulder.

They were walking muffins over to the old farmer. The pond was a detour, but tempting, almost shy-seeming under hanging trees. It was fun to invade its privacy, to part the brush, walk in, and stamp footprints along its stinking rim. The pump throbbed on in the trees. As the water level dropped, it left a rank green line in the bank. Leaves circled in rafts on the surface, round and round, slow and rotting, sliding toward the rusting intake mouth, which was sucking the pond in the middle. Frogs darted and dipped just far enough from the mouth, followed by frog-eaters: ducks and larger birds passing through.

"We'd never swim there!" Mimi yelled. "If it was my pond, I'd fill it with rocks."

When the old farmer went to the doctor one afternoon, the young couple played bullfight in his house. They took turns as bull, bending and pawing the planking, snorting and snapping and rolling their eyes. The matador would pivot from the horns just in time. The forks, sometimes butter knives, were monogrammed, sterling. A towel or rug was the cape. The dog was locked in the bathroom since he harassed the bull, interfered with the game.

❧ —— ❧

Sometimes the bull died fast, but both preferred slow kills: black eyes darting left and right, the picks submerged in the muscular neck, the jugular or carotid. The blood drained. The brain starved slowly. "Please, my love, don't go."

Once the matador stabbed the bull in the eye. Mimi drove Prince to the walk-in clinic. The car aimed for the glow that was town. The land was black, with small lights here and there. Farm windows were blue with TVs flickering, insomniacs, late-shift workers just getting home. The power lines marched toward the river. The hills cut edges into swaths of stars. The radio played one country song, then another, pretty girls and bottles of beer, *goodbye darlin', come back sweetheart.*

The nurse at the clinic gave him eye drops.

"You could have been more careful," Prince said on the way home.

✧ —— ✧

"If there's a God," Prince said one day as he lay waiting to expire in her lap, "he's watching us like Adam and Eve."

The horn had gored him low in the gut. He moaned and squirmed.

"Adam and Eve were the only two people," Mimi said. "God can't watch billions. That's way too many."

"What if God's like sunshine?" Prince said. "Cooking down on everything."

"We're in shadow," she said, petting his wound. "We're thriving seedlings. We take what we need."

"What if God is like a TV show?" Prince said. "In every room. No hiding places."

"There's only us," she said. "The house, the farm, the pond, the dog."

"But I feel something else," Prince said.

His mouth gaping, the matador died, and she noticed how asymmetrical he was, nose askew, left eye a little low and squinty.

Once, they spied a man in the window with a shovel, but with his head in the bushes. It was hard to see him. It might have been the mailbox-mouthed monster, one-eyed but large, the head a gas can or old air tank.

They crouched behind the sofa and zipped their pants up, shaken.

"It was the brother," Prince said. "Gerald's here."

"Gerald's dead," Mimi said with hands on her head. "I've told you and told you."

At his last Farmers' Parade, the old farmer sat with Mimi in the shade of the water tower.

The floats were small but pretty, put together by the families of the seed men, the irrigation outfits, the tractor supply and tack shop, the savings and loan and crop-insurance offices, the fertilizer folks, the insecticide co-op, the crop-dusting inspectors and FAA, the seed bank and prairie-grass historians, the surveyors guild, the beekeepers just back from a nut pollination clinic in California, the topsoil preservationists, all six churches, the bingo and bridge leagues, the entomologist society from the ag school, the cooperative extension, the composters' commune, the triplets who ran the grain elevator. Then came several politicians in antique cars, the 4-H Club on ponies, Scouts of all kinds in sashes and caps—just beautiful, beautiful—the public health nurse with a giant syringe, the Humane Society with adoptables leashed, the Fighting

Gophers Marching Band, the Daughters of the American Revolution passing out candy and voter registrations, the Union locals, though no one liked them, the National Guard reservists in formation, the Masons, followed by Shriners on tricycles. The farmers on tractors got the biggest cheers.

The dunk tank was in the shady town square. The kids did crafts, but there was nothing sellable. Ribbons were given for hot dog eating and the fastest baby still crawling.

"That old man might blow away," said the mayor to Prince. "Is he eating?"

They were watching Mimi with the old farmer in the potluck line. She was spooning food onto the old man's plate.

"He's a slender man anyway," said Prince. "He's been feeling poorly."

"You seem like good people." The mayor nodded at Mimi. "She's a good worker at Town Hall."

"We like it here very much," said Prince, turning red. "Feels like one big family."

Kids raced in potato sacks. They were falling and laughing in piles.

"His color is poor. He's frail," said the mayor. "Why so suddenly downhill?"

"We wonder too," said Prince. "Me and Mimi. We pull our hair out. Almost like someone's out to get him. Poison. Some hard to trace neurotoxin. But death is natural."

The mayor nodded slowly. He asked after rat poison on the farmer's premises. Was it sealed correctly? Put away right in the old man's barn?

"What about the mayor?" Mimi said on the ride home.

"They're trying to figure who we are," Prince said.

"I bet." She checked the rearview mirror. The pavement was fuzzy with heat.

"It's kind of sad," Prince said.

Her fingers fiddled with the radio, then walked up his leg to the belt and button and slipped down in. The car drifted over the centerline, but the road was a flat, lonely ribbon. In a while they swerved back to the proper lane. The dust made a rooster tail behind the car. The wind took the plume higher. It could be seen for miles, anonymous and dry, much taller and grander than dust deserves.

❧ —— ❧

When it got very hot, Prince and Mimi went wading in the pond after all. The dog ran headlong down the slimy slope. The water was cool and thick. They followed the dog and wallowed, but carefully, since the intake mouth could suck a leg in, an arm, a dog, the old farmer had warned them, and irrigation would halt until the line was cleared.

But the dog floated like a cork, swam figure eights. Mimi waded after him, dove.

"When dogs were first domesticated," she called, "they were never allowed to sleep in the teepees!"

"How could you possibly know that?" he called, sitting in slime, swatting bugs.

"Humans had just quit being nomadic!" She paddled after the dog, just far enough from the intake mouth. "We clustered in tribes! Docile wolves lingered near! Lived on scraps and rats in the village dump! Dogs earned their keep! They barked at night and warned the village! I saw a show!"

"Warned the village of what?" Prince called.

"Of enemies approaching!"

They peeled the slugs off after the swim. Checked scalps for ticks. One was headed down Mimi's ear. Prince could've plucked it off the lobe and crushed it, but did not. At night the dog slept in the hallway.

∾ — ∾

The old farmer loved their stroganoff. He said they'd get him fat, but he only got thinner. Prince brought him energy shakes from the pharmacy. They asked his advice about classes at the learning center: Wild Plants: Dos and Don'ts, or Country Life in Five Weeks. Mimi scored better on tests. Prince bought agricultural journals, pamphlets on quicklime, sweet peppers, and genetics for extended seasons.

"You kids are something," the old farmer said, ate and ate.

In those weeks, while he could, the old farmer taught Prince the tractor. Sometimes the seed man dropped in to look around. The mayor watched the house from the road one night. But they saw nothing fishy, they reported to their wives. The old man seemed happy.

"I really like the old guy," said Prince one night. "We could reconsider."

"Sure," Mimi said, climbing on top. "Let's think and think and think and think."

At work, the mayor was demanding, campaigning for a new jail. He wanted perfection. At the pharmacy, the new nail line was arriving with a national spokesgirl to boost rural interest. TV crews were expected after press releases, but a bomb went off in Kansas City. None showed. At night, they fanned themselves on the mattress. They talked about central air, canopies, and mosquito netting. Once, when the old farmer left with the Cross State Choir, they nuzzled in his big breezy bed, under the cross-stitched Ecclesiastes 9:7 hanging above the headboard:

> Go,
> Eat your Bread with Joy,
> Drink your Wine with Merry Hearts,
> For God has Approved
> What You Do.

They sat on his counter, ate his cheese and crackers, unconcerned by crumbs, talked of recent crashes into high-rise buildings, of innocent airplanes used as weapons, of Alis and Mohammeds, their motivations, explosions on train tracks vs. powdery envelopes uninspected vs. rich and poor vs. yes or no vs. maximization vs. potentiation, as they fed each other late-season peas.

"I see why they do it," Mimi said.

"Still, they go too far," said Prince. "Like rabid dogs."

"The deck is stacked," she said. "People have to cheat."

She had ugly traits he'd never noticed: a snout nose, cave-like nostrils, and pygmy fingers in the peas. Her thighs were getting hefty: no beauty queen, no Annie Oakley. They took a walnut highboy from the farmer's attic, and a samovar, which they lugged around the field since the rows were too thick now for walking with furniture.

Once, when they were kissing in the window, a car skidded fast into a telephone pole. "Kids," Mimi said. "They've really smashed it." The car had been too small anyway for all those hollering mouths, too many arms out the windows, the music too loud for such a quiet place this far out. The front end steamed, wrapped around the pole, while the music blared on and a wheel rolled toward town. The old farmer's porch light flicked on.

"Of course," she said. The old farmer was running toward the accident in an old bathrobe. He staggered after his flashlight, which fanned back and forth under purple trees, past the old covered wagon and tractor, all just smudges and spokes at this distance, or maybe bison herds bedded down, Prince thought, or a giant blue squid misplaced at that groggy hour. He shook his head clear.

"Should we go help?" Prince said. "Should we run?"

"Okay, let's run," Mimi said. "Like a fire brigade."

They grabbed towels. Mimi beat the old farmer to the scene, the sirens too and the body bags. But Prince beat Mimi by a mile.

⚜ —— ⚜

There was a story no one knew: how the brother got the land.

While the old farmer had been in ag school, Gerald learned to survey. Lines weren't lining up between counties, which puzzled tax departments and planning offices, so they hired him. He'd found no posts or corners, no markings around the parcels. He'd unfolded maps and compared. Two thousand acres did not exist on paper. He shook the transit, walked to town to phone his brother, and later, together, they had retaken backsights, baselines, and angles to the line of sight, marked meridians, bearings, benchmarks, made adjustments with pencils and fractions. They had walked the tripod on their shoulders. They had sat by the creek and eaten some lunch.

"Who owns anything anyway?" said the old farmer, then just nineteen years old.

"It's ours," Gerald had said.

The land was good and loamy, old river bottom, fine particles to hold the wet, the last uncharted land in either county, in all the continent, maybe, perhaps the last wild land in all the world, excepting some volcanic islands in the Pacific. The brothers laughed at that—a place with little soil and too hot to farm. They'd toasted each other with chocolate milk.

They'd built a house in a clump of trees. The old farmer got married. They built the cottage for Gerald. The brothers slipped cash to the secretary in the records office. Her husband, wounded at Normandy, was legless in the Soldier's Home, then dead. This secretary had mouths to feed. The old farmer never told his wife. He had not known her well enough. Then she'd died. Gerald left before that.

One by one, the old farmer had bought up contiguous parcels. His farm prospered and sponsored Little League teams, gave money to every candidate, sent the high school choir to state competition. He stayed clear of lawyers and auditors. He was engaged to the secretary in the records office, but not for long. No matter that her husband had been buried; everyone felt as though he were still waiting, maimed, for his weekly visit.

The old farmer figured he'd outlive everyone.

       ↝ —— ↜

By August the old farmer wanted apple pie dinners only. Mimi set the thermometer under his old tongue, checked his pulse as she'd learned on a video. He rocked on the swing and talked like he was dreaming: how maybe Gerald had made it to the ocean, to some new wild land where he was mayor. Where everyone was rich or well on their way. Where the guilty paid for their crimes, but fairly and rightly, the old-fashioned way, as Gerald preferred things, the guilty placed squarely face-to-face with punishment, in the public ring, none of this prison foolishness, rather a fight to the death with a bull or a bear, or better yet, with some steel fighting machine of Gerald's invention, the thing huge, tall, and terrible, since brother Gerald could weld anything, and spectators paid a quarter for a front-row seat to best witness the machine's rivets and bolts in action, the claws up close and hideous, enormous ferocious jaws snapping at the small frail man down below in the dirt, helpless, as we all are, every day of our lives, each ticket paid to see life change to death in a moment, as it does, as it will, the old farmer said, the fights to promote repentance only, inspection of soul, the return of salvageable strays to the fold.

The old farmer sucked an apple. Prince was shaking.

Gerald's land was music too, smiles and girls in dresses, food overflowing on every table, fresh fruit, red meat, honey-drizzled bread, fancy chocolates, and dill pickles. Taxation outlawed, he said. Fines paid for the public schools since you can't cheat the kids. Only the best people, the best intentions.

Prince dropped a fine china dish, pie everywhere. "We have to stop," his lips said.

"We just need to speed it up," Mimi's lips said. "He doesn't mind making room."

When the dog started coughing blood, the vet said the disease was mysterious. Parvo or giardia. The dog still wanted to swim in the pond. Prince rented a wheelchair to be ready. One night Mimi woke to Prince kneeling by the mattress with a pillow.

"What are you doing?" she said.

The corn seedlings were ten feet tall and not even done growing yet. They sucked from roots deep and strong. Prince watched all the late-night shows, which he hoped would explain everything explainable. That each silk in the tassel pollinates its own kernel, eight hundred kernels, sixteen rows. That men can survive years at sea. That unexploded bombs sit in fields for decades. Once, Prince was sure he'd seen the tractor running the rows on its own, no farmer in the cab. It stalled and stood there.

He stood at the edge of the field with a machete. He could feel it. The field was the fringe of the mane of some too big Thing.

"I'm ready for you," he panted, facing west, waved the blade at the tractor.

She stood on the porch. "What are you doing?"

"He's booby-trapped it," Prince said. "The storm cellar, maybe, some hidden camera."

"Pull yourself together." Mimi went inside, the screen door slapping.

❧ —— ❧

Prince tried to run away. In the bus station he saw a show on the big TV about a large trash island, the size of fifty Nebraskas, floating east of Japan. It swirled and bunched where currents met, a knot of garbage and aquatic waste: bottles and seal flippers, airplane sections and urchins loosed in typhoons. No country claimed it. The island did not appear on satellite images, which seemed important to Prince: the Invisible Truth. He sat close to the big screen. The bus was leaving. He searched for familiar faces on the island. He saw only himself in the plasma surface.

She picked him up in the car. He was walking out of town by the silo.

To make peace, they took the matching walnut bed frame from the attic. The box spring. They drank boxed wine from the samovar, tried to see the future, played checkers. They slept off the floor from then on, hammered a nail for cross-stitched Psalm 81:10:

> I am the Lord your God
> Who brought You up out of the Land of Egypt.
> Open your Mouth Wide
> and I will fill it.

"It's too late to stop now," she said. They watched the old farmer sip and shrink. They pounded his back when he coughed blood. They said good night at his bedroom door. They called the mayor and others with status reports.

"Someone's getting in my house," the old farmer said one night. "Taking things." He told them where he hid the key, said, "Keep your eyes peeled for riffraff."

"We will. Of course."

The raspberries were getting red. They stood in brambles, stuffed their mouths until their tongues were sore.

"I don't know if I like you," Prince said in the veterinarian's lobby.

"And you're one of those limp modern men," Mimi said.

The nurse called the dog in. The vet shaved the dog to reduce heat stress. "Let him swim in the pond whenever he wants." They shut him in the root cellar that was always cool.

❧ —— ❧

When the old farmer's end was near, the people gathered for a pre-death celebration. They shared happy stories of the past, of antics with Gerald. "Here's to good soil, new seasons, and happy memories!" The old farmer sat in his covered wagon and enjoyed all of it. Mimi passed plates and trays. Prince poured lemonade from their new crystal pitcher. The seed man told how, after the worms, when cremations were just getting big, the brothers brought a crop duster for aerial funerals. The old farmer smiled, remembering. "People wanted to be scattered all over," he said in a tiny voice. "Death is an endless market." People paid extra, he said, for fancy jars, for banners off the tail. Gerald had worn a minister's collar, which made the embalmers mad. The brothers had saved for a new John Deere, jerry-rigged it to do it all: cut the stalks, strip the ears, shell the corn, chop the stalks for silage, which was whisked to a fermenting tank. They did not get a patent for this, either.

All the farmers laughed. "Of course not."

"The city slickers make the millions."

"How they go on and on about this Gerald," Mimi said later that night with her face in his crotch. "Like he's some celebrity. Some Al Capone of the Prairie."

⚜ —— ⚜

The old farmer had never stopped looking for his brother. He had sometimes flown the crop duster, had sometimes buzzed the nuclear station. He kept his eyes peeled for air tanks and rusting raft frames, never saw either.

The river changed each season, with rain and snow levels up and down. Road crews sucked the river for interstate projects. In a cockpit, water level didn't matter. He buzzed low over new islands. He banked at cottonwoods no one cared about. Some flood would take them. Landing was not the problem. The plane could stop and turn on a dime. It was always the takeoff that took yardage, skill, and judgment.

⚜ —— ⚜

An armoire now stood by the bathroom door, which was closed and locked, a wicker-backed chair braced under the knob. Books filled the bookcase, others sprawled open on braided rugs, *Pilgrim's Progress* and *On the Origin of Species*, bookmarked, dog-eared. A set of silver brushes was arranged among nail polish bottles and mascara, all atop a heavy dressing table that was pushed for the night across the door to the hall.

"I wish I knew Gerald," said Prince. "I wish I knew his master plan."

"Don't be a chump," she said. "You didn't believe that aerial funeral story?"

"Of course I believe it," Prince said, pushing her face away. "The whole world's not a liar."

He was in some sort of ecstasy.

In the fall sometimes the heat was unbearable. Prince picked up prescriptions. The vet put the dog down. They trucked the wheelchair to the tree for the burial.

"A good dog," the old farmer said.

Prince and Mimi stayed late at the hospital with him. The doctors shrugged that they didn't know. They slept in the farmer's house due to the robbers. Prince slept as though drugged. He woke sometimes with red patches on his chest as if slugs had sucked there.

The old farmer didn't want cremation. "Life's messy enough. Just bury me."

The nurse was witness when the old farmer signed the will, all on the up-and-up.

After, outside the ICU, Prince folded the paper and stuffed it in his back pocket. They watched the evening news, the weather. A tornado had picked up a house in Indianola, set it down in Simpson. Mimi clicked off the TV. The other visitors drifted off for coffee. Prince scratched his neck.

"You should really pay attention," Prince said.

"Oh?" she said. "What does that mean?"

"You should watch your back," he said. "For tornadoes and such."

Mimi pointed the TV clicker at him. "A good idea," she said. "You too."

The harvest was done, at least. Prince loved driving the tractor. The nurses loved Mimi: her take-charge personality. The mayor and everyone brought a parade of flowers.

"He was so old anyway," people said in the hallway of the morgue.

✕ —— ✕

The last bullfight was on the rim of the pond. This was November. The pump was quiet since the new seedlings were still two seasons off.

The bull seemed sluggish, tampered with. It pawed the ground out of obligation and tossed its dizzy head. Its black eyes rolled, ran at the cape, oblivious to water below, the life proceeding there. Ducks watched the bullfight in flotillas, rested their wings, though their migrational flight was hardly begun. They skirted islands of slush and froth mixed with leaves. They bumped late lily pads, dipped their heads for minnows. The flock parted in Vs for floating objects—barn trash and junk thrown into the pond from cars, twigs and limbs. The first flakes of snow fell onto the slime.

Then, a sound: a shiver on the water's surface. The ducks knew it, lifted up and flew south.

Then the pond began to boil and steam. Pipes appeared on the surface, twisted and kinked. The pump onshore coughed alive. Something large lifted its rusty head from the water, larger and larger. It periscoped up from the center of the pond. Water dripped like oil from its coppery mouth. The neck craned up, link by link, the head fifty feet above the pond and shrubs, stretching up as if to peer over its land, its houses, to watch its sun go down, to bow to deserving comrades, the silo in town, the tall tree on the hill, to dry itself, to stretch its blades and tracks over freezing mud. Then the head turned.

The pair was far below, on all fours now, one-on-one, two nipping beetles.

The head dropped. The jaw cracked open on rusty hinges. An empty belly knows no blame.

Prince saw it coming. It didn't matter.

The teeth were saw blades, splintered and bolted. The tongue was crusty, impervious to the small complaints of minuscule fists, for example, or tiny heeled feet kicking as the gullet swallowed. The head tossed the second meal, lurching to make the catch, down the hatch—a little salty, a fishy flavor—caught for an instant in the riveted throat, the head shaking with the joy of hunger briefly satisfied as the slow grind commenced.

CLIFF ORDEAL

Mr. Ted Wilson stood in the branches. His legs made an uppercase A in the tree, one track shoe on the largest small branch and the other on a middling knot on the cliff wall. The sun was coming up. Mr. Ted Wilson stood perfectly still. He gripped a jut of rock overhead from the cliff first for balance, granite or limestone, who could say which, except for experts, and how could it matter, and second, yes, to take some weight off the largest small branch. Any engineer would have advised it. This tree was far too small for a full-grown man.

He gripped the jut of rock with the longest fingers only. The smaller fingers, the pinkies and third fingers, wagged free, then tucked, then wagged, the fingertips blue. A shorter man, even slightly shorter than Ted Wilson, would never have reached this jut of rock, Ted thought. Standing on his toes, the shorter man would have been obliged to hold the cliff, which was very smooth, a challenge for fingers, or would have cantilevered off in the smaller small branches, thin and soft-skinned and bent over the creek far below, perches for birds. This smaller man's posture would be a lowercase n or h, depending. The muscles would burn and contract, doubled in among the surprising-thick leaves of this surprising cliff. Any lowercase letter would be harder to spot from the old bridge or the road than an uppercase A, Ted concluded. The smaller man could not hold the position, the *n* or *h*, the creek swirled. Ted was sorry for the smaller man.

It had been a miserable night. Cold, hungry, his head bleeding. The cliff—after the hot day—turning cold and then radiating cold. Ted had shivered and tried to be still. He called "Hello!" and "Help!" and his mother's name. He sang "Twinkle Twinkle." He wouldn't worry. Last night Ted Wilson had asked for the wind to stay down and it did, then asked for morning and morning came and that was now.

"Help! Help! Help!" to treetops and the bridge. "Help! Help! Help!" he called.

An engineer would have calmed him. He'd have sat on a boulder below in a windbreaker. He'd have reassembled Ted Wilson's phone that was scattered in the rocks. He'd have called up to the tree, "Hold to the rock! The tree can't be trusted! I've had precipice training!"

"When will they come!" Ted Wilson would call down to this friendly new friend. "I'm getting tired! It's been twelve hours since I fell! I think I have injuries! I'm exhausted!"

"As soon as they miss you! Don't worry! Panic is your only enemy now!"

This engineer was obviously right. The small tree was still in shadow. Mr. Ted Wilson waited calmly for day, the sun that rose off the east rim of the world.

⚬ —— ⚬

Mr. Ted Wilson was very tall and visible anywhere, the engineer would have pointed out, a huge advantage. His tracksuit was blue with orange stripes down the legs and arms, unmistakable, from his alma mater. It still fit him perfectly. June Allison had said so on several occasions, in the office weekends for a Monday deadline. "As late as needed," she had said, "whenever you need me." And there she always was, waiting at the outer desk, Saturday morning with a muffin and coffee as he liked it, she had her own key, the mate to the key on the chain in his tracksuit pocket. It weighed him down. He loved its jingle.

Ted held the jut of rock overhead with both hands, as the engineer would have said. The quarter hours passed. Sometimes, he hung with one hand only if his nose needed scratching, for example, or his belly, which was wet and damp under his tracksuit as if bugs were walking and so the free hand slid under the shirt and smeared the bugs away. Or to wave at a car crossing the old bridge, or to sneeze, his wrist at the nose to hold his head steady, since the small tree shook with sneezes. Or to wave down a van or truck, or any driver, but there were so few cars on this stretch at this hour. Sometimes Ted touched the cliff with his elbow. Or his forearm. This cliff was soft and creamy, average in color and smoothness and only moderately sized for this region of North America where enormous cliffs and huge ledges were the absolute norm. A hundred and fifty feet, a guess. Cliffs dropped off around every seeming corner, Ted thought, like flies or a mouse infestation. Americans lost track. They walked right off, it could happen to anyone.

"I know it!" the engineer would have called up with a thermos. The scent of coffee would swirl up the rock face.

"I'm starving!" Ted would tell the man at breakfast time.

"I'm sure!" the man would say, surely embarrassed to eat and drink before a starving man, but a man must eat and drink.

"I'm not embarrassed about this fall!" Ted would call down to the engineer.

"Of course not! Cliffs and ledges keep people employed. The firemen thrive on search and rescues, we love firemen, firemen should thrive!"

"Yes!" Ted would have called. "It's just geography colliding with carelessness! It's part of the economy!"

"Of course!" the engineer would have said and peeled his muffin, as a doe calls up from below, "Call them 'firefighters,' please."

Now that the new east sun was stronger and older by a few minutes, Ted shifted a foot.

⁂

The creek roared. It foamed between the legs of the A. Ted called out from time to time but thought to save his vocal cords.

It was a fine view, the narrow valley, the mountains, and all the summer's new green to the sea in the distance. Ted watched the confluence of the river and creek where the rainbows schooled for boats. The fishermen will always come.

Ted Wilson watched the old bridge for cars but it was still early, a Saturday, people were home with family and still in bed. Only six cars had passed during the night, five were kids driving too fast, hooting and headlights, and the last was a paddy wagon from the prison heading into Spitfire, fifth largest town in the Frontier State, that Last Frontier.

Ted watched the path up the far side of the creek. It was just a small path dropping down from the pullout at the far end of the old bridge. Walkers would park there, click their locks, leash their dogs, then zag through boulders and shrubs until they would arrive opposite his tree. A passerby could not possibly miss him. Any passerby would do, an early dog walker, a fisherman wading out from the brush, or the fat lady with the ankle weights, but perhaps she was out of town. Ted tried to remember her name. Ted did not want to alarm her. A man in a small tree on a bare rock cliff is hardly expected.

A quarter hour passed. The net of trees atop the opposite cliffs had gone blue from purple and now green from blue.

Ted Wilson craned for a look up at his own cliff edge for a birder or another walker gone wrong at the Y as he had done last evening. It was easy without a sign, no CLIFF AHEAD! in black on orange, no mention of any cliff at all, or a picture of a cliff, or a picture of a person falling through the air, arms and legs kicking, the faller's mouth an uppercase O from a line that meant a cliff into double wavy lines meaning water. The cliff had looked exactly like a clearing. Another walker might think the same up the wrong path from the Y, slapping back branches and jumping puddles. But there was no room for a second man. This tree had grown in the perfect location, ten feet down with branches like a mitt. Only shrubs and grasses for two hundred yards, some nameless flowers like buttons sewn on rock. He watched the confluence again for swimmers but of course there were none at that hour. He checked his watch, but Ted Wilson never wore a watch.

"Good morning, June Allison, how are you? You look bright and shiny."

"I'm A1, Mr. Wilson, as always, I had a great weekend."

"Wonderful, June Allison, I'm happy for you. You deserve to be great."

"But how are you, Mr. Wilson? This cliff is some spot."

"I'm fine, I'm fine, June Allison. I've handled worse things."

"What can I do? Call a search party?"

"Yes, call me a search party."

"It's the least I could do."

"Yes, it's the least you could do, June Allison, or keep me company."

The creek churned gravel, sand, and foam into roar and mist. The wind took the mist to Red Mountain, which still gleamed with old snow that melted in the sun and filled the creek; the current was strong. But for this tree, they might never find Ted's body, a fish would find it, or a whale. It would wash down under the old bridge, dump in the river that turned south then west in a mile behind at the fire hall then to the bend where Spitfire sat then turned fat and flat and fast ten miles downhill to salt water. The blue swath. Ted might smell it too, salt, but that was impossible, his nose was running so. He wiped one nostril on his shoulder stripe.

"Why did the chicken cross the road?"

"I hate that joke, Mr. Wilson."

"Come on, June Allison, I'm stuck in this tree."

"No, I won't say it."

Mountain trees swept by like twigs to the sea. A body might snag in soggy branches with lost fishing poles, bobbers, single boots, and thermos jugs still full and hot and buoyant, last season's rain hats and books and pencils, blurry and logy, all tugged toward deep open water, the urchins and flesh eaters.

"Cut it out!" the engineer would have called up to Ted. "Think positive!"

"When are they coming!"

"They'll be here by ten!"

The wind was calm but would rise with heat, and the bugs would come out and the rainbows would rise up for the bugs. The fishermen would follow, though Ted had not read the most recent fish forecasts, they'd park on the shoulder out of view. They'd zip their life vests at their tailgates. The car doors would slam. "Hello! Hello! Please help me, please." They would walk up the path toward Ted's voice.

"What a big ugly bird!"

"I'll say, Lord!"

"A buzzard."

"Or the world's last dodo!"

Ted would call down, joining in the hullabaloo. He'd be ribbed for life. In business dealings, at high school reunions, as usher in church, ribbed and ribbed but lemonade will come from lemons: the firm will film an ad with Ted in a tree, a clip of the headline after rescue, a fireman and chainsaw, a submarine, and a shark. The clients will swarm.

From the fishermen, a boy runs for help. He will be small and thin. He is the son of the son of the partner in Spitfire's biggest firm, he will sprint up the path on his young-buck legs, a scatterer of rabbits across the road and bridge, a driver of a dirt bike unleashed from a trailer, which coughs awake blue smoke, though the dirt bike is entirely illegal on pavement, a hundred-dollar fine, though the boy has no license yet, it will be years or never, a sudden accident might strike this boy at fifteen, a month before his birthday, a car crash or drowning in riptide, a fall off a cliff on an Eagle Scout outing with a flint in his pocket, the mother bent before the itsy-bitsy casket, though the fire chief could impound the little red dirt bike, or could arrest the sudden change of heart rate, or confiscate the gears and wheels that speed toward safety over clean, blessed pavement, one mile to the fire hall, this still-sweet nubbin, this boy: he'd get a slap on the wrist only. This boy, soon to become a hero of the Famous Ted Wilson Rescue.

⋙ — ⋘

A rabbit was flattened on the bridge. Ted Wilson did not witness the hit-and-run. He'd been planning the day and day-dreaming:

"Life was getting humdrum anyway!" Mr. Ted Wilson decided he would call up to the search party. "Hunger then food, hunger then food, then sleeping, then working and working, and never a break from it! A cliff shakes things up!"

The fire chief would be the first face, the thumbs-up, hands and knees in brush and brambles off his cliff edge. He'd wear a distinctive badge polished with wrinkles and a satellite phone closed in a briefcase. The rookies would follow. They'd mimic the thumb.

"People don't *live* anymore!" Ted decided he'd add. He'd call it out to opposite cliffs for echo and emphasis. "We don't take risks like our ancestors did, like the pioneers did, like the first Atlantic crossers!" The birds would fly up over volunteers and dogs with ladders and ropes. They'd drop a canteen and a rope knotted at the end for a seat. A helmet would fall, splash down, gone like a little yellow boat.

Ted would call up, "I took a wrong turn at the Y!"

"We guessed it!" they would call down.

"This cliff," Ted would call up, "looked exactly like a clearing!"

"Yes, we know, we could tell, it could happen to anyone!" The fire chief would press big, tough buttons on his big, tough headset to the strong, brave cliff crew and the strong, brave dive crew.

"Hang tight!" they'd call down and Ted would call up, "Will do!"

Ted would hold the canteen but not drink. "I'm so grateful! I'll surely up my contribution at the Fireman's Ball!"

Gratitude. Ted would sit somehow on the knot, the rookies who'd hand-over-hand Ted to the edge would marvel at Ted's composure and plan to slap Ted's back. When his track shoelace loops a root, the chief's lieutenant will lean to free it. Another will hold the man's belt. These big, tough, strong, brave men know no fear.

"You are fearless!" Ted will call.

Once aloft on terra firma, Ted will walk the canteen to a new tree twenty feet in, hug the tree, and drink for joy.

⚓ —— ⚓

Time passed, morning, the hours and minutes. This sun slid higher, Ted's stomach growled. He scratched his nose. A leaf had tickled it. Or some mouse. They lived in the cliff edge in a maze of tunnels, though Ted could see only the front doors of thousands. The edge was riddled and bored, these mice must play their little mousy tricks on the big man's nose in the tree to pass the quarter hours that are much more substantial in mouse-time, hours or three hours. Then Ted forgot the mice for the rookies. Since the rookies would strap Ted in a litter, padded, with handles at the foot and head, "One two three lift!"

and float away down the wrong path to the Y to the right path, and turn, the fire chief at the head, explaining the grid search and the Ted-scent and how sniffer dogs had found it from a sock Beth had produced just that morning, and how the dogs had not been fed prior to rescue, a simple coincidence, the fire chief would add, the dogs trained with inaudible whistles of the hardy canine corps, tanned and smooth-skinned and natural athletes every one but with the budget so tight, so many rescues, so many lost people, these dogs and this very corps are next to go, they're all in *jeopardy*.

"In short, we need friends in City Hall," the fire chief would hint.

"You have one in me," Ted would say and shake on it from the litter.

The road would be full of sirens. The fire chief and Ted would fish together in Ted's new speedboat. The chief would catch an octopus.

Ted scratched a mouse-trick.

"Beth called the fire hall. She's coming right out with the kids," the chief would say.

"Wonderful! I have sweet children," Ted would say.

"They send their love," the chief would say. "Beth said to be sure I told you about their love. You are so very lucky, Mr. Wilson."

"Yes, very lucky. I know it. Beth."

"Beth's a fine person," the chief would say.

"Of course, yes."

"A credit to the community, all those boards and committees," the chief would say.

"Yes, yes, yes, I agree one hundred percent," Ted would say.

"Beth's a great mother too," the chief would say.

"Yes, she is," Ted would say. "Beth's a maternal genius."

And the words mixed on the banks of Ted's sandy earlobes: a garble of water, tentacles, and inaudible whistles sloshing with silt and salt and sticky lumps, a jumble of mouse-talk to the opposite cliffs.

"June Allison! June Allison!" Ted called to the cliffs. "Where are you!"

The birds flew up. Ted hugged his branch, which shook, and some rock fell and stones rolled down the cliff, bounced, plunked, and were swallowed. He scrambled back to his A.

At the ambulance the chief will recommend Ted to a local biographer and slide Ted Wilson in. Ted will drink and drink in his bed in the hospital where nurses will dab the hands with salve and wrap that head, which will have stopped bleeding by then, surely. He will be awarded a Rotary Prize and will make a moving speech when accepting it. The kids will sit round the front table with the mayor, Beth and the mayor's wife in matching corsages.

"Congratulations, Mr. Wilson."

"Thank you, Mr. Mayor, I could never have done it without the team." He would squeeze Beth's hand. The book will come out in two years to the day. June Allison will not be mentioned, not even in the index, since she is no one to Ted Wilson, will be hardly remembered, and had nothing to do with this cliff ordeal.

∞ —— ∞

At ten or nine or eleven, the cars became more frequent. It felt like lunchtime but it couldn't be lunchtime since they would arrive by lunchtime and had not arrived. A potato chip van drove by, then a four-door with a missing back bumper, then a cop car from the prison with a full back seat. Ted thought of the peanuts in his leg zip, but didn't dare.

The sun rose over the treetops behind his back. It lanced down the valley, striped the trees and river and the roofs of Spitfire, in the windows to his very own kitchen table, and across to the sea and across into great deep ocean cracks, where it punctured the hulls of submarines with spotlights. His nose bled. He dabbed it with a leaf. Ted's cap lifted off his head. Ted swiped the wind. The cap coptered down and was carried off to the Mariana Trench.

At the press conference in the fire hall they would offer cough drops. The podium would have no microphone but dust and spider sacks from the supply room. The rookies would clean it with rags. The chief would pull down the pull-down map. The chief would point with a pointer at the tree, which will be just an X beside the tiny blue-winding creek on the big map. His friends and neighbors would have gathered with hot dishes and mitts. They'd heard on police scanners. They will use paper plates only.

"Good morning, June Allison, how are you?"

"I'm A1, Mr. Wilson, and you though? This tree is a new one."

"You said that before."

"I'm trying to be friendly."

"You didn't make the press conference."

"It's a long flight. I was there in spirit, by the extinguisher recharge station."

"I could feel you in the back."

The minister would be there too, Beth's mother and father, near the podium, his parents were dead, but his siblings would gather as a group of faces, the dead ones and live ones, then his own mother and father would show up late, in the back, Beth and the kids at the table up front.

"Good morning, June Allison, how was the weekend, did you see your fat lady at the gym?"

"Don't say that, Mr. Wilson, I'm as fat as she is."

"You must look like a whale in Japan."

"So now you've turned nasty?"

"Truth hurts. What's her name?"

"That fat lady? It slips my mind."

"Don't go."

"I'm leaving."

The rookies would feed him orange Popsicles. Pizza would be plentiful from the enormous and overloaded fire hall freezer. Two on every table. Parents would shush the kids. The reporters would ask the spelling of Ted Wilson's name. They would snap pictures and describe his condition. The fire chief will order a warning sign erected at the wrong turn at the Y. The rookies will rush to the rookie truck. At the Y they will pound the posts with sledgehammers and picks, hang the sign with cotter pins since cotter pins will be handy and overstocked in the fire hall supply room. Bolts installed only later.

"Try again, Mr. Wilson."

"OK. Good morning, June Allison, how was your weekend?"

"It was wonderful, Mr. Wilson, church was divine, our minister's expansive, thanks for asking. My friends call me JJ."

"That's repulsive, June Allison. Your name is beautiful."

"Get hold of yourself, Mr. Wilson."

❧ —— ☙

Ted Wilson urinated at ten or nine, or perhaps eleven, or two. He filled one track shoe. The tracksuit dripped off the inner seams.

The sun rose and rose as it does. The mice got working. They sprayed dirt in fine grains on Ted's leaves and he brushed them off as he could. A plane flew over and made a line that faded. A black hatchback stopped at the pullout.

Ted called "Hello!" then "Hello! Hello!" at the man from the hatchback. The birds banked noisily north toward Red Mountain. The man stood at the guardrail. Ted waved an arm. The man did not see. The man was arguing with his mother, Ted could tell, hand to his ear with twisted-mother lips and the angry mother-slam to the roof with his fist, she'd got the last word, Ted felt for this man who turned the key with mother-only-wrath, floored it south, gone and lost, a low point. A rabbit skipped up the path, stopped, then peeled off into ferns, happy or terrified, impossible to know in rabbits.

"Knock, knock."

"No, no."

"Knock, knock, June Allison, it's a good one."

"No, Mr. Wilson, I mean it."

Matching motorcycles sped by. A truck with a silver tank of milk. A truck with tires, a truck with cars, shiny and new, from the outside world, Detroit, Korea, or Tokyo.

"That's a normally very busy bridge," June Allison would have said to the reporters at the press conference, if asked. "I bet twenty cars per hour. And the pullout was always so well advertised. While we lived in the area, this pullout was so popular for families fishing. Marty and I brought the kids for fishing and camping I bet twice a year."

"Not one more word about Marty. I can't take it."

"It's not the same with Marty and you."

"You eat breakfast with him. You share a toothbrush."

"I don't eat breakfast."

The creek rose three millimeters and roared three millimeters louder at ten or ten fifteen or ten thirty-two depending on the time zone. In Topeka it was dark getting darker as the sun touched the farthest leaf on Ted Wilson's tree and the skin on his wrists above the cuffs. An old two-door, puffing blue, crossed the old bridge, a pickup, then a semitrailer with no cargo. If it were Monday, not Saturday, they would have missed Ted at the office already. The search party would gather at the courthouse by noon. They'd find Ted by dinner. The press conference would start by 8 p.m. sharp with the folding chairs where Engine Number Two should park. However, if it was Monday and June Allison was still in Ted's employ, if she had not moved to Japan with her husband and children, if she had not up and packed every belonging not sold at the garage sale (Ted bought the speedboat and Beth bought the bunk beds and the mixer set with American plugs), if she still occupied the outer desk just outside his office door, as a month ago, still tidied his things, still listened to his worries and concerns, if she had not absented herself in this appalling way, then Ted's search party would have come even sooner, earlier than dinner even, but for June Allison's Japan adventure, they'd find Ted in the tree cliff by absolute lunchtime.

Somewhere the tide changed. The jellyfish schooled to the submarine and went in, ten thousand the size of a nickel. They killed a diver through his survival suit. They latched on and ate him in the spotlights.

The tree shook. The wind picked up.

"June Allison."

"What?"

"Nothing."

"What?"

June Allison would have found him by lunchtime. Here's how: June Allison would have arrived at the outer desk at 7 a.m. She'd hello the janitor and the corner assistant who was always early due to a sick child. June Allison the friendly, June Allison the competent, June Allison the beautiful, round-faced and firm-skinned in a North American boulder sort of way. June Allison the sensitive, June Allison the quick of glance, June Allison the *instinctual*. June Allison would have checked his doorknob. Then buzzed him knowing a long shot, no light under the door and getting no answer, and having lost her keys she would pick the lock or break down the door and *find Ted Wilson*. Inquiries and calls by his desk. They will find him by lunchtime.

At lunchtime, up the wrong path from the Y, as they approached his cliff behind the frantic bark of dogs, the fire chief would compliment her intuition, stride for stride, as well as her fit condition, her stamina, but especially the binoculars round her neck, "the astounding clarity of the lenses," the chief would note, binoculars Ted had wrapped up in silver paper one office Christmas as soon as he learned of June Allison's new interest in bird-watching. "I like the little ones best," she had said. He had bought her a field guide too, a good and famous one, he did not recall the name, the cover was a cardinal. The Number One would block the northbound lane. Traffic would stop at the ends of the old bridge and line up to the ocean, maps flapping on the hoods till weighed down by well-wishers with rocks, and the rookies would run with the litter again. Lunch strapped down in the headrest, taped and waterproofed, marked with marks in marker indicating Swiss and ham and tuna salad and three cheese with tomato, made in Wisconsin, not in Japan, not fast asleep with her husband well past midnight.

"But Marty's an engineer. Some fixed-wing jet in Osaka. Japan's his dream."

"He doesn't deserve you."

"I would never leave you otherwise."

Once, he sat in a car outside her house, a rental for incognito. Once he waited for the lights to turn out, and called, but one of the kids answered who passed it to another and Ted hung up. Once Ted watched her kids out the door in the morning, looking for resemblance, once he got hold of her keys and made a copy. He found the condoms in the bathroom trash, a low point, once he sent flowers from Marty, "My darling, I'm so sorry." She did not come to work on Monday. She wore extra makeup. She was sullen.

"Good morning, June Allison."

"I said good morning, June Allison."

"I said 'Good morning' to you, June Allison."

∽ — ∾

A house perched above a mountain creek is a beautiful Home. Heaven, Paradise, Heaven. People save and scrimp their whole lives for a chance like this. They move in with their belongings only when old and stiff and can't enjoy it. How sad how sad how sad!

At eleven came a convoy, or noon, some time. It slowed to cross and crossed the old bridge one at a time. Great yellow earthmovers piggybacked in chains on the beds of the trucks from some finished highway. They rumbled behind the pilot car, which said OVERSIZED LOAD on the roof for oncoming traffic, though there was none for minutes for the orange flags and the blinking hazards.

Ted waved at the driver who smoked out the window and at the loader, two graders, the belly-dump, dirty and dried, etc., dozens of dozers in back-to-back pairs, a cavalry of elephantine mice, tail to trunk floating across the ocean, the Queen Mary, the Hindenburg before the fire, such thoughts. The tires must be $3,000 per spare. The biggest tires were taller than a man is tall, taller than a tall man, or taller than Ted with a second Ted on his shoulders, or a girl on his shoulders. Once, June Allison had stood on Ted's shoulders. They'd gone out for a talk in the alley. They'd locked in both sets of keys. She had climbed onto Ted via a trashcan. Her feet were warm, damp and blissful to his collarbones.

"Can you see up my skirt?"

"I can see up your skirt."

The convoy concluded. The chase car said DO NOT PASS, with more orange flags with no cars to read it, hallelujah, a van drove over. It hauled an old rowboat hardly worth hauling, perhaps inherited by that driver, or sold for parts, or for a fire hall demonstration on burning boats in rivers, or for ocean practice by the rookies in dinghies. The boat said *The Good Luck May* in gold cursive and Ted called out, "The

Good Luck May!" It was something new with good sounds for cross-country travel, "The Good Luck May!" across terra firma across blue oceans, blue islands, blue snorkel masks with blue lunch baskets.

"Lunchtime is the rumble of the stomach!" the engineer advised from below, on a boulder with an apple. "It's science!" His hair was a mess from the wind. "Knock, knock!"

"Who's there!"

"Rumble!"

"Rumble who!"

"Rumble mumble lunchtime bumble! They'll be here by lunchtime!"

"Another!"

"Knock, knock!"

"Who's there!"

"Sandwich!"

"Sandwich who!"

"Sandwiched between a rock and a hard place!"

"Another!"

"Knock, knock!"

"Who's there!"

Morning passed peacefully.

❧ — ❧

Noon is the easiest to calculate. Depends only on time of year, cloud cover, and latitude.

"You should float for a while," she said.

"Men don't float, women float," he said.

"That's a wives' tale, Mr. Wilson."

"I'm starving," he said.

"Trees eat constantly when the sun's shining, I had sushi."

"I'm losing my strength."

"Sharks never sleep at all, did you know that, Mr. Wilson? I read that in the Honolulu airport."

"When are you coming home?"

"Knock, knock, Mr. Wilson, I'm home."

"Shall we kiss?"

"Fine, I'll meet you in the copy room."

They kissed in the tree and Ted's lips cracked. They kissed the tree. Their fingers blued against the jut of rock and the cliff to the knuckles despite the growing heat. Ted lowered one arm and shook it, then the other the same, again, then again. When his arms felt better, he resumed with the jut.

Ted thought of hooks, belts, and inner tubes. He thought of family, his parents and siblings, Beth and the kids. It was perfectly natural to do so, and not disloyal. Three kids crossed the old bridge on bikes. They wore helmets and pedaled hard. A few dog walkers came, they kept to the bridge, the red and tan, the black, and the merle. Perhaps there was a dog show in Spitfire, or farther off, Iceberg, or Klondike, some walkers talked on phones, to themselves, to the dogs while Ted Wilson called out to them.

Ted Wilson would have phoned the fat lady. Ted had seen the fat lady on her phone at the back of Spitfire meetings on trash hikes and potholes too. He tried to picture her name tag, her number on the liquid crystal screen. She seemed civic-minded, in favor of rescues and emergency staff. June Allison knew the fat lady from the women's-only gym, though Ted would never have called June Allison fat, but large-souled, compassionate for Mr. Ted Wilson, eager to fill herself with Ted across his desk behind the door with the knob at the small of her back, which was hardly small, in the alley on the rooftop by the exhaust vent just how he liked it.

"What kinda tree would grow on a cliff?" Ted Wilson would have asked Monday morning to June Allison. Birch, willow, alder were names he knew, but Ted Wilson was not a tree person. A successful businessman and former athlete, but this tree was successful-looking too, how it wrenched out a crack and elbowed vertical. June Allison's amazed eyes would widen. Her amazed hands would cover her amazed mouth, my God: How did this tree anchor? How did this tree cling and hold in wind rain and rockslide? Did its roots root round stones and more stones and roots of other trees with all the advantages of flatness? Flights from Japan were once double-decker. The stewardesses were Oriental and slim as willow with high-buttoned collars and hot wash towels. June Allison would wind back the hand of her watch each hour east. The trees in Japan are weak and small, small and cold, flat like all those small flat faces.

"Good afternoon, June Allison, how was lunch?"

"A1, Mr. Wilson, lunch was divine. How's your cliff ordeal going?"

"A tree on a cliff is a life-changing event."

"I can only imagine."

"I worry for the branches and the smaller twigs. Some damage is not reparable."

"So true. Do be careful."

Long distance. Her voice would be scratchy on his private line.

"Good afternoon, June Allison, how's Japan?"

"Hello, Mr. Wilson, it's morning here."

"Well then, good morning, June Allison."

"Well, how's your scrape? The cliff ordeal."

"I'll pay more attention to trees in the future, you can be sure of it, June Allison."

"I'm so glad, Mr. Wilson."

"What kinda tree would grow on a cliff?"

"Is this a riddle, I hate riddles, ask Beth."

Noon came and went with this chatter.

───✦───

Afternoon, Ted Wilson sat as an *L*. He had tried an *I* after the *A* and before the *L*, but could not hold it. The *I* was the most difficult letter: both track shoes on one branch while hanging still by the fingers from the jut, the feat was impossible, and he could not hold it longer, as if he'd shrunk. He succumbed to *L* then backward *C*, then a *U*, a *Y* but only for seconds, then an *X* for a stretch, then back to the *L*, which was his long-term letter. He wondered if he had spelled anything. *P-E-C-T-O-R-A-L-S, L-U-M-B-A-R, C-A-R-T-I-L-A-G-E, T-H-E-N-E-C-K-T-H-E-N-E-C-K-T-H-E-P-A-I-N-I-N-T-H-E-N-E-C-K.* This wind seemed a dash unkosher. *THEYWILLFINDMEBY TEATIME.*

A station wagon drove over the old bridge with a blinker flashing distress, distress, distress. Ted Wilson wondered and hoped for those sad blinking passengers.

"You see, I thought it was a clearing," Ted would begin to the Blue Ribbon Panel well after Tea Time. "A simple error. I like to see new places and adventure is in my genetic makeup.

Americans are like that. We are a nation of immigrants and risk-takers, we've been naturally selected by transatlantic crossings and umpteen epidemics. My great-great-granddad was a tunneler in the Civil War, for example, the most dangerous job in the Union Army. He died in a pit but had his children before the war so his genes passed on. We have his buttons. It is no wonder about this cliff ordeal."

Afternoon, Ted turned himself upstream for a while, one arm then leg at a time, etc. When he missed the traffic and the old bridge he reversed himself in opposite order. Afternoon, the taxi van came from Spitfire, empty and northbound, then a second van, southbound, with business lettering Ted recognized but could not remember. When the taxi van recrossed southbound it had a passenger who looked familiar. Ted knew everyone this side of Spitfire.

"The Japanese have very little interest in American history, the Constitution, and the cocker spaniels, as you do, June Allison."

"I'm sure I'll be bored to death."

"We'll write."

"We will not write."

Afternoon, the sun rose till then, then hit a cloud that turned silver and rose to another cloud, then the clouds cleared and the sun bit into Ted's large strawberry head. He missed his cap.

Afternoon, a white cat appeared from the brush by the creek. A white dog caught up to the cat, and they followed their miserable cat and dog routine. Its people would not miss the cat. They were pouring milk for children and saying not to spill. They were watching TV on this sunny day.

"Tea Time!" called up the engineer, "is a British term from across the Sea with a capital S!"

"But *Sea* sounds pretentious, I prefer 'ocean' as a term! It's more American not to say sea!"

"I agree completely! Ocean with a capital O, one hundred percent, fine! You are now a capital O!"

"I like you!" called Ted.

"I like you too!" called up the engineer. "You are truly a good guy!"

So they were friends. They called up and down and told comforting stories about flowers and astronauts. When they ran out, Ted told the engineer all about his brother Brian, also an engineer, who, once, at Tea Time, collapsed in the hospital while visiting a friend with a bout of flu. Brian's heart had stopped in the hospital. He lay on the tile by the friend's bed. The doctors and nurses revived Brian Wilson with CPR. They pounded his chest, etc., and by nightfall Mr. Brian Wilson was awake, though he never told his wife. "Never?" called up the engineer, cupping his hands, chewing a sandwich and fries.

"She was young and pregnant! There was no reason to bother her. 'The danger's passed,' he told me!"

"Famous last words. How's your brother's friend!"

"This friend recovered quickly, an airline pilot!"

"Fights from Japan multiple times daily, with connecting flights to Spitfire!"

"Don't get me started!"

"How's the brother!"

"Dead!"

"Like a black-and-white movie!"

"It has nothing to do with me!"

In the afternoon, a passerby might be anyone, they discussed: a trooper with a flat tire, a family with drop lines, catching nothing, luckless. A dog walker prefers afternoons when the dog has digested, when the walker has digested, ditto fat ladies on diets and executive assistants on vacation from the Orient and yellow-vested survey crewmen in helmets with walkie-talkies working Saturday at time and a half, as well as hatchery staffers in jumpsuits with leg pockets for screw-off turbidity cups, slow and heavy-legged, but they would all be along by Tea, they concluded.

"Good afternoon, June Allison."

"Mr. Wilson, hi."

"Perhaps we could go for a walk, I need some files in my car."

"Where are you parked?"

"I'm in the alley."

"I'll meet you at Tea Time."

Ted Wilson rested his throat. It was parched and overtaxed from all this yelling and screaming. The article would describe the throat. In the picture, captioned "Cliff Ordeal," Ted Wilson would stand at the guardrail. An arrow would point out the tree. One of the girls in the office would snip and forward it to Osaka.

"June Allison will certainly send a card!"

"I can't say, I don't know her!" The engineer was eating donuts. "Does this Marty own her! Sounds medieval!"

"No one owns June Allison!"

The engineer stretched and drank from a flask. He offered but Ted couldn't reach.

"My mother was German!" called down Ted. "She was terrible!"

"That explains it!" called up the engineer.

"My mother thought Tea meant four!"

Ted thought of his children, who all had names and faces hard to remember, Dehydration, Exhaustion. Captivation was the youngest one. They fought over the bunk beds. Beth had picked the names, that's how she was.

"I thought it was a clearing," Ted would say to his mother on his private extension. "A fire-burned area, or a burial mound. I'm attracted to such places, as you know, as you know very well."

"He wasn't the first. He won't be the last," his mother would say to June Allison in the alley. June Allison would slap his mother's face.

"She sounds like a moron!" called up the engineer.

"I told her, 'Those Asian men are rather small!'"

"That got her! Hey!"

"Sure, it did!"

"Who will pronounce her name right in that country? Junarrishon Junarrishon Junarrishon!"

"I'm truly sorry for that country! I say it with no hesitation!"

Sometimes June Allison sketched Ted Wilson after dictation. Sometimes after double signatures in triplicate, and after especially difficult closings. June Allison sometimes smoothed his hair at the stairwell vent, or the alley wind or rooftop wind. June Allison sometimes bought him ties or straightened his ties or retied his ties since Beth was laissez-faire on ties. June Allison sometimes stayed late with Ted, "as late as needed," she'd said, but that was clearly falsehood.

"What a lie, June Allison."

A yellow-scarfed lady stopped in a yellow convertible with a black tripod. It was a rental, surely. The wind took the scarf up off to the sea and the jellyfish and scarf-loving sharks. She held the hat with one hand and splayed the tripod legs and posed at the guardrail. If the lens was good, the picture would contain the yellow lady, the red mountain, the green foothills, the foamy creek ascending and noisy, the cliff with the tree with the enormous S floating backward, blue with orange stripes, its mouth wide open, and below, the engineer in a white-ironed shirt smiling and waving. The yellow lady would borrow a magnifying glass from the next-door stamp collector. After a sandwich and the tripod folded, she flung the crusts off the guardrail. The gulls got there first. The yellow rental drove away. Once June Allison said Ted must be French-Canadian. Once she said Ted had an athletic build and was very photogenic, though Beth totally disagreed. Once, June Allison said Ted was probably Cree, given his mother's picture's coloration, his generous but frugal nature, and his attraction to jerky and other smoked meats.

Five skinny deer milled on the creek shore. They ate rotten beechnuts between their skinny legs. They knelt and their legs made twelve lowercase *m*s. Ted blew his nose on a leaf and dropped the leaf between his foaming legs.

"Good afternoon, Mr. Wilson, I knew you would survive it."

"June Allison, you surprised me."

"Is there anything I can do?"

"You could rub my poor shoulders."

"Don't let her touch you!" called up the engineer.

"Be quiet!" Ted called down as she slid onto his lap till the can lid fell, clamored in the alley, anyone could hear it and know.

"It's just geography colliding with carelessness," she said in his ear. "You're just the kind of man for a cliff ordeal."

"You give me such courage."

Afternoon passed.

Late afternoon. The trees on the opposite cliff leaned toward Red Mountain. Ted straightened his head and the trees straightened, the mountain straightened, the opossum straightened, the governor straightened his tie. The trees on the far cliffs were just sapling shadow. The cliff leaked and Ted licked the leak, salt and gritty, his busy birds.

Mr. Ted Wilson would tell the whole ordeal to the Governor, "I misjudged them at first. Those far trees would not have held an opossum."

"The Cree ate willow like aspirin," the Governor would say on his golden throne on the cliff edge. He would look like the fire chief's brother.

"Aspirin is just willow with a modern pharmaceutical name," called up the engineer.

"Here, take one," said the Governor. "It's Beth's fault."

Mr. Ted Wilson put his hand to his mouth. The fire chief would summarize at the press conference with the Governor: "Cliff incidents are only too common in our region, though amateurish. Tourists are the most likely victims, with skiers and hunters in second place for frequency. And for the record," he would emphasize, "ledges and cliffs look exactly like clearings, like house sights, or burn areas, or the end of airports, or tide pools with starfish. People run right to them, as with magnets, people plunge right off them with amazing frequency." To the nodding rookies he'd continue, "I urge compassion: for the teenagers encamped on ledges for the very first time ever, in sleeping bags with bags of stale cookies, licking the plastic innards and crumbs, and for women's groups in pits near old dead soldiers in red hats for whom archaeologists must be called! Newly old men in trees on cliffs are simply run-of-the-mill, though some lost are never found down fouled wells with garbled names, German accents, or new subtle hairstyles. It's no one's fault. Rescues are necessary!"

The reporters would describe the faulty footwear. The search parties would be interviewed about transceivers, ham sandwiches donated from a café down in Spitfire.

A motorcycle girl pulled over at the old bridge. She cut the engine, kicked the stand down, unzipped, unbuckled herself on the way to a bush. Her hair was long and red.

"Hello! Hello! Help me!" called Ted.

She scuffled in the bushes. She walked back to the bridge buckling her belt. She dropped her visor and restraddled the bike. She skidded out and was gone.

"I never gave up," Ted Wilson would say to the Rotary Club as keynote speaker. "But the motorcycle girl's departure was truly a low point."

The motorcycle girl would see him on TV two days later, Ted surmised. That's how she'd realize her intersection with his story.

"I was so surprised," Motorcycle Girl would say in private conference with the Blue Ribbon Chair. They would meet in the bar of a rooftop restaurant. Ted would join them, or even better, in the hotel lounge on cowskin couches, the Chair would grease the wheels of conversation then discreetly leave the two to talk.

"I never even took my helmet off," she'd confess to Ted, smooth her hair, then smooth his. Her name would be Jeannine.

"My name's Jeannine. My mother was French."

"You look French."

"I'm looking for work. I'm a Pisces."

"Cheryl in HR will set up an interview. I'm sure the firm can use you somewhere."

Jeannine's middle name would be Allison. She would take her socks off on the edge of the bed, or in the copy room with a hand on the paper tray for balance. She would buzz Mr. Ted Wilson frequently, check his doorknob when arriving in the a.m.

"Good morning, Ted, how are you?"

"I'm wonderful, Jeannine Allison."

Her stockings will run frequently. She will wiggle on the new pair at the outer desk when she thinks no one's looking. She will like him best in his college tracksuit.

"The stripes are attractive," she will say.

She will massage his feet in olive oil in the supply room. She will feed him smoked meat with creamed fingers, but when her knuckles get rough from windburn Ted will ask her to give up riding, a marvelous typist, good with people, expert in all the programs and spreadsheets, not an ounce of fat on her, who could have predicted this?

"Mr. Wilson, you are working late again?"

"Yes, I'm very busy as you can see, Jeannine Allison."

"Shall I stay again, do you need me?"

"Yes, please, do."

&⸺ ⸺&

A dump truck rolled south, unaffiliated, then a minivan towing bikes on a trailer. A jeep with the top off and music blaring north. A tree swept down the creek, jammed on another and made a V. Some fat deer nibbled just across the creek. They chewed and enjoyed their meal, watching him. The deer scattered when a magnificent black dog galloped up the path, though Ted had not seen the dog or the master coming, no leash, until the deer and dog ordeal was well underway, barking and fur-flying fury.

That's how it passed. How could it have passed that way?

Perhaps the dog was deaf. Perhaps the master was deaf, since Ted could not have yelled or screamed any louder to this deaf man. It was the deer's fault, the dog's fault, the horrible deaf man's fault who did not know how to restrain the magnificent animal.

A blue car pulled away with the dog. When it was gone the birds settled back. Ted doubted the whole thing: the car, the leash. His heels and toes were numb. He ate a leaf. He listened to birds. He was never good with birdcalls, neither *quiki quis* or *kawaki kays*, so many millions. He'd once had a book of birds and birdcalls. In the morning only the crows and magpies had been brave enough to land and see who Ted was, but now, as the sun descended, even the smallest and shiest fledglings came by to foul Ted's tree. Soon, the Allisons will meet on a Pacific atoll, an exclusive place. The two Allisons will be beautiful in silver and gold shimmery gowns. It is a fancy posh place with Rolls and Mercedes. June and Jeannine circle each other, round and round a concrete island with a palm tree near the Lamborghini. The crowd of crows gathers with fresh drinks. Servants in jackets bring folding chairs, Japanese fans, and make a ring. Mr. Ted Wilson blows the whistle.

The Allisons begin to wrestle. A girl in a hat takes bets. It is Greco-Roman Freestyle. There is growling, of course.

The heat makes sweat. One Allison dives for a lightning-fast ankle-pick. The leg is captured for a single-leg takedown that surprises the other wrestler, but she counters. She heaves her hefty legs and weight in the back of the opponent, a nicely executed pancake, which neutralizes the move. The crowd cheers this resurrection. She has flattened the aggressor's face in the parking lot. A nose is bleeding. One Allison complains over the coin toss. The crows throw their sandals. They throw hats and hors d'oeuvres at the clinch on the tailgate.

"This is very exciting!" someone says.

They suck the cherries from their drinks. A tiny umbrella stabs an eye in the crowd. The grapple moves to the shore. The rules are ignored. A dunk-under before the whistle then an illegal full nelson in retaliation and one neck is snapped, but they were warned. The whistle blows. The tide ducks in. Washes red sand.

"I'm dropping a canteen, Mr. Wilson, watch your head."

"Is it poison?"

"Get real, you should conserve your strength. Drink it!"

"As if you care, go away!"

"You look so thirsty!"

"Go away!"

A school bus went by empty over the old bridge, yellow and innocent.

"I have a new assistant."

"Good."

A cow trailer with sheep. The sheep were alive but would soon be dead. This was the thing with sheep in a trailer.

"She's pretty and thin."

"I've lost weight. I look great. I wear a kimono."

A milk truck converted for Volvo house calls, the man waved at Ted and sneered, but Ted knew this was impossible.

"I like her better than you, June Allison," but she laughed and Tea Time passed.

⚜ —— ⚜

There is no name for the time between late afternoon and early evening. The air cools, Ted cooled, the sun was gold and prettiest for photography.

They'll come by nightfall.

At this time a water truck from the prison parked on the end of the old bridge and lowered its nozzle. The driver read a book on the guardrail. The nozzle sucked in water, the creek. The driver looked up a few times but the sun was low with golden glare. He took the calling for coyote or mice or a loose joint rusting. It was an old truck. He reset the nozzle and the truck U-turned toward the prison.

Once Ted hit a dog on the road and it died instantly. Once he unraveled a sweater, hand knitted by his mother.

"What did you do to it?"

"What do you mean?"

A fine mother, an outstanding mother on the mother question, wonderfully motherly, once, he had missed the third-grade play, his daughter was the donkey, a star at nightfall, once, he evicted Beth's brother from the house for singing and playing his guitar too loudly.

"A man's house is his castle."

"He was singing, Ted Wilson. He's my brother. He's happy."

"His voice is only mediocre, I can't take the strumming. Get him out."

Once, very recently, after June Allison's departure, Ted Wilson cut down a tree. Just a small tree, a spruce, it had interrupted their view of the north end of the beaver pond. An odd occurrence followed: when the spruce started to tip and fall, another tree one hundred yards through the woods, a cottonwood of magnificent size, tipped over and fell at the very same moment. This great cottonwood fell with tremendous noise. "They were totally different species," Ted Wilson had said when retelling the story later. "Totally unrelated and unprovoked," Ted Wilson had said, and "there was no scientific way the roots were somehow entangled given the distance and size differential, the Arbor Society confirmed this for us." And now on the cliff, the day ending as it was, Ted Wilson remembered the tremendous noise and thought the whole cottonwood incident over. The cottonwood's root ball was twenty feet high. The cottonwood had fallen with tremendous concussion as well as sound, other trees were smashed in its path, of course, and the enormous scaly trunk was embedded a foot deep in soft spring soil.

How sad how sad.

The neighbors had called. "Did you guys feel that earthquake?" They left messages on their machine, since Ted was still in the backyard, dumbstruck by this fallen giant, Beth was presiding at a Historical Society function, and the kids were on playdates. They had missed the whole incident, And when Beth asked Ted about earthquake messages, "What do they mean by it?" Ted found he was only able to reiterate the facts of the incident to her. He was never able to convey to Beth the feeling the cottonwood incident inspired, or the meaning it seemed to imply.

"My darling, I'm thankful. It's as if this tree had grown there on this cliff for me. Suffered years of rain and wind and gravity just for me at this exact moment. I'm not religious. But it's not easy to be a tree alone on a cliff."

He made himself a W, or an approximation thereof, maybe a letter from a totally new alphabet, and yawned.

"A yawn is a small gasp for oxygen!" called up the engineer. "Yawning has nothing whatever to do with sleep!"

"I'm so tired of this!" said Ted.

"Stay awake till nightfall!" called the engineer.

◆ ─── ◆

In early evening, a car stopped. A boy and girl slid out with two poles from the back seat and a tackle box. They held hands off the bridge, along the creek to the river. Another car came. It parked behind the first. The second kids stood on the old bridge and dropped stones at fish and stones, then the second kids climbed back in their car and U-turned toward town.

Ted tried not to close his eyes, he adjusted a hand on the bark. Ted had never been religious, Ted Wilson's mother had been religious, a Catholic, who loved babies under three and had eight. She worked at the Parish on weddings and baptisms, priests imported from other cities and countries. "Priests are getting rare," Ted's mother had said time and again. She baked them cookies. At home, she rationed orange juice, four ounces round the large kitchen table, Dixie cups to measure. Ted Wilson had always resented his mother, though he'd just learned it in the tree and in the books on maternal resentment that Jeannine Allison would lend him soon: *Hate-As-Action*, the book will say. He made an *H*, which he could not hold, then wedged himself as a period or hyphen, small and stable, against the cliff. After all, he'd done well. These days Mr. Ted Wilson drank as much juice as he wanted, twelve ounces if he wanted, a pint of juice three times daily if he wanted, gallon upon gallon if he wanted. If desired, Mr. Ted Wilson could fill up a tanker with juice and pulp and pump every ounce in the creek, if he chose, thereby changing flow and color for at least a few minutes.

The first two kids returned up the creek from the river, hand in hand. They dropped the poles against a boulder on the far side of the old bridge. They lay together in their jeans and zipped-down sweatshirts. The treetops were purple. Serrated light cut their skin. A siren at the fire hall sounded the shift change.

The kids read their field guide and pointed at birds. They rummaged each other till the boy went to the bridge for the cooler. He left the trunk wide open. They sat together and yawned.

"You see it?" the boy said, pointing.

"No, I don't see it," the girl said.

"Across the bridge to the right," the boy said, "the cliff and over, the third branch up. You can only see the head, a big one."

"I still don't see it," the girl said. "Oh yes, now I see it." The girl marked her book.

Once, when Ted's mother's sister had her first child in Chicago, Ted's mother took the two oldest to the big brick corner to be watched by the nuns. Brian was just an infant so she took him in the backpack to the Windy City, it had once been Teddy's backpack. Teddy Wilson was an early reader and could already read the small ORPHAN sign carved and gold above the door. Mother, children, and backpack ascended the steps.

"I'll see you boys Sunday," their mother had said, but orphans are so suspicious.

The orphan food was served in big orphan spoons at long orphan tables by nuns in long spotless orphan aprons that fell to the black orphan floor. Their giant spoons waved in the air. They turned like shovels onto giant white plates like maps, my God, my God, the orphan meatloaf with ketchup, and he ate, and the lima beans with orphan butter that he ate four at a time, one per tine, though he hated lima beans at home, and when he finished half the plate was piled by shovel and apron with mashed potatoes and more orphan butter, just this much salt please, no pepper, please, no, I do hate pepper, and the nuns were kind and listened to what young Teddy Wilson said. Then pie! Young Teddy Wilson ate and ate. The chocolate milk was last. The glass was filled to the top, which he chewed and swallowed, cut the last into bits in the bottom of the glass with butter knife and fork, to take it slowly, to make it last, this first supper, the prayer at the beginning, a nun at the end with a giant brown pitcher and she sent them to bed at nightfall.

The nuns tucked them in in rows: Timmy and Teddy then another Timmy and another Teddy so on so on so on in ironed-bleached sheets. "You see, Mr. Teddy Wilson was an early reader," said an old dead nun with a crow and cocktail. "Mr. Timmy Wilson, by contrast, was slow with reading. It's made all the difference entirely as outcome."

Night would fall and Mr. Ted Wilson had never told it to June Allison. But how sad and strange to tell the orphanage incident now by transpacific letter, impossible.

"You could always jump!" called June Allison from below with wine and the engineer on a big green waterbed with no headboard or footboard. They floated and sipped.

"Can you believe this woman!" called up the engineer and rolled toward her and she laughed like water.

"But what kind of tree would grow on a cliff!" Ted called down. "I'd like to know it!"

"It's geology and botany joining forces!" called the engineer. "Willows most likely, or some hybrid birch!"

"We'll ask the Arbor Society if such a mix is known to science!" called Ted, "Beth knows those people!"

"Yes, but Beth was against the spruce-cutting scheme all along!" called the engineer, nodding. "A hater of beavers! She's all for cottonwoods!"

"I know that! I know that!" called Ted.

"Marty says every animal eats willow!" called June Allison.

"Marty says willows are the fiercest tree!" called the engineer.

"But a tree on a cliff is eaten by no one!" called Ted. "It's your fault, June Allison!"

The creek would bubble on forever. They linked elbows and would drink from the other's glass.

"You had your chance!" called up the engineer.

They started kissing.

"I could just fall in!" called Ted.

"Sure, you could just fall!"

They proceeded to make out.

— ⚬ —

The boy and girl waved at the jeep, which honked. They ate coleslaw from a plastic tub with a plastic fork. They marked birds then shut their book. The sun sat red on the rim of sky, lit the trunks and the boulders and the cliff face, metallic. The girl collected wood for their fire and the boy struck the match and lit a market receipt, the wrappers from their tea, then twigs when the flame was ready, and the flame jumped up and she fed it more, kneeling with smaller then larger sticks. They warmed themselves by the fire and snuggled. The two began a song but forgot some words and hummed the rest.

> Day is done
> Gone the sun
> So on so on so so so lalala
> All is well
> La la la
> God is la

The boy walked to the old bridge. He swung a yellow backpack from the trunk and slammed it. He checked his headlamp, on then off. The boy walked back to the girl.

The boy said, "You should take off your clothes and swim. We have the fire."

"All right," the girl said, and she turned toward the river. She balled her underpants and T-shirt and dropped them at the boulder. She covered herself with her hands and sandals.

"We might get rain," said the girl.

"No one can live without water," said the boy.

"You're a deep thinker," said the girl.

"We should travel," said the boy, and the girl said, "Yes."

The girl hopped boulders around the fire. She talked about the water as if a student of science, the nature of current as related to the temperature of the upstream source, ice dams and crevasse disasters. She threw the sandals at her clothes.

The boy started the triangle tent in a circle of shrubs. His headlamp lit the blue tarp, a gray rock, a white foot, a white trunk.

The boy said, "You should learn this tent." He fiddled with the poles. The girl sat by the water in a ball and dropped a toe in.

Then the girl said, "I think I'll swim now," and she sat in the creek.

"It's late for swimming," the boy said.

He watched her. They were dark boulders in the deepening blue, the sun was gone. One star appeared.

"It's cold," she said, then she lay down in the creek. They laughed at her surprise. She held herself in the current with her arms locked on two giant boulders. She laid her head in. His headlamp waved across her legs and breasts and the bubbles from nostrils and the girl closed her eyes against his light. Then she released the boulders.

When the girl shot away in the foam down the creek to the mouth of the river, the boy ran after her along the shore. His spotlight wagged rock to rock and jumped from fern to cliff at the corner of the river invisible, panting and calling and footsteps and splashing out digging the river. He even caught her once but she was so slippery round her bare middle and her fingers refused to catch.

At nightfall the clouds came and ambulances. The sirens seemed to calm the wind. The emergency vehicles parked on the old bridge, blocked a lane, flashed the boy's face red and blue. The dive team deployed. A captain examined the bird book and pencil, dropped them in separate plastic bags, which were taped and labeled by underling officers. The detectives talked to the boy. They wrote what he said. They followed him to the car and talked in walkie-talkies. They searched in his car with flashlights and over the guardrail. They made long shadows into the lines of traffic held back by a whistle and the female officer's outstretched hand. It was gloved. One by one it waved the cars by and home. She had a pretty face and a ponytail under her cap but the whistle didn't satisfy her any. What she wanted was a walkie-talkie, anyone could see her suffer for one, a walkie-talkie would be bliss.

The helicopter came. It turned its beam on the tent, which was still sturdy and still in the brush, but for the vestibule, which was never zipped or staked, so flapped. The helicopter circled back again over the fray of tallest trees, now black, cottonwood and birch mixed with spruce, with branches so netted no light could possibly pass. The helicopter swept again and again from the old bridge over the mouth of the creek to the river. The water only seemed to stand still. Ambulances came. The search dogs barked at the outer orbits of their leashes. They sniffed the air of the water along the shore, loping happily, and licking sand for tracks or other indications. Then the dogs looped back toward the creek through the thick, well-watered gnarl of alder and willow toward their masters' clucks and calls and their padded kennels lined on the old bridge.

ALPHA

His blow was overhand, the way a big man swings a hammer, with a machete, yes, but the blunt side only, and it only grazed Donna Rae's ear, then thumped down to her shoulder, and Wally was three inches shorter.

Donna Rae fell anyway. She was tired, just home from the night shift.

She pressed her brow in the hard-packed snow, as if a lump was growing, ass in the air in surgical scrubs.

Wally dropped the machete. He kicked it and it spun toward a tree.

"You've done it this time," she said. "Assault with a deadly weapon."

"I barely nicked you," he said, backing off.

"Better get running," said she. "You'll really hit it off with those Canadians."

It had not snowed in weeks. The crust was the sharp and slick of cold morning. The eight dogs howled on the ends of their chains at the spectacle. They stood on flat-roofed boxes Wally had hammered together with plywood. They yipped and turned, as Donna Rae crawled toward the machete then sat on it by a tree.

"Evidence," she said. "They'll find my blood on the blade."

"There's no blood on the blade," he said. "I drew no blood."

"There'll be blood on the blade," she said. "When the troopers come."

Wally paced the snow. He threw down his cap, picked it up. "You think you can get rid of me," he said.

"Better get going," she said.

"I did my part," he said. "My part of the deal."

"Tell that to the jury."

A glorious new day in the North. The spruce stood tall and straight around the dog lot, a clearing for the small cabin with the tiny porch, the piles of cordwood covered willy-nilly by plastic and sheet metal and rusty roofing, old cars dismantled between trees, snow machines turned over for track work, the parts lost years back, a caribou hide strung between branches, well past dry, cracking, doorframes for the future house leaning on trees, windows, sawhorses, empty barrels for catching water, barrels of dog food, barrels with bottles for shooting practice, trailers with broken hitches, piled with antique stoves and sinks with interlinking pipes, bundles of webbing in stacks of stacks. The Pass presided over all of it. The east glowed with a cold, bored sun. The dogs howled to wake the neighbors, but the neighbors were a mile off and would think their noise was just a bear.

No wind yet.

"I didn't mean it," Wally said.

"Go quick," Donna Rae said. "And I'll wait a few hours before I turn you in."

Wally backed up the narrow path toward the Dump Road. He bumped into a stack of tires, the truck parked just behind it, still warm from her long drive home from Palmer.

"You think you've really got me by the scruff," he said.

"You'll love Canada," she said, standing with the machete, brushing off. "Whitehorse. Winnipeg. Wonderful cities."

Through the trees, a full-up truck rolled up the Dump Road, though the dump was closed on Sunday. The truck crossed the creek, would be back soon just as full.

Wally unplugged the engine block from the power post. The dogs still barked but were getting tired of it. They turned, whined, and pawed the air. The cabin door was open. The phone was ringing.

"I'll go," Wally said. "But I'm taking the dogs."

"Forget it," she said.

Wally opened the door, sat in the truck. His boot was swinging out the door.

"Drive fast," she said. "Tok by noon. Beaver by two."

"If they melted you down," he said, "they'd find a puddle of shriveled-up lemons."

"How you hurt me with your mean, mean words," she said.

She backed to the cabin with the machete. She leaned on the front-porch railing. The dogs barked back and forth between them. The sun stood above the smokehouse on the ridge now, full morning coming, the smokehouse being his newest venture.

The engine turned over. The truck backed onto the Dump Road, the tape deck playing "Purple Haze," his boot still swinging out the door.

"I'm taking my dogs," he said, as the truck rolled away, downhill.

⚓ — ⚓

When the trooper arrived, the cabin door was open, so he started to close it.

"Leave it open," Donna Rae said.

"Close to zero," said the trooper.

"Don't touch the door," she said. "I need to see if he's coming."

A big blue lump rose above her right eye now. Blood on the blade, blood on her scrubs, down the side of her face. She handed over the machete with a rag.

"I'm sure it's got fingerprints," she said.

The trooper looked the machete over. The cabin was one room so they sat very close, she on the bed, he in a chair. There was a closet behind a hand-sewn curtain. Plans for a house were pinned on the wall. The bed pressed between the dry goods shelf and the table and chairs. The outhouse was just out the back window. No door. Wally had cut the seat with plywood and blueboard.

"We need to warm up this place," he said.

He balled up newspaper, struck a match, went out for an armful of wood, which got the dogs barking again.

"They're jumpy," said the trooper.

"My alarm system," she said.

He took his notes with gloves on. He turned his back while Donna Rae changed out of scrubs and underthings, pulled on snow pants, washed her face in a bowl in the sink. He took the scrubs. He labeled a plastic evidence bag.

"You took care of my mother," he said.

"I've taken care of everyone's mother," she said.

The fire was slow to get going, so the trooper knelt down on hands and knees. He added cardboard after paper, then slivers that caught well, burned hot enough to encourage, then larger sticks, blew in sometimes, then a crisscross of small dry logs when the flame was strong.

"You still work at the Pioneer Home?" he said.

"Twenty-two years," she said. "I eat dinner at 5 a.m. Sleep all day. Breakfast at dinnertime. Needles, blood, and bedsores. Kids who want mom to keep going. Others who want to unplug her for money. Bedpans and bibs. Lost TV clickers. Lost books. Lost glasses. They can't remember my name, though I feed them, change them, wipe their asses. Twenty-two years of bringing home the bacon to old Wally, there at the stove in his apron."

"A good nurse," he said.

"They all die anyway," she said.

"I heard Wally's quite a cook," he said. "A happy guy. I took him to jail once."

"He bashed me in the head today," she said.

"Quite a bruise," he said. "But the skin's not broken. Seems like a machete would break the skin."

"Who knows about tropical weapons," she said. She pulled the quilt over her legs.

"Where's the blood come from then?" he said.

She showed him her mouth, the bloody space where the tooth was missing.

"How does a machete do that?" he said.

He stood at the stove. He found no faucet to fill the kettle. She pointed to the five-gallon jugs along the wall.

"No well yet?" he said.

"We drilled three times," she said. "Hauling water's OK."

He poured hot water over tea bags. The bed creaked when she stirred in honey. She looked out the window. Her words were clear and calm as he took her statement.

"We'll keep an eye on the border," the trooper said, closing his notebook. "Tok Station has his plate and description."

"Ace police work," she said.

The trooper opened closet curtains, dresser drawers.

"How much cash does he have?" he said. "Credit card?"

"How should I know?" she said. "He takes everything."

"A number would be helpful," he said. "Got a stash? Something under the mattress?"

"I got nothing under my mattress now," she said.

"Why didn't you just divorce him?"

"I'm not willing to split it."

There was a puddle of ice on a low spot on the plywood floor. He followed the ice to its source, the gray-water bucket under the sink, found it overflowing, island of foam on the top, slid the bucket out, careful not to spill it, lifted the bucket out the door, and emptied the mess off the porch.

"You're welcome," he said, and she said, "Thank you."

He chopped clean snow and filled a baggie. She pressed it to her lump. He stood at the woodstove and warmed his hands. He called Tok again. He called the Pioneer Home for a substitute for night shift. He dropped the machete into an evidence bag.

"This here's my first machete at a crime scene," he said.

"He got the machete for the fiddlehead project," she said.

"Axes and mauls are more the norm," he said.

The trooper was tall and dimpled. His boots were sheepskin.

"Better come with me," he said. "That bump. However you got it."

"I told you how I got it," she said. "You wrote it down."

They stood. She held the door for him and he stepped to

the porch. The radio cracked in the cruiser. He shoved the pen down his pants to keep the ink from freezing.

"My mother would want me to insist," he said.

"Your mom was demented when I knew her," she said.

She allowed the trooper to examine her rifle. He set his eye to the sight, scanned the clearing from left to right. The thermometer read twelve in the sun. The dogs panted in their doorways. The trooper handed the weapon back.

"I sure hope he's gone," he said.

"Yep," she said.

"You're not strictly in our jurisdiction," he said.

"Nope," she said.

"I can't make you come," he said. "It's a free country."

"It sure is," she said.

The trooper walked the path to the cruiser. His face was red. A moose stepped onto the Dump Road and hung its head on the centerline. The dog sniffed the air. The cruiser's radio snapped again, some garbled language.

"Last chance," he said.

"You have the report," she said. "I have your number."

"Call me if he comes back," he said.

❧ —— ❧

The dogs were jumpy all day. They watched the trees and howled. They bared their teeth and chewed their legs to raw skin. They would have nipped each other if their chains had let them. They lunged at foxes, real and imagined, at birds and rabbits flying over, at Donna Rae, the Pass, clouds, trucks that rumbled up and down the Dump Road.

"Quiet down," Donna Rae said from time to time, but they never did.

The lump rose to bust her skull. She should have thought of this idea before, twenty-two years ago. She'd got work at the Pioneer Home right off the bat, nice old folks and Death with Dignity. The dogs were part of their long-term plan. A dollar per dog per day and she paid it. Rehab funded his syrup projects, the experiments with brine, the advanced taxidermy training, but she had funded everything else. He ordered relish jars from an outfit in Portland. Aprons. Business cards once per year, always a new logo.

She might have bashed her head with a pipe along the pipeline sooner. Sufficient pipes lay around everywhere. She chewed six vitamins. She dragged a lawn chair out and sat among the dogs, rifle between the knees of the snow pants, a sleeping bag over her shoulders. The phone rang from time to time, but it was none of its business.

In the afternoon she went to the cabin and stuffed in cordwood. She boiled water, filled beer bottles with it. She found corks, whittled them to fit and returned with the bottles to the lawn chair. She tucked a bottle under an arm, the crook of a knee, the small of the back. When they cooled, she walked back to the cabin to reheat, uncork, refill. The sun soaked the white world, burnt the dirt rings around the dogs' houses. She checked the water jugs each time in. Four full ones. Twenty gallons total, enough to hole up for a week, if careful. She could melt snow for the dogs. She thought of the trooper's mother, who'd been only slightly addled. Donna Rae had liked her especially.

"You're not the first woman to marry a drone," the old woman had said, who'd lived behind an oxygen mask, steaming and clearing. They played checkers at midnight on the dinner tray. They read *National Geographic* about faraway lands without IV tubes, ice cubes, or morphine.

"Learn to laugh at pain as quick as you can," the old lady said. "Dead parents, lazy husbands, childbirth."

"How fast?" Donna Rae had said.

"I've got it down to five minutes."

Now, in the lawn chair, Donna Rae finally got laughing. The warm bottles dropped free and rolled toward Egypt, the closest dog, who pawed a bottle like a ball.

As she doubled over, tossed her head back, the dogs stopped barking. They stood alert on their chains. She spit some blood out, wiped, felt the place where she had knocked the tooth with his rock-cutting hammer.

She laughed again. Howled.

"I don't see what's so funny," Wally said from the trees.

He was running well on the crust in snowshoes, wearing a parka she'd never seen before, staying low, darting lithe from tree to tree, like all his Vietnam movies. Rambo. Colonel Kurtz. He had some sack he was filling, dropping in and out of view, dashing to piles around the dog lot. The rifle fired first into trees, kicked her shoulder. He disappeared behind the caribou.

"You can't shoot for shit," Wally said from behind the clamming buckets.

He ran behind the old dip nets, upright against the sugar shack roof. Still no wind to push the cold away. No need to raise the voice in crystal air. She turned the crosshairs as he found the perimeter, round the cabin to the outhouse, to the old fridge draped in a tarp, round the tractor from Missouri from his farming stage, to a pile of skis for a future fence, behind the greenhouse with ten-foot weeds still standing to the roof inside, since no wind could ever knock them down. Her arm got tired as he circled.

"Keep the nose up," he said. "Can't shoot straight with a dipping muzzle."

He ran behind the greenhouse, then the greenhouse scattered. The weeds stood inside it like nothing happened.

"OK," he said. "You killed the greenhouse."

"Go to goddamn Canada," she said. "Do like you did for Vietnam."

He waited behind the old fridge. The door hung off the top hinge. The sun was dropping toward the Pass. This far north, winter evenings started at three—pink and orange, tropical. He slipped off toward the Dump Road with his sack, zigzagging for cover from tree to tree till he was out of range and walked in the open, then got smaller and smaller until he was gone. The phone was ringing and ringing. She thought to call her sister. When she got to the cabin the ringing stopped.

She balled up paper, struck a match. She drank tea at the table, chewed more vitamins and salmon oil capsules. At nightfall, the dogs wagged and whined. They were going crazy at something in the shed. She wound through their houses with a Maglite, circled the shed, checked the lock. She listened for his clumsy sounds inside. The shed's window was busted— how had she not heard it? A pile of necessities forming below: several old water jugs with missing caps, a sleeping bag, the tent bag and poles, several coils of rope, the awl kit, the camp stove and gas, and eight harnesses, she counted them. The sled between some birches. She waited on the tractor seat, the rifle ready. His leg came out the window first, then a second leg, then his coveralls slithered out, just barely, Wally being born again, arms, shoulders, then his cap hopped down.

She dropped her flashlight. She lost him in the eyepiece. Her second shot hit the old Singer. He scrambled for the dog gear, caught the rope to the sled, which fishtailed behind him.

"Might hurt the dogs with ricochet," he said behind the old fridge, panting.

"If you're so worried about them," she said, "go to Canada."

"I cut every board," he said. "Dug every shithole."

"I paid for the shovel," she said.

She postholed to the fridge after him, but was no way fast enough.

"The troopers are coming," she said.

"Sure, they're coming," he said.

She stopped to rest at the caribou, then at the halibut crate filled with bricks and rocks. She postholed back to the shed. She kicked the pile of camping gear together. She unlocked the shed lock and found a gas can. The camping gear fire was wonderful and warm. She sat for the fire on the old Singer. The sleeping bag jumped like kindling. The tent burned fast and hot. The poles melted a little, bent, contorted. She dragged a pallet and tipped it on. Sparks flew up. The dogs barked. The Singer was an old iron treadle, which was cold to sit on. He'd got it at a garage sale from an old miner touting pedal power. "Good for sewing on doomsday, during wars of all magnitudes, and power outages." In summers, Wally had set the machine among the dogs. He sewed shirtless, pumping with his right boot, the left foot bare in the weeds. He sewed singing, swatting mosquitoes as required, always enjoying, no matter if justified. He hemmed curtains and stitched booties for the dogs for races, thirty-two pairs, to have a stock of extras. He raced the dogs while she was sleeping. He fed them and trained them at the same time. He'd always wanted to learn to sew, he said. To push an awl through leather. To build. To dip for fish on big silty rivers—knock the fish out with a rock before gutting, heading, slicing fins. Now that's living. To smoke the fish after, to "feel the river enter my body," he said, as he smoked his best homegrown weed, his only lucrative trade till he was busted. In jail they taught him knitting and taxidermy, how to replace coyote eyes with marbles. The phone was ringing.

"You were born in the wrong century," she would tell him someday, if things simmered down, blew over.

"I was making this century fit my needs," he'd say.

The camp stove only turned black in the fire, but several gas canisters exploded, arching down to the shed roof. When she woke, the shed was cool rubble. At the cabin, the door was open, the woodstove nearly out, the four water jugs gone, a pillowcase too. The bread and tea. The noodles in a pot on the range. His sheepskin hat and gloves were missing. Jam and iron fry pan, every jar of pickles, can opener, batteries, extra shells. The thermometer, the clock above the sink window. The propane tank. The salt and pepper and the phone.

She dropped to hands and knees at the woodstove. Nearly no more paper. She balled up socks from the closet, struck a match, then another. She peed in a jelly jar, tightened the lid, stuffed the jar down her coat. The ice must be creeping up his beard. She wrapped a sweater around her face. The lump seemed bigger than her head was now. On the porch, the Pass was black on blue, the moon coming. The footsteps on the switchback were light and dreamy, like a bear sniffing for a den, or a man making camp on the ridge in a smokehouse.

"You can't stay in the smokehouse," she said slow, tongue-tied. "I can't allow it."

"These dogs are hungry," he said from high on the hill.

"Go to Canada," she said. "And then I'll feed them."

She tried to read a book in the porch light. Soon, the single window in the smokehouse glowed. The air smelled like jerky. Hypothermia sets in soon as your body temperature dips below ninety-five degrees Fahrenheit, any nurse in the North knows such numbers. Night is slowest when it's eighteen hours. Solstice. December. Christmastime. She had not always minded his skinny legs, tiny paychecks. He did not mind her looks at first. "This, what we're doing, is women's lib," he'd said. But what she'd most wanted was a lie detector: a portable model for the kitchen table, with a handle and a mouthpiece for talking into, a green light for true, red for false. Is there such thing as love? True or false. Till Death Do Us Part? Yes or no. At the border the Mounties wear all brown: "Good evening, sir. How long do you intend to stay in Canada?" "I'm never leaving," Wally would say, then, "Where's the gas? My truck is low, a place with an engine block plug-in." He'd knitted her hat, wool with twisted colors on the rim. What happened at ninety-four degrees? She found a joint under the mattress, warmed her lungs in and out. She threw the butt in the woodstove, added his balsa airplane from the rafters, a wedding picture in a burl frame he'd fashioned, his favorite slippers. That trooper was handsome. She'd met him at the funeral and before that. Maybe in a year or two. "Come on out. I'll make you dinner for all you did on that cold hard day."

On the hour, she walked the dog lot, like the Mounties at Beaver Station: "Pull forward, sir. You'll find the first fuel in two thousand meters. But we call it petrol here." The truck would roll across a line sunken by permafrost, the yellow paint meaning *my side, your side*. The Canadian pavement would be smooth. WELCOME TO THE YUKON—LARGER THAN LIFE! The Welcome Center would serve him free coffee. The soap dispensers would be full and dripping. To wash the face. To soak the hands. To pull the boots off and submerge the foot. The pain of thaw would be exactly like burning. Then the other foot, then the knees and hips, till the whole body was down the drain to someplace warm and dark, a septic tank, a pipe to Calgary. She stirred the fire with an iron poker, though only smoke. He'd hammered the poker in a blacksmithing seminar, $350 by check, their joint account. "Canada the Beautiful," the Mountie would say. "Drive on, sir. Enjoy your visit. Our enormous country."

She walked the porch back and forth. She thought to goose-step or click her heels. She walked the dog lot, counting dogs: Egypt, the biggest, came from Missouri with the tractor. Shamrock, the white, found on St. Patrick's Day with Bonnie and Clover. Mazy, the red one, culled from an Iditarod kennel, worth money. Elva for Elva Creek. Lucky, the littlest, black, white, and shy. Lucy, the old lady with mange.

The moon came up. Still no wind.

"You always thought you were smarter than me," his voice said from the smokehouse. "That hurt me."

She chopped an icicle from the eave and sucked it. She sat on the step, pried gloves with her teeth, blew on her hands, entwined the fingers in her crotch. With her sleepy, frozen, swollen ears, his voice was everywhere, flying, circling. The dogs moved in moony tangles of moon, shadow and branches and unnameable shapes. Their chains clinked on chain. She caught the pairs of eyes in the Maglite, some green some gold that turned away.

"I am smarter," she said.

The chains were quiet after that.

On the hour, she found the three abandoned chains. She walked the perimeter calling names out, though her head was such that she was not sure which. The crust was hard now and easy walking.

"You can't have them."

"You better eat something," he said. "You're getting too weak to defend your position."

He was cooking bread or cake up there in the smokehouse. He was singing something toward Canada, symphonic, eight minus three is six. She was sure of it. She took the Maglite to the Dump Road, to wait for a truck, to wave in some help, till she heard the dogs behind her burst into crazy. She ran, if she could run, up the path to prevent a kidnap, the rifle leading. She caught him red-handed over Egypt's chain, Shamrock already running free—romping and teasing the others. Egypt leaping beside Wally—happy and free—headed toward the switchbacks. The third shot was wild, but Egypt yelped. He spun on his back leg as if caught in a snare.

"You shot Egypt like a rat," he said and swept the dog under his arm, seventy pounds up the switchbacks. He rested behind a tree in gray light turning blue.

"Is he dead?" she said in a while.

"None of your business. That's a forfeit."

At first gold dawn, Donna Rae smelled bacon, ham, and potatoes. She smelled her mother's apple pie, heard the phone ringing, turned from the ridge, stood to answer, another glorious new day in the North.

"You always thought you were better than me," he said.

"I am."

At true orange dawn, she counted dogs again. The three wagged, hungry, thirsty, and uncertain. She doled out icicles to chew and roll. They dug the snow and ate it. Full blue morning was leaning in, and she chewed snow to moisten her tongue. She searched the cabin. She looked for paper, for cardboard and lint, one match. She searched for an egg or bread or jar of salmon. She searched the trees, the birches. Once, Wally stayed up for a week solid with the birch trees. He said they did it in the Tet Offensive and "Hell, Donna Rae, it's sugar season!" The buckets on the taps were overflowing, and a big order, the prison in Whitehorse where he had connections. His pot was a cauldron next to the shed. His stirring stick was four feet long, his apron with his name on the pocket. A floating thermometer. The birch trees dripped, clear as water and almost tasteless, a hundred gallons for one gallon of finished product. He drank the sap from a mason jar. "This is the best day ever!" He said it daily, even when syrup prices bottomed out, when the shops in Tok returned the overstock, when boxes piled on the porch, when squirrels got into them.

He was behind the old fridge again.

"Give me three and I'll go," he said.

"Three?" she said.

"Three dogs," he said.

"That's all the dogs," she said. "That means you get all of them."

"That's my suggestion," he said. "Then peace and good riddance."

For an answer, she aimed at the red dog, the nearest one. With this fourth shot, the red jaw flew off its hinge, flopped with canines and molars hanging. The body leaned on the chain, then wrenched, surprised. The head shook as if to shake the jaw off. The blood was bright on dirty snow, Wally running in from the fridge.

She rounded the red dog for the black and white, a clear shot, the fifth of the day, the decade. The black and white, coward, tucked her tail and dipped in her doorway. Donna Rae had to haul her out, fist by fist, by the chain. The muzzle blew at an awkward angle. Then the black and white lay quiet.

Wally crouched behind the wheelbarrow.

Donna Rae stepped around the black and white to the mangy one, Lucy, who snarled and drooled, with snagged yellow teeth and sagging gums.

"You," she said.

The bitch snapped and lunged at her leg.

Donna Rae kicked the dog. "You always did like him better."

The rifle lifted for number six, but a pipe flew from the wheelbarrow, clipped her face. Then a log flew next and she fell again, her mouth rebleeding.

"This will get in the papers," Wally said.

"I told you," Donna Rae said, rubbing her jaw. "You can't have them."

❧ —— ☙

A truce followed. They sat on opposite sides of Lucy's house, just a tuft of tail peeking out. Donna Rae searched for a marble in the snow. Wally squatted, stroking red fur, speaking softly, before he found the pipe and finished the job.

"I'm cold," Wally said. "I'm thirsty. I'm sorry for my part."

"Canada has plenty of water," she said.

Eight dogs minus four dogs, minus two. Math was too difficult this near to Canada. A border does not require a line. Just cross the line and walk to town. In that town are Canadians, full of them. Say to them: "I've just walked down from that Pass. I'm hungry." Show your snowshoes and pack. Peel open your pack and show your lackings to all the Canadians. The totality of your actions. The implications for freedom. Canadians understand everything. It is a tremendous-sized nation full of wind and geese. The Canadians are the best people. The Canadians make sense of things.

Wally blew on his hands. Donna Rae peeled her coat off.

"Don't do that," Wally said. "That's the cold playing tricks."

She pulled her boots off, her socks, and sunned her skin.

"Are you sorry for anything?" Wally said. "If so, this is when you should say it."

"I did right," she said. "I did everything you asked me. This is your fault."

"OK then," he said.

While Wally seemed to sleep, Donna Rae crawled on to Lucy's house, where she unclipped Lucy. She dragged the dog by the chain to the cabin, up the steps, in the door, shut it, shoved the bed in front of the door, undressed, and lay on top of the quilt. Her legs were doll's legs, dead and floppy. Lucy squeezed under the bed, chain dragging over plywood.

Lucy scratched at the door, since any sled dog loathes a cabin.

She slept for only thirty seconds, she was sure of it. Sleep is just a natural process. The bed snored and swelled, bedsores and waves. The human body was made for the tropics, where we lost our pelts due to lack of need. We moved north for elbow room, for other continents, for other ideas: sinks and soap dispensers, steel and saltpeter and oxygen masks. In thirty seconds she would ball up paper. Lucy was no Harry Houdini. A cabin is safety, a box with a door, while this cold was nothing really, just air and a number, since the lowest temperature ever recorded in North America was at Snag Airstrip just outside Beaver Station, Yukon Territory, on February 3, 1947. Minus 81.4°F, Beaver hunched in a low spot, no wind ever, so the cold of a continent settles there—a respectable number, but nowhere near the Siberian record.

When the bed moved, she did not wake, but watched him. She watched Wally enter their cabin, squeeze between the door and the jamb and push the bed a little farther, and she slid as if on a magic carpet.

"Come on," he said and Lucy bellied out.

He unclipped the chain. It fell to the plywood. Lucy skittered through the door as Wally shivered and went about his business, turned over boxes, thumbed envelopes, fingered jars. He found her stash in a Band-Aid box, mostly fives and tens. He located the caramel candies, his most recent batch, hard but good for sucking on, to warm the gut while walking far, or driving, stuffed five sets of dog booties in his big pockets, long underwear over his shoulder. A lung is just a dense balloon. He found his insulated coveralls, stepped in, zipped.

He listened for her breathing, then unfurled an old blanket and flung it over her.

He replugged the phone. Followed Lucy.

He left the door ajar, to knock, knock, knock the bed all the day, every day from now on, tapping. Dogs barked far off, somewhere near the Dump Road, a truck parked. Rifles popped far off, fire set to rock ground to a pulp, and flammable.

Some girl practicing.

ACKNOWLEDGMENTS

There's the popular view of the solitary writer, writing her stories in a bunker in the desert, in a cabin by a frozen lake, at a picnic table in the wilds of Alaska or Canada, geese flying over. Those images were actually kind of true for the making of these stories, but they are also terribly incomplete. Writing, for me, is a team sport. These stories have been tinkered with, petted, praised then beat up by many brilliant, patient, ruthless writers who read draft after draft, and thereby pushed these stories into viability. Joyfully, I get to acknowledge all your efforts now, and thank you, Sandra Jensen, Nancy Foley, Tim Sutton, Julie Himes, Claire Burdett, Lauren Johnson, Carol Keeley, Kara Lindstrom, Charlie Watts, Susan Tacent, Melanie Manual, Lizzy Bradbury, Michael Carolan, Dona Bolding, and Lynn Grant. I'm especially grateful to you, Chris Bachelder, Jodie Angel, Joanna Scott, Hannah Tinti, and Jim Shepard.

The team lives all over, formed all over, in writing hives across the land: Tin House Writers Workshops, Sirenland/ Wishingstone, New York Summer Writing Institute, GrubStreet. I'm so thankful to UMass Program for Poets and Writers, BOA Editions, Burlington Writers Workshop, The Loft, Hugo House, Mount Holyoke College, and the Nevada

State Libraries and Nevada Writers Hall of Fame, especially Shaun Griffin and Robin Monteith, for long term support of my writing. Thanks to *Cincinnati Review* and *Copper Nickel* for publishing several stories in this collection.

For notions that bloomed to stories: Christina, Ulrik, Oscar, and Emma. Jerry and Derick. Betsy Vielhaber *et al* in Heidelberg. Jerel Vinduska. Chris Rose. The Copper River. The beasts of Alaska, the desert, and everywhere. Carolina McLean Marshall, for general long-term trickster sass, and for the title.

And one needs folks back home to just help you live. Mike and Rosie, you were with Pearl and me for this whole thing. Margaret Eagleton, Melissa Guerra, Melinda Haas, and all my family, blood and chosen. I've needed each and all.

Mom and Dad.

Stephanie Steiker. This collection is how I found you. All else follows.

To Jerry for strength, love and wisdom always and when it was needed most.

To wonderful Jeremy Davies and the spectacular gang at And Other Stories—Stefan Tobler for starting this amazing whole-planet press, Tom Flynn, Javerya Iqbal, Emma Warhurst, Nicky Smalley, Michael Watson, and Tara Tobler—for believing in my stories, the long and the short, for your love and toil for books and the literary world.

Dear readers,

As well as relying on bookshop sales, And Other Stories relies on subscriptions from people like you for many of our books, whose stories other publishers often consider too risky to take on.

Our subscribers don't just make the books physically happen. They also help us approach booksellers, because we can demonstrate that our books already have readers and fans. And they give us the security to publish in line with our values, which are collaborative, imaginative and 'shamelessly literary'.

All of our subscribers:

- receive a first-edition copy of each of the books they subscribe to
- are thanked by name at the end of our subscriber-supported books
- receive little extras from us by way of thank you, for example: postcards created by our authors

BECOME A SUBSCRIBER,
OR GIVE A SUBSCRIPTION TO A FRIEND

Visit andotherstories.org/subscriptions to help make our books happen. You can subscribe to books we're in the process of making. To purchase books we have already published, we urge you to support your local or favourite bookshop and order directly from them – the often unsung heroes of publishing.

OTHER WAYS TO GET INVOLVED

If you'd like to know about upcoming events and reading groups (our foreign-language reading groups help us choose books to publish, for example) you can:

- join our mailing list at: andotherstories.org
- follow us on Twitter: @andothertweets
- join us on Facebook: facebook.com/AndOtherStoriesBooks
- admire our books on Instagram: @andotherpics
- follow our blog: andotherstories.org/ampersand

THIS BOOK WAS MADE POSSIBLE
THANKS TO THE SUPPORT OF

Aaron Bogner
Aaron McEnery
Aaron Schneider
Abbie Bambridge
Abigail Gambrill
Abigail Walton
Adam Lenson
Adrian Kowalsky
Ajay Sharma
Alan Raine
Alastair Gillespie
Albert Puente
Alec Logan
Alex Fleming
Alex Lockwood
Alex Pearce
Alex Ramsey
Alex von Feldmann
Alexandra Kay-Wallace
Alexandra Stewart
Alexandra Tammaro
Alexandra Tilden
Alexandra Webb
Ali Ersahin
Ali Smith
Ali Usman
Alia Carter
Alice Radosh
Alice Toulmin
Alice Wilkinson
Alison Hardy
Alison Winston
Alistair Chalmers
Aliya Rashid
Alyssa Rinaldi
Amado Floresca
Amaia Gabantxo
Amanda

Amanda Dalton
Amanda Fisher
Amanda Geenen
Amanda Read
Amber Da
Amelia Dowe
Amitav Hajra
Amy Benson
Amy Bojang
Amy Hatch
Amy Tabb
Ana Novak
Andra Dusu
Andrea Barlien
Andrea Oyarzabal
    Koppes
Andrew Lahy
Andrew Marston
Andrew McCallum
Andrew Place
Andrew Reece
Andrew Rego
Andrew Wright
Andy Corsham
Angela Joyce
Angelica Ribichini
Angus Walker
Anita Starosta
Ann Rees
Anna French
Anna Hawthorne
Anna Milsom
Anna Zaranko
Anne Boileau Clarke
Anne Carus
Anne Edyvean
Anne Kangley
Anne-Marie Renshaw

Anne Ryden
Anne Withane
Annette Hamilton
Annie McDermott
Anonymous
Anonymous
Antonia Lloyd-Jones
Antonia Saske
Antony Pearce
April Hernandez
Arathi Devandran
Archie Davies
Aron Trauring
Arthur John Rowles
Asako Serizawa
Ashleigh Phillips
Ashleigh Sutton
Audrey Mash
Audrey Small
Aurelia Wills
Barbara Mellor
Barbara Spicer
Barry Norton
Beatrice Taylor
Becky Cherriman
Becky Matthewson
Ben Buchwald
Ben Schofield
Ben Walter
Benjamin Judge
Benjamin Pester
Bernadette Smith
Beth Heim de Bera
Beverley Thomas
Bianca Duec
Bianca Jackson
Bianca Winter
Bill Fletcher

Bjørnar Djupevik
  Hagen
Blazej Jedras
Brenda Anderson
Briallen Hopper
Brian Anderson
Brian Byrne
Brian Conn
Brian Isabelle
Brian Smith
Brianna Soloski
Bridget Prentice
Briony Hey
Buck Johnston &
  Camp Bosworth
Burkhard Fehsenfeld
Caitlin Halpern
Caitriona Lally
Cameron Adams
Camilla Imperiali
Campbell McEwan
Carla Castanos
Carole Parkhouse
Carolina Pineiro
Caroline Perry
Caroline West
Carolyn A Schroeder
Catharine Braithwaite
Catherine Barton
Catherine Campbell
Catherine Lambert
Catherine
  Lautenbacher
Catherine Tandy
Catherine Williamson
Cathryn Siegal-
  Bergman
Cathy Galvin
Cathy Sowell
Catie Kosinski
Catrine Bollerslev
Cecilia Rossi

Cecilia Uribe
Chantal Wright
Charlene Huggins
Charles Fernyhough
Charles Kovach
Charles Dee Mitchell
Charles Rowe
Charles Wats
Charlie Levin
Charlie Small
Charlie Webb
Charlotte Furness
Charlotte Coulthard
Charlotte Whittle
Charlotte Woodford
Chenxin Jiang
Cherilyn Elston
China Miéville
Chris Blackmore
Chris Johnstone
Chris Lintott
Chris McCann
Chris Potts
Chris Senior
Chris Stergalas
Chris Stevenson
Chris Thornton
Christian Schuhmann
Christiana Spens
Christine Bartels
Christopher Allen
Christopher Smith
Christopher Stout
Chuck Woodman
Ciarán Schütte
Claire Adams
Claire Brooksby
Claire Mackintosh
Clare Young
Clare Wilkins
Clarice Borges
Cliona Quigley

Colin Denyer
Colin Hewlett
Colin Matthews
Collin Brooke
Courtney Lilly
Craig Kennedy
Cris Cucerzan
Cynthia De La Torre
Cyrus Massoudi
Daisy Savage
Dale Wisely
Dan Vigliano
Dana Lapidot
Daniel Axelbaum
Daniel Gillespie
Daniel Hahn
Daniel Jones
Daniel Oudshoorn
Daniel Sanford
Daniel Stewart
Daniel Syrovy
Daniel Venn
Daniela Steierberg
Darcie Vigliano
Darryll Rogers
Dave Lander
David Anderson
David Cowan
David Gould
David Greenlaw
David Hebblethwaite
David Higgins
David Johnson-Davies
David Leverington
David F Long
David Richardson
David Shriver
David Smith
David Smith
David Thornton
Dawn Bass
Dean Taucher

Deb Unferth
Debbie Enever
Debbie Pinfold
Deborah Green
Deborah Herron
Deborah McLean
Deborah Wood
Declan Gardner
Declan O'Driscoll
Denis Larose
Denis Stillewagt &
  Anca Fronescu
Derek Sims
Diane Salisbury
Diarmuid Hickey
Dietrich Menzel
Dinesh Prasad
Dirk Hanson
Domenica Devine
Dominic Nolan
Dominic Bailey
Dominick Santa
  Cattarina
Dominique Hudson
Dornith Doherty
Dorothy Bottrell
Dugald Mackie
Duncan Chambers
Duncan Clubb
Duncan Macgregor
Duncan Marks
Dustin Hackfeld
Dyanne Prinsen
Earl James
Ebba Tornérhielm
Ed Smith
Ed Tronick
Edward Champion
Ekaterina Beliakova
Elaine Juzl
Elaine Rodrigues
Eleanor Maier

Eleanor Updegraff
Elena Esparza
Elif Aganoglu
Elina Zicmane
Eliza Mood
Elizabeth Braswell
Elizabeth Coombes
Elizabeth Draper
Elizabeth Franz
Elizabeth Guss
Elizabeth Leach
Elizabeth Seals
Elizabeth Sieminski
Elizabeth Wood
Ellie Goddard
Emiliano Gomez
Emily Paine
Emily Williams
Emma Bielecki
Emma Louise Grove
Emma Morgan
Emma Post
Eric Anderson
Eric Weinstock
Erin Cameron Allen
Esmée de Heer
Esther Kinsky
Ethan Madarieta
Ethan White
Evelyn Eldridge
Ewan Tant
Fawzia Kane
Fay Barrett
Felicia Williams
Felicity Le Quesne
Felix Valdivieso
Finbarr Farragher
Fiona Mozley
Fiona Wilson
Forrest Pelsue
Fran Sanderson
Frances Dinger

Frances Harvey
Frances Thiessen
Francesca Brooks
Francesca Hemery
Francesca Rhydderch
Frank Curtis
Frank Rodrigues
Frank van Orsouw
Freddie Radford
Gail Marten
Gala Copley
Gavin Aitchison
Gavin Collins
Gawain Espley
Genaro Palomo Jr
Geoff Thrower
Geoffrey Cohen
Geoffrey Urland
George Stanbury
George Wilkinson
Georgia Shomidie
Georgina Norton
Gerry Craddock
Gill Boag-Munroe
Gillian Grant
Gillian Stern
Gina Heathcote
Glenn Russell
Gloria Gunn
Gordon Cameron
Gosia Pennar
Graham Blenkinsop
Graham R Foster
Grant Ray-Howett
Gregor von dem
  Knesebeck
Hadil Balzan
Hannah Freeman
Hannah Harford-
  Wright
Hannah Jane
  Lownsbrough

Hannah Rapley
Hannah Vidmark
Hanora Bagnell
Hans Lazda
Harriet Stiles
Haydon Spenceley
Hazel Smoczynska
Heidi Gilhooly
Henriette Magerstaedt
Henrike Laehnemann
Holly Down
Howard Robinson
Hugh Shipley
Hyoung-Won Park
Iain Forsyth
Ian McMillan
Ian Mond
Ian Randall
Ida Grochowska
Ines Alfano
Ingrid Peterson
Irene Mansfield
Irina Tzanova
Isabella Garment
Isabella Weibrecht
Ivy Lin
JE Crispin
Jacinta Perez Gavilan
  Torres
Jack Brown
Jacqueline Haskell
Jacqueline Lademann
Jacquelynn Williams
Jake Baldwinson
Jake Newby
James Attlee
James Avery
James Beck
James Crossley
James Cubbon
James Elkin
James Greer

James Higgs
James Kinsley
James Leonard
James Lesniak
James Portlock
James Ruland
James Scudamore
James Silvestro
Jamie Mollart
Jan Hicks
Jane Dolman
Jane Leuchter
Jane Roberts
Jane Roberts
Jane Willborn
Jane Woollard
Janis Carpenter
Janna Eastwood
Jasmine Gideon
Jason Montano
Jason Sim
Jason Timermanis
Jean Liebenberg
Jeanne Guyon
Jeff Collins
Jen Hardwicke
Jenifer Logie
Jennie Goloboy
Jennifer Fosket
Jennifer Higgins
Jennifer Watts
Jennifer Yanoschak
Jenny Huth
Jenny Newton
Jeremy Koenig
Jerome Mersky
Jess Hazlewood
Jess Wilder
Jess Wood
Jesse Coleman
Jesse Hara
Jessica Gately

Jessica Laine
Jessica Mello
Jessica Queree
Jessica Weetch
Jethro Soutar
Jill Harrison
Jo Heinrich
Jo Keyes
Jo Pinder
Joanna Luloff
Joao Pedro Bragatti
  Winckler
JoDee Brandon
Jodie Adams
Joe Huggins
Joel Swerdlow
Joelle Young
Johannes Holmqvist
Johannes Menzel
Johannes Georg Zipp
John Bennett
John Betteridge
John Bogg
John Carnahan
John Conway
John Gent
John Hodgson
John Kelly
John McWhirter
John Reid
John Shadduck
John Shaw
John Steigerwald
John Wallace
John Walsh
John Winkelman
John Wyatt
Jolene Smith
Jon Talbot
Jonas House
Jonathan Blaney
Jonathan Fiedler

Jonathan Gharraie
Jonathan Harris
Jonathan Huston
Jonathan Paterson
Jonathan Phillips
Jonathan Ruppin
Joni Chan
Jonny Kiehlmann
Jordana Carlin
Jorid Martinsen
Joseph Camilleri
Joseph Thomas
Josh Sumner
Joshua Davis
Judith Gruet-Kaye
Judith Hannan
Judith Virginia Moffatt
Judith Poxon
Judy Davies
Judy Rich
Julia Foden
Julia Rochester
Julia Von Dem
  Knesebeck
Julienne van Loon
Jupiter Jones
Juraj Janik
Justin Anderson
Justine Sherwood
KL Ee
Kaarina Hollo
Kaja R Anker-Rasch
Karen Gilbert
Karin Mckercher
Karl Chwe
Karl Kleinknecht &
  Monika Motylinska
Katarina Dzurekova
Katarzyna
  Bartoszynska
Kate Beswick
Kate Carlton-Reditt

Kate Shires
Kate Stein
Katharine Robbins
Katherine Brabon
Katherine McLaughlin
Katherine Sotejeff-
  Wilson
Kathleen McLean
Kathryn Burruss
Kathryn Edwards
Kathryn Williams
Kathy Wright
Katia Wengraf
Katie Brown
Katie Cooke
Katie Freeman
Katie Grant
Katy Robinson
Keith Walker
Ken Geniza
Kenneth Blythe
Kent Curry
Kent McKernan
Kerry Parke
Kevin Tole
Kieran Rollin
Kieron James
Kirsty Simpkins
Kris Ann Trimis
Kristen Tcherneshoff
Kristen Tracey
Krystale Tremblay-Moll
Krystine Phelps
Kylie Cook
Kyra Wilder
Lacy Wolfe
Lana Selby
Larry Wikoff
Laura Ling
Laura Murphy
Laura Newman
Laura Pugh

Laura Zlatos
Lauren Pout
Laurence Laluyaux
Lee Harbour
Leona Iosifidou
Leonora Randall
Liliana Lobato
Lily Blacksell
Linda Lewis
Linda Milam
Linda Whittle
Lindsay Attree
Lindsay Brammer
Lindsey Ford
Lindsey Harbour
Linnea Brown
Lisa Agostini
Lisa Dillman
Lisa Hess
Lisa Leahigh
Lisa Simpson
Liz Clifford
Lorna Bleach
Lottie Smith
Louise Evans
Louise Greenberg
Louise Jolliffe
Louise Smith
Luc Verstraete
Lucinda Smith
Lucy Huggett
Lucy Moffatt
Lucy Scott
Luise von Flotow
Luke Healey
Luke Murphy
Lynda Graham
Lyndia Thomas
Lynn Fung
Lynn Martin
Lynn Grant
Madden Aleia

Madison Taylor-
  Hayden
Maeve Lambe
Maggie Humm
Maggie Livesey
Marco Medjimorec
Margaret Dillow
Margaret Wood
Mari-Liis Calloway
Maria Ahnhem Farrar
Maria Lomunno
Maria Losada
Marie Donnelly
Marie Harper
Marijana Rimac
Marina Castledine
Marion Pennicuik
Marja S Laaksonen
Mark Reynolds
Mark Sargent
Mark Sheets
Mark Sztyber
Mark Waters
Martha W Hood
Martin Brown
Martin Price
Martin Eric Rodgers
Mary Addonizio
Mary Angela Brevidoro
Mary Clarke
Mary Heiss
Mary Wang
Maryse Meijer
Mathieu Trudeau
Matt Carruthers
Matt Davies
Matt Greene
Matthew Banash
Matthew Black
Matthew Cooke
Matthew Crossan
Matthew Eatough

Matthew Francis
Matthew Gill
Matthew Lowe
Matthew Woodman
Matthias Rosenberg
Maura Cheeks
Maureen Cullen
Maureen and Bill
  Wright
Max Cairnduff
Max Longman
Maxwell Mankoff
Meaghan Delahunt
Meg Lovelock
Megan Taylor
Megan Wittling
Mel Pryor
Melissa Beck
Melissa Quignon-
  Finch
Melissa Stogsdill
Meredith Martin
Michael Aguilar
Michael Bichko
Michael Boog
Michael James
  Eastwood
Michael Floyd
Michael Gavin
Michaela Goff
Michelle Mercaldo
Michelle Mirabella
Michelle Perkins
Miguel Head
Mike Abram
Mike Turner
Mildred Nicotera
Miles Smith-Morris
Molly Foster
Mona Arshi
Morayma Jimenez
Moriah Haefner

N Tsolak
Nancy Jacobson
Nancy Kerkman
Nancy Oakes
Nancy Peters
Naomi Morauf
Nargis McCarthy
Natalie Ricks
Nathalie Teitler
Nathan McNamara
Nathan Weida
Nicholas Brown
Nicholas Jowett
Nicholas Rutherford
Nick James
Nick Marshall
Nick Nelson & Rachel
  Eley
Nick Sidwell
Nick Twemlow
Nicola Cook
Nicola Hart
Nicola Sandiford
Nicolas Sampson
Nicole Matteini
Nicoletta Asciuto
Nigel Fishburn
Niki Sammut
Nina de la Mer
Nina Todorova
Nina Nickerson
Norman Batchelor
Norman Carter
Odilia Corneth
Ohan Hominis
Olivia Clarke
Olivia Powers
Olivia Scott
Pamela Tao
Pankaj Mishra
Pat Winslow
Patrick Hawley

Patrick Hoare
Patrick McGuinness
Paul Cray
Paul Ewing
Paul Flaig
Paul Jones
Paul Munday
Paul Nightingale
Paul Scott
Paul Stallard
Paula McGrath
Pavlos Stavropoulos
Penelope Hewett-
  Brown
Peter Edwards
Peter and Nancy Ffitch
Peter Gaukrodger
Peter Goulborn
Peter Griffin
Peter Hayden
Peter McBain
Peter McCambridge
Peter Rowland
Peter Wells
Petra Stapp
Phil Bartlett
Philip Herbert
Philip Warren
Philip Williams
Philipp Jarke
Phillipa Clements
Phoebe McKenzie
Phoebe Millerwhite
Phyllis Reeve
Pia Figge
Piet Van Bockstal
Prakash Nayak
Rachel Adducci
Rachael de Moravia
Rachael Williams
Rachel Gregory
Rachel Van Riel

Rachel Watkins
Ralph Cowling
Ralph Jacobowitz
Raminta Uselytė
Ramona Pulsford
Rebecca Moss
Rebecca O'Reilly
Rebecca Peer
Rebecca Roadman
Rebecca Rosenthal
Rebecca Servadio
Rebecca Shaak
Rebecca Söregi
Rebecca Starks
Rebecca Surin
Rebekka Bremmer
Renee Otmar
Renee Thomas
Rhiannon Armstrong
Rich Sutherland
Richard Clark
Richard Ellis
Richard Gwyn
Richard Mann
Richard Mansell
Richard Shea
Richard Soundy
Richard Stubbings
Rishi Dastidar
Rita Kaar
Rita O'Brien
Robert Gillett
Robert Hannah
Robert Weeks
Roberto Hull
Robin McLean
Robin Taylor
Rodrigo Alvarez
Roger Newton
Roger Ramsden
Ronan O'Shea
Rory Williamson

Rosalind May
Rosalind Ramsay
Rosanna Foster
Rose Crichton
Rosie Ernst Trustram
Ross Beaton
Roxanne O'Del Ablett
Roz Simpson
Rupert Ziziros
Ruth Deyermond
Ryan Day
Ryan Oliver
SK Grout
ST Dabbagh
Sabine Griffiths
Sally Baker
Sally Warner
Sam Gordon
Samantha Pavlov
Samuel Crosby
Samuel Stolton
Samuel Wright
Sara Bea
Sara Kittleson
Sara Sherwood
Sara Unwin
Sarah Arboleda
Sarah Brewer
Sarah Duguid
Sarah Lucas
Sarah Manvel
Sarah Pybus
Sarah Spitz
Sarah Stevns
Sasha Dugdale
Scott Astrada
Scott Chiddister
Scott Henkle
Scott Russell
Scott Simpson
Sean Kottke
Sean Myers

Selina Guinness
Serena Brett
Severijn Hagemeijer
Shannon Knapp
Shauna Gilligan
Sienna Kang
Simak Ali
Simon Clark
Simon Malcolm
Simon Pitney
Simon Robertson
Stacy Rodgers
Stefano Mula
Stephan Eggum
Stephanie De Los
  Santos
Stephanie Miller
Stephanie Smee
Stephen Cowley
Stephen Pearsall
Stephen Yates
Steve Clough
Steve Dearden
Steve Tuffnell
Steven Norton
Steven Williams
Stewart Eastham
Stu Hennigan
Stuart & Sarah Quinn
Stuart Wilkinson
Su Bonfanti
Sue Davies
Susan Edsall
Susan Ferguson
Susan Jaken

Susan Winter
Susan Wachowski
Suzanne Kirkham
Tallulah Fairfax
Tania Hershman
Tara Roman
Tatiana Griffin
Teresa Werner
Tess Cohen
Tess Lewis
The Mighty Douche
  Softball Team
Theo Voortman
Thom Keep
Thomas Alt
Thomas Campbell
Thomas Fritz
Thomas Smith
Thomas van den Bout
Tiffany Lehr
Tim Kelly
Tim Nicholls
Tim Scott
Timothy Cummins
Timothy Moffatt
Tina Rotherham-
  Winqvist
Toby Halsey
Toby Ryan
Tom Darby
Tom Doyle
Tom Franklin
Tom Gray
Tom Stafford
Tom Whatmore

Tracy Birch
Trent Leleu
Trevor Wald
Tricia Durdey
Turner Docherty
Val & Tom Flechtner
Vanessa Baird
Vanessa Dodd
Vanessa Fernandez
  Greene
Vanessa Heggie
Vanessa Nolan
Vanessa Rush
Veronika Haacker
  Lukacs
Victor Meadowcroft
Victoria Goodbody
Vijay Pattisapu
Wendy Call
Wendy Langridge
Will Weir
William
  Brockenborough
William Franklin
William Leibovici
William Mackenzie
William Richard
William Schwaber
William Sitters
William Orton
Yoora Yi Tenen
Zachary Maricondia
Zachary Whyte
Zoe Taylor
Zoë Brasier

ROBIN MCLEAN worked as a lawyer and then a potter in the woods of Alaska before turning to writing. Her debut novel *Pity the Beast* was chosen in multiple Best Books of 2021 lists in outlets such as the *Guardian*, *Wall Street Journal* and *The White Review*, while the American Booksellers Association chose it as an Indie Next pick. She teaches writing across the U.S. and internationally, and currently lives in the high desert West.